A Maverick for Her Mom

STELLA BAGWELL

HARLEQUIN

SPECIAL
EDITION

Special thanks and acknowledgment are given to Stella Bagwell for her contribution to the Montana Mavericks: Lassoing Love miniseries.

HARLEQUIN®
SPECIAL
EDITION™

Recycling programs for this product may not exist in your area.

ISBN-13: 978-1-335-59420-4

A Maverick for Her Mom

Harlequin Enterprises ULC
22 Adelaide St. West, 41st Floor
Toronto, Ontario M5H 4E3, Canada
www.Harlequin.com

Printed in U.S.A.

MONTANA MAVERICKS

Welcome to Big Sky Country, home of the Montana Mavericks! Where free-spirited men and women discover love on the range.

LASSOING LOVE

After years away, some of Bronco's most memorable sons and daughters have returned to the ranch seeking a fresh start. But there are some bumps along the road to redemption. Expect the unexpected as lonesome cowboys (and cowgirls) discover if they've got what it takes to grab that second chance!

Baker Kendra Humphrey is a whiz when it comes to desserts, but she's lost her confidence when it comes to love. She's determined to teach her daughter, Mila, they don't need a man to be happy. Once Dale Dalton swaggers into her bakery, however, Kendra finds her resolve wavering. The charming rancher is giving her all the feels...

Dear Reader,

When rancher Dale Dalton walks into Kendra's Cupcakes, he isn't looking for love. Especially not with a divorced mother of a seven-year-old daughter. But one look at the pretty baker has him deciding one or two dates with her couldn't possibly put his bachelorhood in jeopardy.

After a short failed marriage, Kendra has moved to Bronco, Montana, for a fresh start in life. Presently, she has no wish to jump into another relationship. Her life is consumed with raising her young daughter, Mila, and running her bakery. She doesn't have time, or courage, to search for love. But when Dale walks in to collect an order of cupcakes, she takes one look at the sexy cowboy and begins to dream about having a big, loving family.

Meanwhile, Mila wants a father and the child is interviewing any and every bachelor who crosses her path for the job. Trouble is, the girl thinks cute cowboy Dale is all wrong for her mother. Can he prove to Kendra and Mila he's the right man for the role of father and husband? He believes so—until Kendra's ex-husband shows up in Bronco and puts the meanings of love and family to the test.

I hope you enjoy visiting Bronco and dropping into Kendra's Cupcakes for a tasty treat while you read Dale and Kendra's love story.

Best wishes,

Stella Bagwell

After writing more than one hundred books for Harlequin, **Stella Bagwell** still finds writing about two people discovering everlasting love very rewarding. She loves all things Western and has been married to her own real cowboy for fifty-one years. Living on the south Texas coast, she also enjoys being outdoors and helping her husband care for the animals on the small ranch they call home. The couple has one son, who teaches high school mathematics and coaches football and powerlifting.

Books by Stella Bagwell

Harlequin Special Edition

Montana Mavericks: Lassoing Love

A Maverick for Her Mom

Men of the West

A Ranger for Christmas
His Texas Runaway
Home to Blue Stallion Ranch
The Rancher's Best Gift
Her Man Behind the Badge
His Forever Texas Rose
The Baby That Binds Them
Sleigh Ride with the Rancher
The Wrangler Rides Again
The Other Hollister Man

Rancher to the Rescue

Montana Mavericks: Brothers & Broncos

The Maverick's Marriage Pact

Visit the Author Profile page
at Harlequin.com for more titles.

To the big sky country of Montana and the rugged cowboys who work the open range.

Chapter One

Dale Dalton was a cowboy. He wasn't the kind of guy who walked into a bakery and asked for cupcakes. If he wanted dessert, he'd eat whatever his mom served at home on the ranch, or order pie at one of his favorite restaurants.

But Dale wasn't making this stop at Kendra's Cupcakes to satisfy his own personal sweet tooth. He was doing it as a favor to his brother Morgan and sister-in-law, Erica. Otherwise, he'd hardly be wasting his time driving the streets, searching the upscale business district of Bronco Heights for a fancy bakery-café.

He located the shop in a narrow building jammed between an antique store and a beauty salon. The front was constructed mostly of plate glass framed with red brick. The words *Kendra's Cupcakes* were painted in red cursive lettering across the wide window, while a second sign with the same name hung beneath a small red-and-white-striped awning that shaded the entrance.

Inside the bakery, Dale took his place behind a line of customers and glanced curiously around the spacious room filled with the mouthwatering smells of baked goods and deep-fried pastries. The floor was a checkerboard of red and white tiles, while on the left side of the room, several wooden tables and chairs were grouped in front of the plate glass window that overlooked the sidewalk. Presently, all the tables were occupied, and that surprised him. He didn't have any idea cupcake shops were such social spots. Did they serve beer in this joint?

He was studying a large menu displayed on the wall, when the person ahead of him moved forward to give Dale a direct view of a long, glass display case. But it wasn't the sweet treats inside that caught his immediate attention. It was the blond woman working behind the counter that had him staring and wondering.

Who was *she*? And why hadn't he seen her around Bronco before now? Because she was married? He didn't want to consider that possibility.

Standing in line normally irritated the heck out of Dale, but this evening he was more than happy to endure the wait. It gave him more time to watch the woman as she sacked up treats and dealt with the cash register.

Even though he was several feet away and peering around the heads of the customers in front of him, he could see she was darned attractive. The top of her head would probably reach the middle of his chest and her slender curves would fit right into his hands. Wavy blond hair was pinned atop her head in a messy bun, but he could easily imagine pulling the pins and coaxing the silky strands to fall upon her shoulders. A red-and-white-striped apron covered most of her blouse and jeans, yet as far as Dale was concerned, the casual clothing only made her sexier.

As customers collected their orders and departed the sweet shop, Dale mentally went over every line he'd ever handed a woman, but once his turn came to step up to the counter, all he could do was stare at her sky-blue eyes and the smile tilting the corners of her plush pink lips.

"Hello," she greeted. "May I help you?"

He cleared his throat, but the reflexive action didn't seem to help loosen his partially paralyzed tongue. "Uh—yeah. I'm here to pick up an order."

"Name?" she asked.

"Oh. Yes. My sister-in-law—she called in the order."

The pretty blonde continued to smile at him and Dale could see a bit of humor had crept into her expression. Did she think he was funny-looking or something?

"And your sister-in-law's name?" she prompted.

Dale felt hot color creeping up his neck. "Uh—sorry. Erica. Erica Dalton."

Nodding, she said, "Oh sure. I have her order ready."

She turned away from the counter and walked over to a long table situated against the wall behind her. Dale used the moment to slide his gaze over her pert little bottom and shapely legs inside the skinny jeans.

That part of her looked more than fine, he thought. But he still hadn't had a chance to get a full view of her left hand. If he spotted a wedding ring, then all his admiring and ogling would be for naught.

She returned and placed a large paper bag with the name *Kendra's Cupcakes* stamped on the side onto the checkout counter. "Two dozen cupcakes of mixed flavors," she stated, then asked, "Is there anything else you'd like?"

Dale could think of plenty of things he'd like from her, none of which he could say out loud. The decadent thoughts were going through his head as her left hand finally came into view. Ridiculous relief poured through him as he saw there was no ring or even a pale circle of where one used to be.

Without bothering to consider what he was actually doing, he gestured to the glass display case situated on the right side of the checkout counter. "You know, I'm feeling mighty hungry this evening. You might box me up a dozen of those cupcakes with the swirly stuff on top."

She stepped over to the case and slid open a door at the back. "The chocolate or vanilla?" she asked.

"Uh, which one tastes the best?" He realized there were customers behind him and he was taking up her time, but he had to grab the chance to talk with her. Even if the conversation was only about cupcakes.

She let out a soft chuckle and the sound floated over him like a warm, dreamy cloud. What in heck was wrong with him, anyway? He'd been around plenty of attractive women. So why was this one making him feel like an addled fool?

"Depends on a person's taste," she told him. "Frankly, I like the vanilla, but I'm a plain Jane."

Her comment very nearly made him laugh, but he stifled the reaction. There was nothing plain about this lady. "Okay, I'll try the vanilla."

She quickly placed the cupcakes in a special holder, then carefully eased the whole thing in a sack that matched the one with Erica's order.

When she stepped over to the cash register and began to punch the keys, she said, "So you're Erica's brother-in-law?"

Could she possibly be the teeniest bit interested in him? He could only hope. "Yes. I'm Dale Dalton."

"Nice to meet you. I'm Kendra Humphrey."

She totaled up the amount due for his order and he handed her enough bills to cover the cost.

"Kendra," he repeated thoughtfully, then his gaze fell to the name on the sacks and the connection clicked. "You own this bakery?"

"I do." Her smile was edged with pride as she counted his change. "I hope you enjoy your cupcakes. Thank you for coming in."

Dale was all set to continue their conversation, but she was already moving over to where the next customer was eyeing rows of apple fritters.

Realizing the short moments he'd had with her were over, Dale turned away from the counter feeling oddly bereft. He'd exchanged a handful of words with a woman he'd never met in his life, yet he felt like he'd just said goodbye to one of his arms or legs.

Damn! He must be losing it, he thought. Love at first sight didn't happen in real life. Especially not to Dale Dalton. He was too happy playing the field. Still, a date or two with the pretty baker would be mighty nice.

As Dale skirted around the line of waiting customers and made his way to the front, he was so preoccupied with the notion of asking Kendra Humphrey for a date that he very nearly collided with a little girl who'd pirouetted directly into his path.

Somehow he managed to do a quick sidestep to avoid the crash, while the child, seemingly unaffected by the near miss, stopped and stared curiously up at him. Dale's first instinct was to hurry on past her and out the door. He wasn't good with kids. Except for the limited time he spent with his nieces and nephews, he wasn't around children very often. But something about this girl's sweet little face made him pause.

"Hello," she said brightly. "What's your name?"

Somewhat nonplussed by her bold approach, he answered, "Dale Dalton. And let me guess. Your name is Princess."

Her little nose wrinkled with disapproval. "My name isn't Princess. Why would you think that?"

A fluffy pink skirt partially covered the top portion of a pair of black jeans, while a purple T-shirt with a cartoon dinosaur in bright lime green completed her colorful wardrobe. A small rhinestone tiara adorned the top of her blond hair.

He gestured to the head decoration. "You're wearing a crown. Princesses wear those things, don't they?"

Her expression said she'd already summed him up as being a silly man and as Dale noted her wavy blond hair and blue eyes, he was knocked a bit off-kilter. This girl clearly resembled the owner of the bakery.

Quick to correct him, she said, "This is not a crown. It's my tiara. My name is Mila Humphrey and I'm seven. Do you live around here?"

"I live on a ranch. Dalton's Grange. It's a few miles out of town," he answered, while the child's last name spun through his head.

Dale glanced over his shoulder to where Kendra continued to take orders from the waiting customers, then back to the charming child standing in front of him.

Mila didn't give him a chance to question the connection—she lifted her chin to a proud angle and stated, "That's my mommy and this is her bakery. She makes money selling good things to eat."

So Kendra had a daughter. Did that mean she was married? In spite of her not wearing a wedding ring? He could ask the girl an offhand question about her father, but that would make Dale a creepy jerk. Besides, there were plenty of reasons Kendra might not be sporting a ring. She might be allergic to precious metals. Or maybe she didn't want to get her diamonds all gooey when she mixed pastry dough. And no doubt her wedding ring would be full of diamonds, he thought. A man lucky enough to have her for a wife would give her nothing less.

Realizing his mind was on a runaway fantasy, he gave himself a mental shake and smiled at the child. "I'm sure everything your mommy bakes is delicious."

The girl regarded him skeptically. "Are you married?"

A bit taken aback, he said, "No. Are you?"

"I'm too young," she explained. "And I don't have a boyfriend yet."

"I'm sure you'll have one soon enough," he told her.

She tilted her little blond head to one side as she continued to regard him with big blue eyes. And even though Dale was telling himself he needed to be headed home to the ranch, there was something about Mila that made it impossible for him to walk away.

"I'll bet you have lots of girlfriends," she said suddenly. "Cute cowboys usually do."

Was that how this rosy-cheeked cherub saw him? He was thinking she might be smarter than he first imagined when she promptly added, "My mommy goes on dates—sometimes. But I don't think you should bother asking her to go on one."

Dale was thrilled to hear Kendra Humphrey was single and dated occasionally. But he wasn't at all sure he liked having a seven-year-old read his mind. And where did she come off giving him romantic advice?

"Why not? I'm a nice guy."

She shrugged. "You're just not her type. She likes men who wear glasses and read books."

The nerdy type? Kendra hardly looked like a woman

who'd want to spend an evening discussing literature with a man, Dale thought. It was difficult for him to imagine those luscious pink lips talking instead of kissing.

He said, "Uh, don't you think you should let your mommy decide whether she likes cowboys?"

She shrugged both shoulders, then reached up and carefully adjusted the rhinestone tiara on her head. "Well, she might like cowboys. But only the kind who want to settle down and have kids. And you're not that kind. I can tell."

Dale had to admit there was nothing bratty or purposely impolite about Kendra Humphrey's daughter. But just the same, her comments were pushing his buttons. How did this child know he was the free-roaming type? Did he have it written across his forehead? And even if he did, could a seven-year-old read?

He was wondering how he could respond to the girl, or if he should even try, when a soft, female voice sounded behind him.

"Mila! Are you harassing Mr. Dalton?"

Dale glanced over his shoulder to see Kendra, looking somewhat exasperated, hurrying toward them. At the same time, he noticed the customers had cleared away from the display counters and now the only patrons left inside the bakery were the ones seated at the tables.

"No problem." Dale flashed Kendra his most charming grin. "Your daughter and I were just having a— Well, an enlightening discussion about cowboys."

Groaning with embarrassment, she leveled a stern look at her daughter, then turned an apologetic smile on Dale. "I'm so sorry, Mr. Dalton—"

"Oh, no one calls me Mr. Dalton. I'm Dale to everybody."

Smiling, she took a step closer and rested a hand on her daughter's shoulder, and as Dale took in the image of the two of them together it was hard for him to imagine why there wasn't a man in the family. What kind of fool would give up these two? Or perhaps he'd not given them up. Maybe the man had died an untimely death.

"Okay, Dale. And I apologize for Mila. She can be, uh, very pushy sometimes and unfortunately she says exactly what's on her mind."

Which appeared to be screening men for her mother's potential boyfriends. Judging by the way Mila was carefully taking in everything he and Kendra said to each other, she probably held these question-and-answer sessions with suitable male customers on a daily basis.

"Don't give it a second thought. I welcome a girl's dating advice no matter what their age," he joked.

Kendra let out another embarrassed groan. "I'm sorry about this, Dale. Please let me give you some extra cupcakes to make up for my daughter's behavior."

"That's thoughtful of you, Ms. Humphrey. But it's not necessary," he told her.

The smile she flashed him said she was grateful he wasn't taking Mila's chatter to heart. It also told Dale he couldn't possibly rest until he saw this woman again. Especially without a seven-year-old chaperone.

"Call me Kendra. And it's necessary to me," she said. "I'll be right back."

While Kendra went to fetch the cupcakes, Mila used the time to practice her pirouettes, only she wasn't balanced on the toes of ballet flats, she was wearing a pair of sparkly pink cowgirl boots. Dale couldn't imagine how it would be to parent such a precocious child. His brother Morgan did a great job dealing with his little daughter, JoJo. But Dale had never imagined himself as a daddy.

"I've been taking dance lessons," she told Dale. "Someday I might dance on a stage. Mommy says anybody can do what they really want if they try hard."

"Your mommy is right."

She stopped her whirling and leveled a curious look at him. "Are you trying to do something?"

The simply spoken question caught Dale off guard. What was he trying to do in the greater scheme of things? Sure, he was helping to keep the family ranch, Dalton's Grange, intact and profitable. He was doing his part to make sure his mother remained healthy and happy. But in regard to his own life, he couldn't think of one single thing he was trying to do, except enjoy himself.

"Well, I guess I try to do lots of things," he told her. "When I'm at work on the ranch."

She didn't appear to be all that impressed with his answer, but she remained silent. Probably because her mother had just walked up to join them.

"Here's the extra cupcakes, Dale." She handed the sack to him and he could tell by the weight that she'd been very generous. "I hope my pestering daughter won't keep you from visiting the bakery again."

He could tell her that a herd of wild horses couldn't keep him away, but he kept the thought to himself. He didn't want to give Mila reason to shoot him a look of disapproval, or give Kendra the impression he was overeager.

"Like I said, she hasn't been a bother. You'll be seeing me again. And thanks for the extra cupcakes."

"You're welcome," she told him, then purposely wrapped a hand around Mila's shoulder. "Come on, sweetie. I have a job for you back in the kitchen."

Mother and daughter walked away and Dale forced

himself to leave the bakery, but as he made the long drive to Dalton's Grange, he continued to think about Kendra and little Mila. A fact that surprised him. He'd never thought of himself as a family man, yet something about Kendra and her daughter had him wondering how it might feel to be a husband and father.

The kitchen area at the back of Kendra's Cupcakes wasn't large, but the space was efficiently equipped with everything Kendra and her helpers needed to get the daily baking done. At this time of the evening, the ovens and deep fryers were shut down and Jackie, a twenty-five-year-old woman with vivid red hair, cut in a pixie style, was busy mopping the floor.

She looked up as Kendra marched Mila over to the end of a work counter and lifted her onto the top seat of a step chair.

"Uh-oh. Looks like someone is in trouble," she said slyly. "Who did she ambush this time? A married minister?"

"I only wish it had been," Kendra told her assistant. "This time Mila had to pick on one of the Dalton brothers. An unmarried one."

Shaking her head, Jackie leaned on the mop handle. "You made a big mistake, Kendra, when you allowed Mila to go with you to Audrey Hawkins and Jack Burris's wedding. Now the child has weddings on the brain."

Unfortunately, Jackie was right. Ever since they'd attended Audrey Hawkins and Jack Burris's beautiful wedding, Mila talked incessantly about brides and grooms, flower girls and ring bearers. Each time an opportunity presented itself, she announced to their friends, and even strangers, that her mommy was going to get married— soon! It was beginning to be a very frustrating problem for Kendra. Especially when she had no plans to even look for a boyfriend, much less get married.

"Well, that can't be all bad," Jackie said. "The way I remember, there's not one ugly Dalton in the bunch."

Kendra helplessly rolled her eyes. "Jackie, you're no help at all!"

With a mischievous chuckle, Jackie continued with her mopping, while Kendra turned an admonishing look on her daughter.

Mila carefully smoothed her pink tulle skirt before she leveled an innocent smile at her mother. "What do you want me to do sitting here, Mommy?"

"I want you to explain what you were doing with Mr. Dalton. I know you haven't forgotten what I told you about talking to the male customers—about asking them personal and embarrassing questions. I've told you it's rude and not to be doing it. So what do you have to say for yourself?"

Seemingly unfazed by her mother's interrogation, Mila said, "I wasn't being rude. Dale liked talking to me. I could tell."

The moment Kendra had spotted the Dalton brother sauntering into the bakery, she had to admit, she'd taken a second and third peek at the tall, good-looking cowboy. Dark hair, blue eyes and a killer smile. He'd had that look of a charming rascal. Exactly the sort of guy she didn't need in her life. But that hadn't stopped Kendra from snatching a few more glances at the man while she'd tended to the other customers.

While she'd dealt with Dale's order, he'd been polite and friendly. He hadn't ogled her as if he wished she was a part of the dessert menu and Kendra had appreciated his gentlemanly attitude. So when she'd looked up a few moments later to see her daughter had waylaid the sexy cowboy a few feet from the door, she'd been totally mortified.

Turning her focus back to Mila, she asked, "Really? How did you decide that Dale liked talking to you?"

Mila's lips pursed together before she finally spoke. "Well, he was smiling and he wasn't saying anything mean. And he wasn't rolling his eyes or looking bored."

Kendra let out a long sigh. She didn't know where her daughter had gotten the ability to size up people, but usually Mila was spot-on in her assessments. And to be fair, Dale hadn't appeared to be all that irritated with Mila's foolishness.

"And I suppose you asked him if he was married or had a girlfriend."

Mila nodded. "Why not? He's cute. We needed to know if he had a wife. And he doesn't. But don't worry, Mommy. I already told him that he wasn't your type."

Oh Lord, this was worse than Kendra had first thought. "Mila, you didn't!"

Seeing the anger on her mother's face, Mila held her palms up in a defensive gesture. "Well, I had to set him straight. Because I could see he wasn't the kind of guy who'd want to get married and have kids."

There was no point in asking her daughter how she'd reached such a conclusion about Dale Dalton. Frankly, Kendra had concluded the same thing, but that hardly meant it was right or proper for her daughter to be discussing such issues with a strange man.

"Mila, I realize you'd like to have a daddy and that you want brothers and sisters. But you need to understand how things like this work. You can't just go around picking out a man to be your mommy's husband. It doesn't work that way. A man and woman need lots of time to discover if they're compatible and if there's chemistry between them before they can, um, get together."

A puzzled frown wrinkled Mila's forehead. "Does that mean you need to find out whether you like each other?"

"Well, that's a simple way of putting it, but yes. And finding out whether you'd like someone for a lifetime doesn't happen overnight."

With an exaggerated sigh, Mila folded her arms across the dinosaur on her chest. "Well, it won't happen with you at all, Mommy, 'cause you're too busy. That's why you need me to help you find a boyfriend. One that'll want to be my daddy."

There was no way Kendra could stay angry with her daughter. Hearing Mila's wish for a father always tore at her heart. It also left her feeling like a failure.

Damn Bryce! She'd given her ex every opportunity to be a part of Mila's life. She'd tried her hardest to make him see how much his daughter needed her father. But he'd always been too self-absorbed to ever acknowledge Mila, much less give her attention and support.

Sighing, Kendra reached out and patted Mila's cheek. "I know you mean well, sweetie. But you need to let me choose my own boyfriend. Okay?"

Mila frowned. "Okay. But I don't think you'll really start looking for one."

Her daughter knew her well. Kendra had little interest in finding a boyfriend. Her marriage to Bryce had been humiliating and heartbreaking. He'd broken every promise he'd ever made to her and squashed every dream she'd ever had for a family. She didn't need a man waltzing into her life and messing it all up for a second time.

Hearing the jingle of the outer door of the bakery,

Kendra quickly lifted Mila off the seat and set her back on the floor. "Come on. We have customers waiting."

Three hours later, Smitty, the young man who worked as the bakery-café's barista, along with Andrea, a part-time college student who worked as a server and all-around helper, had already left for the night. Kendra was getting ready to close up shop when she spotted a frequent patron attempting to enter the bakery. Because the woman was elderly and walked with the aid of a cane, she oftentimes struggled with the door, so Kendra hurried over to give her a helping hand.

"Let me hold the door for you, Mrs. Garrison. The wind is strong tonight."

"Bless you, Kendra. Are you about to close?"

"Don't worry. You have plenty of time to get whatever you'd like," Kendra told her.

Just as the woman hobbled over the threshold, an orange cat zoomed past her legs and straight into the bakery, causing both women to let out shrieks of surprise.

"Oh my goodness!" Mrs. Garrison cried out.

Kendra stared after the flash of ginger fur racing across the bakery floor.

"It's that darned cat again!" she exclaimed.

Racing after the animal, Mila shouted, "Mommy, it's the orange kitty! He's come back to see us. Can I pick him up?"

"No, Mila!" she called out, but Mila was already chasing the cat around the display cases and through the door of the kitchen.

With the customer safely inside, and the door shut behind her, Kendra said, "Excuse me for a minute, Mrs. Garrison, I'd better see about our unannounced visitor."

Kendra hurried back to the kitchen to find Mila peering beneath a rolling cart that was sandwiched between the refrigerator and a cabinet.

"He's hiding under the bottom shelf, Mommy!"

Jackie, who was standing directly behind Mila, glanced over her shoulder as Kendra approached them. "I don't think the cat is too happy about being in the kitchen," she told her.

Kendra walked cautiously over to the cart and squatted on her heels to get a better look at the cat. At the moment, the animal was peeking timidly out at the unfamiliar surroundings.

"Hello, pretty guy," she gently said to him. "What are you doing? Looking for a meal, or a girlfriend?"

The cat's big green eyes blinked once as he made a skeptical study of Kendra, but he didn't make a move to crawl from his hiding place to greet her.

"Can I give him some milk, Mommy? It might make him come out and let me pet him."

Kendra had seen the cat at the back of the bakery on different occasions. Probably because Mila had been secretly tossing it food. And once he'd dashed into the bakery's entry, but during those visits, he'd never stuck around long enough for the animal-rescue organization to catch up with him.

"Okay. A small bowl of milk. But don't scare him. Animal rescue needs to collect him."

"I'll pour the milk for Mila to give him," Jackie said. "Go ahead and finish whatever you were doing."

"Thanks, Jackie."

Kendra returned to the front to deal with Mrs. Garrison. The woman's order turned out to be an extra-large one and Kendra carried everything out to the woman's car.

Once she helped the faithful customer to her vehicle,

Kendra waved goodbye, then hurried back inside to call animal rescue. When a man answered, she quickly related the situation.

"The cat you're describing sounds exactly like Morris. The feline who went missing in July."

"Morris," Kendra repeated thoughtfully. "Yes, I recall seeing a poster on a missing cat by that name. You think this might be him?"

"Possibly. We've been getting calls of sightings around town, but no one has managed to corner him," the man replied. "He escaped an apartment fire and hasn't been located since."

"Morris or not, this cat is right here in my kitchen," Kendra explained. "It's past closing time, but I'll be glad to stay here until the rescue unit arrives to collect him."

"Thank you, Ms. Humphrey. Someone will be there in just a few minutes."

At some point during the phone call, Mila had appeared at Kendra's side. Now, as Kendra hung up the phone, her daughter tugged on the leg of her jeans and looked up at her with pleading eyes.

"Mommy, why does someone have to get the cat? Why can't we take him home with us? He looks nice. And remember, you said I could get a pet pretty soon."

Kendra wearily pushed at the strands of hair that had tumbled loose from the bun atop her head. She'd been going since four o'clock this morning and the day had been a long one. Now, with a wily cat to deal with, the day was growing even longer.

Suppressing a sigh, she looked down at her daughter's eager face. "I haven't forgotten my promise to get you a kitten or puppy. But this cat belongs to someone else. He's been lost and people are looking for him so they can take him to the home where he belongs."

Mila looked crestfallen. "I guess he does need to be with his family. But he should've walked to his own house instead of coming to the bakery."

"He's probably confused and doesn't know where his house is." Kendra patted her shoulder. "Now I need to finish packing up the leftover pastries. You'd be a big help if you'd go sit by the door and watch for the animal-rescue people."

"Okay, Mommy."

While Mila stood sentinel at the door, Kendra went to work. Each night, on her way home, Jackie dropped off the surplus of baked goods at a local charity house or nursing home. Kendra liked to think the donated food was enjoyed by folks who were especially in need.

As she packed up a cardboard box, Kendra's thoughts unwittingly drifted to Dale Dalton. Until he'd walked into the bakery, she'd never seen the man before. But that was hardly surprising. She was usually too busy to attend many social events around Bronco and those that she did take in were usually family-type outings. Not the sort of entertainment a good-looking bachelor like him would find interesting.

Before he'd explained to Kendra that he was picking up his sister-in-law's order, she would've never guessed he was a member of the Dalton family. Except for Morgan Dalton, who was married to her friend Erica, she wasn't personally acquainted with the Dalton brothers. She'd often heard Erica talk about living on Dalton's Grange with her husband, however, Kendra had never seen or visited the property located on the outskirts of Bronco. From Erica's comments, Kendra knew the ranch was very large and supported huge herds of livestock.

During Mila's earlier chatter about Dale, Kendra had

learned he worked on the ranch. Which meant it was probably safe to assume he lived there too. He'd also told Mila
he didn't have a wife, which hardly surprised Kendra.
From the looks of him, she figured his romantic involve-
ments were the brief kind without promises or strings.

*Kendra, why are you thinking about Dale Dalton? He
isn't your kind of man. Besides, you don't want a man
in your life, remember?*

Pushing back at the annoying voice in her head, she
started to carry the box of leftovers back to the kitchen,
when Mila sang out.

"Those people are here, Mommy! And they have a
little cage with them!"

After placing the box on the counter, Kendra walked
to the door to meet a young man and woman, both wearing polo shirts with emblems that read Bronco Animal
Rescue.

"Thank you for coming so quickly," Kendra told
them. "The cat is in the kitchen—hidden under a table.
Follow me and I'll show you."

The group entered the kitchen and Mila immediately
pointed to the table where Morris had remained since
the rescue service had been called.

"He's under there," Mila told the rescue workers. "We
gave him a bowl of milk and he drank all of it. He was
hungry."

The man cautiously approached the rolling cart, then
kneeled down and looked under the bottom shelf. "I
don't see any kind of cat under here."

"What?" Kendra practically shouted the word. "He
was there not more than five minutes ago. I saw him.
A big orange cat."

Mila raced over to the cart and, lying flat on the
floor, peered beneath it. "He's not here, Mommy!"

"Well, he has to be here in the kitchen somewhere," Kendra said. "He couldn't have gotten out."

She'd barely spoken the words, when Jackie entered the back door of the building. The redhead was carrying a large plastic bucket. She glanced nonchalantly at the group.

"Did you get the cat?" she asked.

Kendra walked over to where Jackie was placing the pail in a storage closet. "No. The cat isn't under the cart, where we left him," Kendra told her. "Have you seen him?"

As she waited for Jackie to answer, the rescue pair began to search the small nooks and spaces around the room.

Puzzled, Jackie nodded. "He was here a couple of minutes ago. I saw him before I went out to the dumpster. Maybe—" Her mouth formed a perfect *O*. "Do you think he might have run out the door?"

Kendra passed a weary hand over her forehead. "Did you leave the door open while you went out?"

A look of guilt crossed the redhead's face. "I'm sorry. I wasn't thinking. I mean, we don't normally have a cat in the kitchen."

"We don't normally have *any* animal in the kitchen!" Kendra exclaimed, then, with a rueful shake of her head, she patted Jackie's arm. "Don't feel badly. I imagine the cat will turn up somewhere sooner or later."

Hearing Jackie's admission about the door, the two rescue workers decided to search the back alley, but several minutes later they returned to announce Morris was nowhere to be found.

After the rescue workers departed and Jackie left with the box of pastries to be donated, Kendra began locking the doors for the night.

Mila trailed after her. "Mommy, why did Morris run off? Didn't he like us?"

Pausing, Kendra stroked a hand down the back of Mila's blond hair. "Well, he wasn't with us long enough for him to decide whether he liked us. And I suspect he's just trying to find his way back home."

"Like we found our home here in Bronco?"

Smiling now, Kendra bent down and placed a kiss on her daughter's forehead. "That's right, princess."

Mila giggled. "Dale said my name was Princess. Because I'm wearing my tiara. That's funny."

Kendra slanted her a curious glance. "I thought you decided Dale wouldn't make a good boyfriend for me."

Tilting her head from side to side, she said, "Well, he wouldn't make a good one for you. But he is cute."

Yes, Dale was charming, cute and sexy, Kendra thought. Everything she didn't need in her life.

Chapter Two

By the time Dale drove home to Dalton's Grange, and then headed to Morgan's house, night had fallen and so had the temperature. Long before he pulled to a stop in front of the rock-and-log structure, he spotted smoke spiraling up from the chimney. Dale hardly considered the weather cool enough this late summer evening for a fire, but the air was a bit chilly, and he figured his brother had built it for Erica. With her being pregnant with their second child and currently on bed rest, Morgan was doing all he could to make his wife comfortable.

Dale walked across the wooden porch and knocked briskly on the door, then, without bothering to wait for an answer, stepped inside.

"Hey, anyone home?" he called out.

From his seat in a large leather recliner, Morgan motioned for Dale to join him. Dale walked over and deposited the large sack of cupcakes on a low, pinewood coffee table, then eased onto the end cushion of a long couch.

"You've surprised me," Morgan said. "I thought you'd stay in town and have a beer or something before you came back to the ranch."

"I wasn't much in the mood to hang around town," Dale told him. "And I didn't want to drag in here with the cupcakes about the time you and Erica were getting ready to go to bed."

Morgan pulled a rueful face. "Erica is already in bed. Remember?"

Dale nodded. "I haven't forgotten. How's she doing?"

"Okay. Just tired of being in bed and staring at the walls. She watches TV, reads, eats and does it all over again."

Dale could see the worried look on his brother's face, and he knew the situation with his wife and unborn baby had to be putting a load of stress on Morgan's shoulders. He was crazy in love with Erica and this second baby she was carrying was the first biological child for him. Not that this child was any more precious to him than little Josie, or JoJo as everyone called her, who'd been born shortly after Morgan and Erica had married.

Dale admired his brother for being such a good, dedicated family man. Dealing with his little daughter seemed to come natural to him. So did his ability to keep a loving smile on Erica's face. But Morgan's success at being a family man didn't necessarily mean Dale was cut out for such a life. No, sir.

Dale replied, "Well, as long as she and the baby are healthy that's all that matters."

"Exactly. Just getting them safely through the next few months means everything." Morgan raked hands through his dirty blond hair, then rested his elbows on his knees and looked at Dale. "Seen Holt or Boone today? I was out most of the day riding fence on the north range. Did Holt go to the horse sale at Kalispell? He was all worked up over that cutting horse he'd found in the consignment catalog."

Dale's chuckle was wry. "He'd need more than that to get worked up. That mare will probably bring six figures. The ranch can't afford her and neither can Holt. But, yeah, I think he went to the sale. I saw Boone earlier this morning. He was headed into town for vet supplies."

Like Morgan, both Holt and Boone were older than Dale and, like Morgan, were married to women they were gaga about. Boone had married Sofia Sanchez, a fashion stylist for BH Couture, a high-end fashion boutique in Bronco Heights. Holt was married to Amanda Jenkins, who worked in marketing. Together they were raising Holt's ten-year-old son, Robby.

Presently, Dale and Shep, the two youngest sons of Neal and Deborah Dalton, were the only ones who were still single and living at home. And though Dale couldn't speak for Shep, he had no intentions of changing the direction of his life anytime soon. Even though their dear mother would love to see the last of her boys married and raising babies of their own.

In an effort to push that unwanted scenario from his mind, Dale glanced around the room and noticed the TV was on, although the sound was turned down too low to hear. A coloring book and a box of crayons were on the floor in front of the fireplace, but JoJo was nowhere to be seen.

"Where's my little niece?" he asked.

"She took her mommy a plate of cookies for dessert. But you can bet JoJo will do all the eating," he said with a fond smile. "When she finds out you've delivered the cupcakes, she'll be begging for one. By the way, thanks for picking them up for me."

JoJo was starting her first day of nursery school tomorrow and she was supposed to take cupcakes. Since Erica was on bed rest and Morgan couldn't cook a piece of toast without ruining it, they'd called in an order to Kendra's Cupcakes.

"No problem," Dale said. "In fact, the bakery trip turned out to be a pleasure of sort."

"Oh. Let me guess. You bought a half-dozen donuts and ate them on the way home?"

Dale grinned and waggled his eyebrows. "No. But I met the tasty-looking blonde who owns the bakery."

"You're talking about Kendra?" Morgan asked.

Hearing his brother speak the woman's name caused Dale to sit straight up. "Yeah, that's who I mean. You know her?"

"Only slightly. Erica knows her very well. She's been going to the bakery since Kendra first opened it."

Dale felt like groaning out loud. Three long years Dale could have been walking into Kendra's Cupcakes and getting to know her. So much wasted time.

"Do you know anything about her?" Dale asked him.

Morgan shrugged. "Not much. Erica said she's been divorced for a while. And she has a little girl. I saw her once when we ran across them at a burger place in town. Cute kid."

Yes, Mila was a mini-replica of her mother, Dale thought. Which made her very cute. But he considered her far too precocious for a child of her age.

Dale said, "I met Mila this evening when I stopped by the bakery. I've never met such an outspoken kid. She gave me an earful."

Puzzled, Morgan asked, "What was she doing having a conversation with you?"

Dale grimaced. It still got his goat to think how the

seven-year-old had ruffled his feathers. He was a grown man, for Pete's sake. A child's opinion should roll right off his back, not stick him like a knife blade.

"Apparently when she grows up she has plans to write an advice column for the lovelorn," Dale answered wryly. "She informed me that I'd be wasting my time to ask her mother for a date. I was cute, but not the sort of guy her mother goes for."

Morgan threw back his head and laughed. "Must be a smart kid."

"Hey, hey, Morgan. This is your brother, Dale, you're talking to. What's wrong with me?"

Morgan shook his head. "Nothing. You're just not Kendra Humphrey's type."

Dale snorted. "Mila implied her mommy wants a husband and babies."

Morgan shot him a droll look. "And what's wrong with the woman wanting those things? You'd rather Kendra be the one-night-stand type?"

"No!" The mere notion of that blond angel flitting from one man to the next made Dale a little sick to his stomach. "Not at all. But what would be wrong with her liking a gentleman cowboy? Enough to go on a date with him?"

"Nothing. If that's all you wanted from her."

Morgan's comment caused Dale to pause and stare at his brother. Did he think sex was all he ever wanted from a woman?

Well, to be fair, you sure aren't looking for love or marriage. What's left? Conversation and hand-holding?

Dale gave himself a mental shake in an effort to rid his head of the annoying voice.

"You make me sound like some sort of playboy," Dale said distastefully. "I'm not that kind of guy."

"I'm glad to hear it. Because I don't think Kendra needs another heartache."

Dale arched his eyebrows at Morgan. "Another heartache? You're implying she's already had one."

Morgan shot him an impatient look. "She's gone through a divorce, Dale. Don't you figure that was a heartache? Or maybe you consider the end of a marriage a laughing matter?"

Shaking his head, Dale said, "Oh, come off it, Morgan. I mention a woman and you start giving me a moral lecture. What's wrong with you, anyway?"

A resigned grin on his face, Morgan rose to his feet. "Sorry, Dale. I guess I've forgotten how it is for a man to be single and looking. And you're my brother. I don't want to see you get tangled up in a relationship that might hurt you."

"Don't worry about me. I'm not going to get tangled, period."

"Good. So let's go to the kitchen. I'll make coffee and you can have a cup with me before you head home."

Chuckling, Dale rose from the couch. "Wrong, brother. I'll make the coffee. You can't boil water."

A few days later, on a sunny, but particularly cool day for the first Saturday in September, Kendra parked her white SUV a couple of blocks away from the city park, which was located across the street from the city hall. Bronco's back-to-school picnic was held every year around this time and the event was something that Mila waited eagerly to attend. Her daughter loved being outdoors and especially enjoyed the chance to see all her friends she'd be reuniting with once school opened.

Kendra had to admit there was still enough of a kid in her to enjoy going to the park. And this particular gathering gave her a chance to chat with friends and acquaintances she didn't get to see on a regular basis.

"Maybe you'll run into plenty of cute guys at the park today, Mommy. I'll bet they'll all be looking at you too. 'Cause you're so pretty."

Kendra doubted there would be many single guys present today. Not unless they were widowed or, like her, divorced and a single parent.

She glanced over at Mila, who was happily swinging her arms to and fro and alternating her forward movement with a skip and a walk.

"I think you're a little biased, sweetie. But thank you for the compliment."

Mila looked at her. "What does *biased* mean? Does that have something to do with chemistry and compat-i— Well, whatever that word was?"

So her daughter had listened to at least part of the lecture she'd given her over this idea she had of finding Kendra a husband. She could only hope that enough of these talks would convince Mila to drop this obsession she had of getting her mother married. "Not exactly. It means you think I'm pretty just because I'm your mommy."

"That's not being bad, Mommy. You are pretty. And you wore your sweater today that I like the best."

Kendra glanced down at the Fair Isle sweater she'd pulled on over a pair of flare-legged jeans. The jewel-necked garment was done in autumn shades of gold and brown that complemented her blond hair. At least, that's what her friends told her. Kendra had donned the sweater mostly so she'd be comfy and warm without having to wear a jacket. She'd certainly not dressed to attract a man's attention.

For some reason she didn't want to analyze, the idea

of attracting a man had her thinking of Dale Dalton. Since he'd come into the bakery to pick up Erica's cupcakes, he'd not returned. Not that she'd expected him to show up again. It had been fairly obvious that he wasn't a bakery-café-type guy. Still, she had to confess that a few times this past week, she'd caught herself glancing around and hoping she might see him walk through the door.

"Oh wow! Look at all those people!" Mila exclaimed. "I'll bet lots of my friends are here. Louisa and Violet said they would be here. Do you think we can find them?"

The park consisted of a wide expanse of lawn area surrounded by tall cedars and thick fir trees with a few hardwoods mixed in. Presently, there were crowds of people milling about the lawn and gathered beneath the trees. At one end of the park, portable tables had been erected to hold food and drinks for anyone who wished to partake. From the looks of things, there were plenty of people piling finger food onto paper plates and filling foam cups with soft drinks.

Kendra reached for Mila's hand just to make sure the girl didn't dash into the crowd ahead of her. "We'll work our way around the park," Kendra told her. "I'm sure we'll run into your friends along the way."

More than a half hour passed before the two of them reached the opposite side of the park. By then, Kendra had spoken with several of her daily bakery customers and a neighbor who lived across the courtyard from her in the same apartment complex. Mila had run into Violet, and the two girls had chatted up a storm until Violet's parents had announced they had to leave.

"Gosh, the picnic is just getting started," Mila complained as she watched her friend disappear into the crowd. "I wanted Violet to stay longer."

"I know you did. But Violet's mom and dad had an important appointment they couldn't miss," Kendra explained. "I'm sure you'll find another friend. Are you getting hungry yet? We could walk over to the refreshment tables."

"Okay. But I'm not hungry yet. Do we have to eat right now?"

"No. We can eat later. But most of the picnic crowd is gathered around the tables. Maybe you'll run into Louisa or some of your other friends over there."

They had almost reached the refreshment area when Mila pulled her mother to a stop and pointed toward another group of people gathered near a stand of tall fir trees. "Mommy, look at that pretty black-and-white dog. Wow, I'd really love to have a dog like him."

"He is very pretty." Kendra gave her an indulgent smile. "What happened to wanting a cat like Morris?"

Her daughter continued to gaze longingly at the energetic dog, which looked to be a border-collie mix. At the moment, the canine was zooming in happy circles around a boy, who appeared to be somewhat older than Mila.

Flashing Kendra an impish grin, she said, "Well, a dog would be good too. But a dog *and* a cat would be the best!"

With a hand on her shoulder, Kendra urged her daughter forward. "That's a pretty tall wish, but we'll see. Come on. Let's walk on and maybe you can get a closer look at the dog."

The two of them were maneuvering through the people scattered across the open lawn when Kendra lifted her gaze to the distance and spotted *him*.

Black cowboy hat, broad shoulders covered with a blue plaid Western shirt and long legs encased in faded denim, he stood out from the rest of the crowd.

Dale Dalton.

What was he doing at a picnic for schoolchildren? More importantly, why was her heart suddenly beating a mile a minute? Other than his name, she hardly knew the man.

Mila must have spotted him too. She stopped in her tracks and pointed in Dale's direction.

"Mommy, there's Dale. The cowboy in the bakery."

Kendra was staring directly at him when he suddenly turned his head and looked straight at them. Did he recognize her and Mila? she wondered. Or had he already forgotten his visit to the bakery?

She didn't have long to wonder as he suddenly lifted a hand to acknowledge them.

"We don't want to talk to him," Mila said and gestured to a spot at the opposite end of the park, where only a handful of people were milling about. "Let's walk down there and sit on a bench."

Since Mila rarely wanted to sit for any reason, Kendra knew she was purposely trying to avoid Dale. It wasn't unusual for her daughter to develop strong opinions about people, but Kendra found it a bit odd that she viewed Dale as a threat to the wedding plans she'd been making for her mother.

Kendra tried to keep her admonishment gentle. "Walking away from a friend who greets you is rude behavior, Mila. What if you waved at Violet and she took off in the opposite direction?"

"I'd be sad. I'd think she didn't like me," Kendra answered.

Hoping Mila was getting the message, she said,

"Okay. We don't want Dale to think we don't like him. So let's go say hello."

Mila hesitated. "Mommy, do you like Dale?"

Even though Kendra was puzzled by her daughter's question, she tried not to show it. "Why, yes, Mila. I do like him. He seems to be a nice guy."

Mila shrugged both shoulders. "I guess he's nice. But he doesn't look anything like my daddy."

Kendra wasn't expecting that sort of thing to come out of her daughter's mouth. Mila hadn't seen her father in a long time. Not since they'd moved to Bronco. Yet, in spite of his neglect, Mila had this fairy-tale image of her father. She often gazed at his photo and talked about how perfect it would be if the three of them were a family again.

The idea sickened Kendra, but she made sure she didn't criticize Bryce in front of her daughter. Mila needed to learn for herself exactly what sort of man her father really was.

"No. Dale doesn't look like your father. He's not supposed to." She gave Mila's hand a little tug. "Come on. Let's go say hello."

Chapter Three

Attending the back-to-school picnic at the Bronco town park had never been something on Dale's to-do list. Especially since he had no children of his own. But this year, Holt and Amanda had invited Dale to join them and their ten-year-old son, Robby. And because he hadn't wanted to let down his nephew, Dale had made an effort to make an appearance at the function.

He'd not planned to spend the whole day at the picnic and had been on the verge of telling Holt he was going to head back to the ranch when he'd spotted Kendra and Mila in the distance.

If Dale had been thinking clearly, he would've already guessed that she and her little girl would be at the picnic today. Now, as he watched the two of them turn and walk in his direction, he was so thrilled he wanted to shout with joy.

When they finally reached him, he encompassed

them both with a friendly smile. "Hello," he greeted. "I wasn't expecting to see you two here today."

Kendra smiled back at him. "We weren't expecting to see you, either."

From the corner of his eye, Dale could see Mila was sizing him up, as if she wasn't quite sure she was in favor of spending any time in his company. The idea annoyed him. Especially when he'd not done one single thing to make the child dislike him. Other than be a cute cowboy, he thought wryly.

After clearing his throat, he said, "Well, I'm here for my little nephew, Robby. The brown-haired boy with the dog. I imagine by now you've seen the two of them running around here somewhere."

"Actually, we have. Mila was infatuated with the dog."

"That's Bentley. He's quite a character," he said, then asked, "How's the bakery business been going?"

Kendra said, "The bakery has been extremely busy. I think the cooler the weather gets, the more people want to eat sweets and drink coffee."

Dale didn't know what it was about this woman, but the moment he'd first spotted her behind the counter, he'd felt extraordinarily close to her and he was getting that same odd feeling today. It made no sense whatsoever.

"The cupcakes were delicious," he told her. "I shouldn't admit it, but I ate all of them except for the two Mom ate."

Her gentle smile was full of appreciation. "I'm glad to hear it."

Dale leveled a friendly smile on the girl. "Hello, Mila. Are you excited about starting school?"

Mila nodded. "Yes. I get to see my friends and learn all kinds of new things. And I got a bunch of new school clothes to wear."

Dale glanced over at Kendra's amused expression.

"You can't leave fashion out of the equation," Kendra explained.

As Dale's gaze swept over Kendra, he thought how she looked as warm and inviting as a fire on a cold night. He could only imagine how it would feel to cuddle her close and have her soft lips pressed to his.

"Mila would probably enjoy spending time with my sister-in-law, Sofia. She's a fashion stylist at BH Couture. Ever shop there?"

"Only occasionally. Whenever I need something sort of fancy to wear. Otherwise, I stick to discount stores in Bronco Valley."

He winked at her. "Smart girl. The discount stuff looks just as good to me. But I'm only a cowboy. I don't know a thing about clothing. Except that my mother enjoys filling her closet. And Dad enjoys giving her the money to do it."

She smiled. "Your father must be a thoughtful man."

Thoughtful? Yeah, Dale thought bitterly. Neal was considerate of his wife's feelings now. But it had taken nearly losing her to teach him a hard lesson. After Deborah had learned her husband had cheated on her, she'd suffered a heart attack and Neal had spent the past several years trying to make the mistake up to her.

"He, uh, I guess you could say he's learned how much his wife means to him." He inclined his head toward Holt and Amanda, who were seated several feet off to their left. "My brother and sister-in-law are Robby's parents. I'd like for you to meet them. Or maybe you already know Holt and Amanda."

"I think I remember seeing Amanda and Robby in the bakery," Kendra admitted. "But I've never actually met them, or Holt."

They began walking over to the seated couple, but

before they reached them, Robby and his border collie raced up to the group.

"Who's your friends, Uncle Dale?"

Dale quickly introduced his nephew to Kendra and Mila.

"Kendra owns Kendra's Cupcakes," Dale told the boy. "Bet you'd like her cupcakes. You should try them. They're yummy."

A thick fringe of brown hair hid the boy's eyebrows as he rolled a pair of blue eyes at his uncle. "Gosh, Uncle Dale, you need to go to town more often. Me and Mom go in the bakery all the time and eat cupcakes."

Dale shot Kendra a helpless look. "I'm always out of the loop. I guess I spend too much time on a horse."

Kendra chuckled, while next to her, Mila let out a squeal of joy as Bentley approached her with a wildly wagging tail.

She looked eagerly at Robby. "Is it okay to pet your dog?"

"Sure. Bentley loves attention," Robby told her. "He won't bite or anything. That why my parents let me bring him to the picnic."

Mila bent down and gave the dog a hug around the neck. In turn, he let out a happy bark and ran excited circles around her.

"I think Bentley has found a new friend," Dale said to Kendra. "Does she like animals?"

"Oh my. *Like* is an understatement. She's been begging me for a dog or cat. And after today my promise to let her have one is going to be even harder to put off much longer."

"When you do decide to get Mila a pet, you might want to consider adopting one from Happy Hearts Animal Sanctuary. Daphne Taylor Cruise owns the place, and she's always looking to find good forever homes for her animals."

Kendra nodded. "That's a nice thought, Dale. I'll do that," she said, then smiled a bit sheepishly. "Whenever I get myself psyched up to take on the added responsibility of caring for an animal."

He flashed her an encouraging smile. "Take it from a man who cares for animals every day of his life. I can promise you, Kendra, the affection they give back to you makes all the extra work worthwhile."

One of her winged eyebrows arched slightly upward. "I'm surprised to hear you say that."

"Why?" he asked wryly. "Didn't you expect me to have pets?"

Since the cool wind had already stung her cheeks with color, it was impossible to tell if the deepening shade of pink was caused by a blush. Either way, she sure was a beauty, Dale thought.

"Coming from South Beach in Florida, I don't know much about ranchers. I understand there are plenty of ranches in the state, but I was never near any. I just assumed you were all about raising livestock. I guess I never thought of you having pets. The image of you cuddling up to a cat or dog never crossed my mind."

"I see. Well, ranchers aren't any different than regular folks. Except we spend most of our time outdoors and do lots of work from the back of a horse."

In spite of the faint smile on her face, Dale got the impression something had flustered her. Him? What had he done? Grinned in a lecherous way? Said a wrong word? He'd not thought so, but women were sensitive creatures. Any little thing could set them off. Or so it seemed to him.

Hell, Dale, why should it matter to you what Kendra

is thinking? It's just like Morgan told you. Kendra isn't your type. Trying to do or say the right thing to her isn't going to win you any favors.

Doing his best to dismiss the pessimistic voice in his head, Dale gestured to his relatives. "Come on. My family is right over here."

She glanced over her shoulder at Mila. The girl was a few feet away, running and romping with Robby and his dog.

Dale said, "She's having fun. I wouldn't bother her with stuffy introductions."

She laughed softly and Dale decided it was a sound he'd like to hear every day of his life.

"You consider introductions stuffy?" she asked.

"I did when I was Mila's age. Especially when I had to stand still and behave politely in front of my elders."

The corners of her lips tilted upward impishly. "You must have been quite a little rounder when you were a child."

He let out a short laugh. "All of us Dalton brothers were little rounders."

"All? How many brothers do you have?"

"There are five of us. I'm second from the youngest, and Holt, who you're about to meet, is second from the eldest."

When they neared Holt and Amanda, the couple rose to their feet and eyed Kendra with friendly curiosity.

Dale quickly introduced her. "This is Kendra Humphrey. She runs Kendra's Cupcakes in Bronco Heights."

"Hello, Kendra. Nice to meet you," Holt greeted, while Amanda tacked on another hello.

Turning to Kendra, he said, "This homely guy is my brother, Holt. And his saint of a wife is Amanda. I call her a saint for putting up with him."

Tall with dark wavy hair and brown eyes, Holt and Dale faintly resembled each other. But as far as their personalities, Holt had turned into a real family man, whereas Dale ran from any woman who mentioned the word *marriage*. Still, the two brothers shared a love of horses and making Dalton's Grange the home their mother deserved.

Holt reached out and gave Kendra's hand a friendly shake. "I should warn you not to listen to Dale. He'll have you believing all of us Daltons are wild guys."

Amanda leveled a pointed look at her husband. "Would he be all wrong?" she joked.

Holt groaned and Dale was glad to see Kendra was taking their teasing banter in stride.

Smiling warmly, Amanda reached for Kendra's hand and gave it a friendly squeeze. "I've seen you working behind the counter at the bakery, but you were always so busy I never had a chance to actually meet you. It's nice to see you again."

Kendra returned the woman's smile. "When we ran into Robby a few moments ago, I thought I recognized him from the bakery."

Raising her hand, she let out a guilty laugh. "Yes. We come in far too often," she admitted. "You make everything far too tempting."

"Thanks for the compliment," Kendra told her, then explained, "I see so many faces in the bakery I can't remember them all, but when I saw Robby and then you my memory clicked."

Dale wasn't sure why Kendra had recognized him among the sea of faces here at the park. But he was thrilled that she'd not only recognized him, but had also agreed to spend these few minutes with him.

"Kendra has a daughter—Mila," Dale told Holt and Amanda. "That's her playing with Robby and Bentley."

"Oh, she's a cutie," Amanda said.

"Mila's only problem is that she's terribly bashful," Dale added, unable to help himself.

Kendra shot him a befuddled look before she burst out laughing.

"Dale is pulling your leg," she said. "Mila never meets a stranger. Unfortunately."

"I wouldn't say that. She might grow up to have an important job in communications," Amanda said.

Kendra darted a glance at Dale. "Well, Mila certainly has a knack for talking. But it's usually at the wrong times."

"Robby is our son," Amanda told her. "He'll be starting fifth grade this year."

"Mila will be a second-grader," Kendra replied.

While the two women continued to discuss the children and the coming school year, Dale remained out of the conversation. But once he caught a short lapse in their talk, he gestured to a park bench a few feet away.

"Would you like to go sit down for a few minutes, Kendra? Looks like Mila is still having a good time with Bentley."

She glanced around to see the children playing fetch with the border collie. Judging by Mila's happy squeals, she was having the time of her life.

"I imagine if I tried to pull her away from that dog right now, I'd never hear the end of it." She gave Dale an agreeable nod. "I suppose I could sit for a few minutes. It's not something I often get to do."

Dale cupped a hand beneath her elbow and internally shouted with triumph when she didn't pull away from his touch. And as they strolled over to the bench, he was struck by the warm scent drifting from her hair and the feel of her arm as it brushed against his.

"It turned out to be great weather for a picnic," he commented. "The wind is a little chilly, but the sun makes up for it."

They reached the bench made of slatted wood and Dale quickly brushed off the seat before she sat on one end.

"It's a lovely day," Kendra agreed. "Mila and I don't get to spend much time outdoors, so it's nice for us to visit the park."

He eased down next to her, but was careful to keep a small space between them. He didn't want to blow this opportunity by giving her the impression he was a wolf in cowboy clothing.

"You don't have a yard where you live?" he asked curiously.

She let out a long sigh. "Yes and no. We live in an apartment complex in Bronco Valley. Everyone's back door opens up to a large courtyard with a lawn. It's better than having no yard at all. But I'd like it better if we didn't have to share it with a dozen other renters. Don't get me wrong. All my neighbors are great people. I like them. But— Well, privacy can be a great thing."

"Sure," he told her. "I'm not sure I could get used to having neighbors living right next to me. If me and my brothers couldn't yell at each other across the ranch yard, it would drive me crazy."

She laughed softly and then her blue gaze momentarily locked with his and Dale's breath lodged in his throat. What was it about this woman that made him feel so connected to her? he wondered. What made being with her feel as if he'd known her all of his life? It made no sense. And if he was being honest with himself, it scared the heck out of him.

She said, "Well, we're fortunate to have any kind of yard and Mila is thrilled that the complex allows pets."

Today her long golden hair had been let loose of its bun to fall freely around her shoulders. Presently, the wind was whipping the silky strands across her face. As Dale watched her fingers tuck the wayward tendrils behind her ears, he was once again surprised to see no engagement or wedding ring.

Morgan had said she was divorced and that was even more difficult for Dale to imagine. Why or how could any man have given up this woman? He must have been the biggest fool to walk the earth, Dale thought. If she was his wife…

Dale's thoughts came to a screeching halt. There was no chance Kendra would ever be his wife! He didn't even want a wife. So why had the idea even entered his head?

"So you're a part of a big family," she said thoughtfully. "I can't imagine having so many siblings. I only have one brother, Sterling. He's a few years younger than me. He lives in South Beach, not far from our parents."

So her parents and brother still lived in Florida, yet she'd chosen to move way out here to Montana. Three thousand miles wasn't a little move, it was a major one. He couldn't imagine her doing such a thing just for a change of scenery. Might her ex have been involved in her decision? he mused.

"You must miss not being around your family."

She shrugged. "I do. But we stay in touch regularly. And like I said, Mila and I love it here. The small town feel of the place is nice and the people are generally friendly and helpful."

"Sound like you've been here in Bronco long enough to make friends and really call the town home," he said.

"A little more than three years. Fortunately, it only took a few days to find the ideal spot for my bakery, so I started the business right after I negotiated the deal for it. And, yes, Bronco is definitely our home now."

He couldn't believe how interested he was in her life. How much he wanted to know every little detail about her. This wasn't his normal MO with an attractive woman. No, he usually skimmed over the personal and got right down to the physical attraction.

"Were you already experienced with bakery work?" he asked. "I'll be honest, other than my mom, I don't know any women who love to bake."

She chuckled. "I've always enjoyed it and always wanted my own business. I had my own bakery in South Beach and it did very well. And so far, Kendra's Cupcakes has been equally successful, for which I'm very grateful. The people around Bronco have been very supportive of my business."

"Hmm. You made quite a change," he remarked. "From the hot sand and the surf to the cool, rugged mountains. I'm glad the move has turned out good for you."

She cast him a curious glance. "Have you always lived in the Bronco area?"

He shook his head. "No. We moved here about five years ago. Another branch of the Dalton family has a ranch over in Rust Creek Falls, about three hundred or so miles from here, but our dad wanted a bigger place to raise cattle and horses. He liked this area, so when he happened to come into a large sum of money, he bought the property that's now Dalton's Grange."

She seemed genuinely interested in his background and the fact gave him a bit hope. Maybe if he got up the nerve to ask her for a date, she wouldn't laugh in his face.

"So you and your brothers were living with your parents back then?" she asked.

He shook his head. "No. We were all kind of scattered around the state, doing our own thing. But when Dad bought Dalton's Grange, he asked for our help and Mom needed us too. So we all decided to move here."

"Do your brothers like living on the ranch?"

Dale let out a wry grunt. "In the beginning we were all a little reluctant to uproot and move here to Bronco. But it didn't take long for the situation to change. See, none of my brothers were married when we first settled on Dalton's Grange. But then Morgan found Erica and they got hitched. And as you've seen, Holt and Amanda are married. Then Boone and Sofia tied the knot. I'd say my brothers are all happy about the move here—now."

Her smile was thoughtful. "What about you and your single brother? You don't have the urge to take a wife?"

Dale very nearly squirmed, but somehow he managed to keep his ankles crossed casually in front of him.

With an awkward chuckle, he said, "I can't speak for Shep. Except that he's twenty-nine and thinks he's way too young to take on a wife."

"And you?"

His laugh this time was worse than awkward. It sounded more like a painful gurgle.

"I guess I never met a woman who'd be willing to take me on a permanent basis," he said, attempting a joke. "You know the old saying about bachelors. It's hard to change a man who's already set in his ways."

"I hope a woman never changes you, Dale," she said gently. "That would be a shame."

Momentarily stunned by her remark, he stared at her. "A shame? Really?"

Her smile deepened, and then to his great surprise, she reached over and softly laid her hand over the back of his. The touch was as soft as a dove's wing and he tried not to think of how it might feel to have her hand gliding over his body.

"I like you just as you are," she said gently.

Dale's chest swelled to the point that he feared the snaps on the front of his shirt were going to pop wide open.

"That's, uh, nice of you, Kendra. And in case you haven't noticed, I like you too."

"Thank you, Dale. A person can't have too many friends."

He was thinking he could sit on this park bench with her for hours and still not want to move when Mila suddenly came trotting up to them.

Dale couldn't help but notice how the girl's keen gaze went straight to her mother's hand resting atop his.

"Did you get tired of playing with Bentley?" Kendra asked her.

Mila grimaced. "No. But Robby left to go find his friend and Bentley went with him."

Kendra slowly eased her hand from Dale's and he was immediately struck by the loss of connection.

"Well, we'll go look for Louisa in a minute or two," Kendra told her daughter. "She might have brought her dog with her."

Mila sidled closer to her mother's knee and Dale could see she was weighing the situation carefully. Obviously, the girl wasn't accustomed to seeing Kendra sitting next to a man. At least, not as close as she was to Dale's side.

"She won't have Samson with her, 'cause her parents told her she couldn't bring him to the picnic." She purposely clamped her hand around Kendra's wrist. "But we should walk around, Mommy, and talk to some other people. If we see Mr. Drake he might ask you for another date." She looked directly at Dale. "He's one of the nicest teachers at school."

So Mila was trying to make sure Dale knew he had competition. He had to admit the girl was far from bratty, but underneath her polite manners, there was a wily little mind at work.

Kendra let out a groan of frustration.

"This Mr. Drake must not be a cute cowboy," Dale said to the girl.

Mila looked properly offended. "Of course, he's not a cowboy. He's a teacher."

Dale looked at Kendra and winked. "Guess a guy can't be both things at once."

Groaning again, Kendra shook her head. "Mr. Drake is just a casual friend and that's all he'll ever be." She leveled a pointed look at her daughter. "Remember what we talked about this morning while we were getting ready to come to the park?"

Scuffing her toe on the ground, Mila met her mother's disapproving gaze. "Yes. You said we weren't going to the picnic to hunt a boyfriend. And I'm not supposed to ask any man questions about being married or having kids."

Mila hardly sounded apologetic. But Dale figured the girl didn't believe she was doing anything to be sorry about.

Kendra nodded. "You do remember. So why are you saying such things about Mr. Drake?"

Mila glanced innocently at Dale, then back to her mother. "Well, this is a school picnic and Mr. Drake is a teacher. And lots of teachers are here."

With a hopeless sigh, Kendra rose to her feet. "Looks like it's time Mila and I move on," she said to Dale. "I'll go say goodbye to your brother and sister-in-law."

Dale realized he'd been lucky just to garner this much of Kendra's time. But that didn't stop a wave of disappointment from washing over him.

Rising from the bench, he cupped a hand beneath her elbow. "I'll walk you over."

Once she'd said her goodbyes to Holt and Amanda, she turned a faint smile on Dale.

"Goodbye, Dale. Maybe we'll see each other again sometime."

Maybe? Sometime? Dale was so busy wondering how soon he could walk back into Kendra's Cupcakes without looking like an eager fool that his tongue suddenly forgot how to work.

Finally, he managed a reply. "Yeah. See you around, Kendra."

She walked off with Mila in tow. Behind him, Holt chuckled.

"That was some real cool maneuvering, brother. 'See you around?' Was that the best you could do?"

As he glanced at his brother, Dale could feel his face turning red. "Look, Holt, I can't be Mr. Cool all the time. Besides, Kendra is different. She's not the sort to appreciate a glib line."

Holt exchanged a pointed glance with his wife before he turned an amused grin on Dale.

"Yes. We can see Kendra is *very* different."

Chapter Four

Darkness had already fallen when Dale finally parked his truck in the Dalton's Grange ranch yard. After a hard day of fence building in the warm sun, the night had turned cold. Now the brisk wind penetrating his denim shirt drew his eyes up to the chimney on the sprawling rock-and-log structure he called home. With no sign of smoke, he supposed his father had been too busy to build a fire in the fireplace.

Do you and your brothers like living on the ranch?

The question Kendra had posed to him during the school picnic drifted through Dale's mind once again as he slowly walked to the back of the big ranch house.

Dale realized he'd given her a pared-down answer. He hadn't explained that since his three brothers had married, they'd moved into their own houses on Dalton's Grange. Dale and Shep were the only brothers still residing in the ranch house with their parents. Nor had he told her how all five brothers had frowned upon going into the ranching business with their father. Admitting that tidbit of truth would have required him to explain why, and he wasn't quite ready to talk to Kendra about his father's infidelity. He hardly wanted her thinking like father, like son.

Actually, the only reason Dale and his brothers had agreed to move to Bronco and throw their efforts into building Dalton's Grange was because of the deep love they all had for their mother. At that time, Deborah's health had been fragile and, for her sake, Dale and his siblings had felt like they needed to show a united front. As a result, she now had the home she'd always wanted, and thankfully, their father had kept his promise and turned over a new and better leaf.

At the back of the house, Dale crossed the porch and entered a door that led directly into the kitchen. Except for his mother, who was busy at the counter putting leftovers from the evening meal into plastic containers, the room was empty.

She glanced over her at him as he hung his hat on a peg by the door. "I'm glad you're home. I was beginning to worry."

He walked over and planted a kiss on her cheek. "Now why would you worry about me? I'm too mean to get hurt."

"Ha! There isn't a mean bone in your body. Not since you grew past the age of thirteen," she teased, then asked, "Neal said you and Shep were fencing all day. Is that why you were late getting back to the ranch?"

"Yes. We had to finish one section before we could let the cattle back into the pasture. And Dad has decided to replace more cross fence than he'd first planned."

Deborah shook her head. "I told Neal he should hire a fencing crew instead of putting the load on you and

Shep. It's very nearly fall roundup time. You two need to be getting ready for that job."

"Fence builders are an expensive luxury," he told her. "It isn't going to hurt me and Shep to work until dark."

He peered over her shoulder at the food she'd put into a large container. "Is that Swiss steak? Smells like it."

She flashed a smile at him. "It is. And since your dad and I are the only ones who've eaten, there's plenty left of everything. Want me to fill a plate for you before I put everything in the fridge?"

In her early sixties, his mother was still an attractive woman with a slender build and blond hair worn in a smooth bob. At one time, before she'd met Neal, she'd had a job in the corporate world. But most of her adult life had been spent as a wife and mother to her five sons. If Dale ever did get the crazy notion to look for a wife, he'd want one as loving and devoted as Deborah had been to Neal. But finding a needle in a haystack would be easier than finding that kind of love and devotion, Dale thought.

"I'd appreciate it, Mom. But I can take care of myself. You go sit down with Dad or whatever you need to do."

"Neal is in his study. Talking on the phone with a cattle broker."

"Oh? Buying or selling?" Dale asked.

Deborah chuckled. "Buying, of course. Your father is always thinking in bigger terms. But he promises not to make any deals without all of you boys involved first." She made a shooing gesture with her hand. "Go on and wash. I'll take care of heating your supper."

Dale went to the mudroom, which was located just off the kitchen. After using the deep double sink to wash his hands and face, he returned to find his mother had already placed the warmed plate of food on the table, along with a long-necked bottle of beer.

"You're an angel, Mom. Thanks."

"Just doing my job." She carried salt and pepper shakers over to the table and took a seat in the chair opposite his.

Even though his mother had once had a promising career in business, Dale supposed being a mother had become the most important thing in Deborah's life. She'd always put all of her energy into caring for her husband and children. As a mother, she'd never been overly strict. But she'd not let any of her boys go unpunished if they crossed the boundaries of right and wrong.

The thought made him wonder about Kendra and the relationship she had with Mila. He supposed if it came right down to it, Kendra would choose her daughter's happiness over her own. Never being a parent himself, Dale was hardly in a position to know whether that was good or bad. But it made him wonder how Kendra could possibly find a man to love if she allowed Mila to dictate her life.

He glanced at his mother. "Speaking of Shep, has he shown up tonight? Earlier this afternoon, he left the area we were fencing to go into town after more supplies."

She said, "He stopped by the house to change his dirty shirt for a clean one and told me he'd grab a burger or something in town. I don't think he's gotten back from Bronco yet."

"Probably ran into a girlfriend." And if that was the case, he most likely wouldn't be back to Dalton's Grange until the wee hours of the morning, but his mother didn't need to be reminded of her sons' carousing ways. At least, not her single sons. Although, Dale had to admit it had been a while since he'd even gone on a date. For some reason, the idea of calling up one of his old girlfriends for a night out on the town just didn't hold any appeal. Not since he'd met Kendra.

Damn. Was he turning into a sap, or what?

Deborah rested her chin on the heel of her palm as she slanted Dale a thoughtful look. "Son, there's something I've been wanting to talk to you about."

He shoveled up a forkful of the smothered steak. "Okay, shoot, Mom."

"It's about all those cupcakes you've been bringing home from town. I think it's extra nice of you to want to save me from baking, but, Dale, we can't possibly eat all of them. I'm going to have to freeze that last bunch you brought in yesterday and save them for later."

Dale felt his cheeks growing warm. Since the picnic in the park, he'd visited the bakery a couple of times. Once on Monday morning, when he'd run an errand in town for his father, and last evening after making a trip to the feed store for vet supplies. And during each visit, he'd purchased two dozen cupcakes in assorted flavors.

"Sorry, Mom. I guess I didn't realize just how many I'd been buying."

She reached over and patted his arm. "Honestly, Dale, I'm surprised that you've been bothering to stop by a bakery. I've never known you to be so into cupcakes."

He downed a few swallows of beer, then gave her a lopsided grin. "Okay, Mom. I need to fess up. I've been stopping by Kendra's Cupcakes. And I had to buy something or I'd look like a jerk or worse. Because—Well, the woman who runs the bakery—she's really special. And I'd like to get to know her better."

Deborah's eyebrows arched with faint surprise. "You mean you'd like to ask her for a date?"

"Exactly. But I'm not sure— Heck, Mom, I'm afraid if I do ask her, she'll turn me down."

Frowning, she studied him for a thoughtful moment. "This isn't like you, Dale. You've never exactly lacked self-confidence."

"No. But Kendra is different. She's been married before and she has a seven-year-old daughter. And the child thinks I'm all wrong for her mother."

Deborah continued to frown. "How do you know the child thinks that about you?"

"Because she told me directly to my face."

She shook her head with wry amusement. "Nothing like the honesty of a child. But, Dale, I wouldn't worry about what the child thinks. If you believe you have a chance with Kendra, then go ahead and ask her for a date. The worst she can do is say no."

Dale reached for his beer. "Yeah, but once she says no that might be the only answer she'll ever give me."

"The way I see things, Dale, if she's not smart enough to see what a great guy you are, then you need to find a gal who does."

"I don't want to find anyone else."

The admission was out of him before he could stop the words, and from the look on his mother's face, he could see she was somewhat surprised.

"I'm curious now," she said. "Is this woman from around here?"

Dale continued to eat. It was easier to keep his eyes on his food than to deal with his mother's searching gaze.

"She moved here a little over three years ago from South Beach, Florida."

"Hmm. Quite a switch from there to here. What made her come to Bronco? Does she have relatives here?"

"No. She just wanted a change, I think. Although, I wonder...well, I wonder if—"

"She's running away from something?" Deborah asked, finishing for him.

He didn't know how his mother managed to do it, but she always seemed to be able to put her finger right on the spot that was itching.

"Sort of," he admitted. "I've only talked to her a couple of times. Mostly when I went to the school picnic with Holt and Amanda. She never mentioned she wanted to get away from her ex or anything. But I keep asking myself why she'd need to move three thousand miles. And maybe none of that should matter."

"You know, I think what you just said makes the most sense. If you like this woman, then none of that should matter. She'll share things about her life with you eventually."

"You mean, if she agrees to date me?"

Smiling, Deborah gave his arm another pat. "I'd be very surprised if she turned you down. But, Dale, I don't think you should keep buying cupcakes to impress her." She flashed him a smile. "Maybe next time spend your money on a few maple bars or apple fritters for a change."

Dale chuckled. "Good advice, Mom."

The next evening, as closing time was drawing near, Kendra was getting ready to package the unsold cupcakes when the door chimed and she looked up to see Dale entering the bakery.

This was the third visit he'd made to Kendra's Cupcakes this week and she had to admit that each time she saw him she was thrilled just a little more. Now, as she gazed at his smiling face, something snapped inside her and she suddenly felt as soft and gooey as the inside of a chocolate bismarck.

"Hi, Dale. You're out late this evening."

He glanced at the clock hanging on the wall behind the checkout counter. "Oh. Are you about to close?"

"I've sent my barista home and Andrea has left. You're the only customer I've had in the last thirty minutes. In fact, I was about to lock the door and help Jackie with the cleaning."

He looked totally crestfallen and she couldn't help but laugh. "Don't worry. I'll lock you inside and let you out whenever you're ready to leave."

He chuckled. "So in other words I won't be held captive?"

"Not against your will." With a light laugh, she gestured over to the empty tables and chairs. "Would you like to sit down and have a cup of coffee? I'll make us a fresh cup and there are plenty of leftover goodies."

A wide grin dimpled his cheeks. "Sounds great. Thanks."

She grabbed her keys from under the checkout counter, then went to the front door. As she locked it, she said, "Sit at any table you'd like. They've all been wiped down. What would you like to eat? A cupcake?"

His chuckle held a sheepish sound. "No. I think I'll go for something different. Other than cupcakes, what's your specialty?"

"Well, I like to think everything I serve tastes good. So I'll just surprise you," she told him. "Make yourself comfortable and I'll be back in a couple of minutes."

As Dale took a seat, Kendra hurried to the kitchen. Jackie was already starting her nightly cleaning routine by washing the empty display trays. She shot Kendra a puzzled look when she saw her making coffee at the pod machine they used for their personal use in the kitchen.

"I thought you were going to lock the door."

"The door is locked. But I have one customer I've invited to have coffee."

Jackie's expression turned shrewd. "Dale Dalton?"

Kendra smiled. "How did you guess?"

Jackie rolled her eyes. "Let me see. The cowboy has been here three times this week. And I don't think he's showing up because he has a sweet tooth."

Kendra wasn't going to argue Jackie's point. She was beginning to believe Dale had developed a crush on her and the notion made her so ridiculously happy, she felt like laughing and crying at the same time.

"I think you're right, Jackie. And you know what— it feels good to have a guy like him look at me like I'm an angel."

Jackie sighed. "Maybe one of these days I'll discover how it feels to have a hunky cowboy look at me like I'm something special. But for now, I'm just glad Mila is at the sitter's. Otherwise, she'd be wedged between the two of you."

Kendra groaned. "Don't remind me."

Carrying the two coffees, she headed out of the kitchen and paused at the display cases long enough to place the cups and several bakery items on a serving tray.

When she approached the table where he was sitting, he immediately rose and pulled out a chair for her. "You're making me feel special, Kendra. Or do you often do this for cowboys you feel sorry for?"

The idea that he thought she probably had lots of suitors was a compliment, she supposed. Yet, the notion of her having the time or inclination to flirt with male customers was laughable.

What do you think you're doing now, Kendra? Aren't you flirting with Dale?

Doing her best to ignore the provocative questions swirling through her mind, she placed the tray on the table.

"Actually, I don't do this sort of thing, period," she told him. "And what makes you think I might feel sorry for a big strong guy like you?"

His low chuckle was more like a purr. "Maybe because I look like a lost and lonely pup," he joked.

He was standing directly behind her with his hands resting on the back of her chair, yet she could easily imagine their warmth curling around her shoulders, drawing her closer.

Her throat suddenly tightened, forcing her to swallow before she spoke. "Are you always so funny?"

He moved around the table and took the chair opposite hers. "Believe it or not, I have my serious moments. But my motto is that life is mostly meant to be enjoyed. I like to laugh and be happy. Don't you?"

She handed one of the coffees to him, then poured a dollop of cream into her own cup and slowly stirred the steaming liquid.

"Sure. Sometimes it's not always easy to put on a happy face, but I try. Especially for Mila's sake." She pushed a brownie topped with chopped walnuts toward him. "If you like chocolate, try a bite of this."

He bit into the brownie and as Kendra watched him chew, she couldn't help but think how different he was from her ex-husband. Bryce considered roughing it in the outdoors to be playing eighteen holes of golf. The man handled little more than an ink pen, a cell phone and the keyboard of a computer. Whereas Dale worked in the harsh elements. His hands were tough and strong from handling ropes and saddle leathers. He nurtured the land and the animals on it, because it was something he loved, instead of a means to make money.

Yes, Dale was different in the best kind of way, Kendra thought. But would he be best for her?

"Mmm. This is delicious," Dale commented after he'd swallowed a couple of bites of the brownie. "Mom was right when she told me I needed to buy more than just cupcakes."

Kendra slanted him a quizzical look. "Your mother told you that?"

His grin was sheepish. "She thought I was overdoing things with all the cupcakes. Guess I'm a little too obvious, huh?"

Kendra couldn't explain the attraction she felt toward Dale. Over the years, she'd been around good-looking men with plenty of sex appeal, but none of them had left an impression on her. Not the way Dale had firmly stuck in her mind.

"To tell you the truth, I'm enjoying you being obvious."

He blew out a heavy breath. "Whew! That's a relief."

She could have told him she was completely endeared by his effort to spend a few minutes with her. She could confess how each day this week, she'd watched for him to walk through the door. And then she'd be the one looking totally obvious.

But suddenly none of that mattered, and before she could analyze what she was about to do, she reached across the table and placed her hand over his. "I think you're very nice, Dale. And I'm wondering if you'd like for us to go out one evening? Maybe have a burger or pizza together?"

His blue eyes stared at her in complete fascination. "Are you serious?"

Her fingers tightened around his hand and just like the day in the park, it felt good to touch him. It felt right to be connected to him even in this simple way.

"Absolutely, I'm serious," she answered. "Why? You don't think you'd like to go out with me?"

He opened his mouth to speak, but when nothing came out, he turned his head to one side and coughed. After clearing his throat a second time, he said, "Sorry. I promise I'm not coming down with the flu. You shocked me, that's all. I was thinking— Well, I've been wanting to get up enough nerve to ask you for a date. But I thought you'd probably turn me down."

At some point since she'd met this man, she'd memorized everything about his features. The stubborn jut to his chin, the faint lines fanning from the corners of his eyes, the deep grooves in his cheeks whenever he smiled and the sparkle in his vivid blue gaze. His was a face to remember.

"Why would you think such a thing? I haven't been cold or distant, have I?"

His short laugh was a sound of disbelief. "Not at all. But I'm just a cowboy. And you're beautiful and successful and, well, Mila doesn't exactly consider me Mr. Right for her mother."

He could never guess just how much his unassuming attitude drew her to him. Yet she wanted him to know he was just as good, or better, than any man she'd ever met.

"Listen, Dale, Mila is a child. She doesn't pick my friends. Furthermore, don't ever call yourself *just a cowboy*. Your job is as admirable and as important as mine, or anyone's." She leaned slightly toward him. "So what's your answer about the date?"

His hand shifted beneath hers and then his fingers were sliding intimately between hers. The contact sent a flood of heat up her arm and straight to her face. The gentle touch also filled her with an odd sense of belonging.

"Would it embarrass you if I stuck my head out the door and let out a happy howl?" he asked.

Smiling, she gestured toward the door. "Be my guest. If anyone happens to be walking by, they'll just think you've eaten one of my special 'happy' cupcakes."

His skeptical expression made her chuckle.

"You make 'happy' cupcakes?" he asked. "What sort of magic ingredient do they have in them? Bourbon? Rum?"

"I was only teasing about the cupcakes," she confessed. "But I'm glad I made you happy."

His blue eyes sparkling, he asked, "So when would you like to go on this date? Is tomorrow night too soon?"

She pretended to ponder his question for a moment before she answered. "Let's see, tomorrow is Saturday. The bakery is closed on Sunday and Mila doesn't have to go to school. I think tomorrow night would be perfect. Will that fit in with your schedule?"

The grin he gave her very nearly melted her bones. And for a split second she wondered if going out with Dale might be worse than playing with fire. On the other hand, why should she be concerned about getting her wings scorched? She wasn't going to allow herself to get close enough to the man to risk getting burned.

"No worries. I'll make it fit." Reaching inside the front of his jacket, he pulled out a cell phone. "I'd better put your address in my phone so I won't forget it."

He punched in her private cell number, along with her address, and was slipping the phone back into his jacket when the sound of the kitchen door opening caught their attention.

"Don't mind me," Jackie sang out. "I'm only going to pack up the leftovers."

Kendra glanced at the clock and was shocked to see she'd been sitting here with Dale much longer than she'd thought.

"I didn't know it was so late," she told Jackie. "But there's no need for you to deal with the leftovers. I'll take care of them later."

Jackie continued to pull out the trays of unpurchased pastries. "Finish your coffee, Kendra, and let me take care of this. The nursing home is expecting me in about thirty minutes. A patient is having a birthday and the staff wants to treat her with special refreshments."

Sizing up the situation, Dale gulped down the last of his coffee, then rose to his feet. "I'm keeping you from your work."

"There's really no need for you to rush off," Kendra told him. "And you haven't finished your brownie."

He winked at her. "I'll take it with me. I have chores waiting on me at the ranch. And it's past your closing time. We'll talk tomorrow night."

Disappointed, but doing her best not to show it, she stood and gathered what was left of his brownie and the other desserts he'd not yet sampled. "Okay. Give me a minute and I'll put these in a container for you."

Kendra walked behind the display counters and over to a wall of storage cabinets. As she fished a foam box from a shelf, Jackie sidled up to her and silently mouthed, *I'm sorry.*

Shaking her head, Kendra said under her breath, "Don't be."

After Kendra put Dale's treats in the take-out box, she walked over to where he was waiting for her to unlock the door.

When she handed him the container, he said, "This feels too heavy."

"I added a few more brownies—for your mother," she explained.

He gave her a grateful smile. "Thanks. I'll be sure and let her know you sent them to her." He pushed the door partially open with his shoulder, then paused. "I'll see you tomorrow. Six thirty okay?"

The very thought of being alone with Dale sent a silly little thrill rushing through her. "I'll be ready. Goodbye for now."

He lifted a hand in farewell, then slipped out the door. Kendra didn't linger to watch him leave. As soon as she carefully locked the door behind him, she hurried over to where Jackie was still working to clear the trays.

The redhead cast a rueful grin at Kendra. "I'm so sorry, Kendra. I didn't mean to interrupt your coffee date, but I had to come out here and get these things."

"Don't be silly," Kendra told her. "You're only doing what you're supposed to be doing."

Jackie waggled her eyebrows in a suggestive way. "So how did your coffee with the cowboy go? From what I could see, you two were looking extra chummy."

Kendra couldn't stop a smug grin from crossing her face. "We're going on a date tomorrow night."

"Oh. So he finally decided to ask you out," Jackie said as she hurriedly placed the last of the maple bars into a cardboard box. "That's great, Kendra."

"Before you get the wrong idea," Kendra said, "Dale didn't do the asking. I did."

Jackie gasped and whirled around to stare at her. "*You?* Pardon me if I faint! What's come over you, Kendra?"

If anyone knew how hard Kendra worked at the bakery, and how rarely she took time off for any kind of entertainment, it was Jackie. The young woman also knew how Kendra had become gun-shy of dating and how mistrustful she'd grown of men since her divorce from Bryce.

"Honestly, I can't explain it," Kendra told her. "Something about the man gets to me. And when I talk with him, he, uh, well, he seems very sincere."

Jackie tapped a forefinger against her chin. "In other words, you don't think he's faking his niceness?"

She shrugged. "I'll admit I don't know much about him—yet. Mila keeps telling me that Dale isn't my type. And maybe she's right. Heaven knows, she's been right about people before. But I need to find out for myself if he's all wrong for me."

"Sure," Jackie said slyly. "After all, there's nothing wrong in having a little fun while you're getting to know the man."

Kendra wasn't looking for fun with Dale. Nor was she searching for everlasting love from the sexy cowboy. She simply wanted to feel like a desirable woman again without having to worry about commitments or promises.

"I'm not sure I remember how to have fun with a man, Jackie. And there's something else about this date that I'm a bit concerned about."

"Oh? What's that? You're wondering what to wear?"

Kendra rolled her eyes toward the ceiling. "I wish that was my only concern."

Jackie picked up the large box of baked goods she'd gathered for the nursing home, then she turned a knowing look on Kendra.

"Mila?" she asked.

Kendra nodded as she tried to imagine the look on

Mila's face when she heard her mother was going on a date with Dale Dalton.

"Yes, Mila." Kendra sighed. "She tells anyone who'll listen that I'm going to get married and give her a daddy. And I keep telling her it's not that easy."

"So? You don't think Dale would make Mila a good daddy?"

Kendra's mouth fell open, and laughing, Jackie hurried out the door.

But later, as Kendra finished closing up and turning off the lights, she thought once again about Jackie's loaded question.

When Dale had talked about his three brothers finding wives and making families of their own, he'd not exactly stated he was against the idea for himself. But he'd implied he was perfectly happy as a bachelor.

Which meant their time together tomorrow night would be nothing more than fun and laughs. But that was just fine with her. In spite of what Mila was broadcasting to all their friends, Kendra wasn't looking for a husband. So she and Dale should make the perfect match.

Chapter Five

The next evening, Dale was walking across the ranch yard to his truck when Morgan stepped out of the barn and intercepted him.

"Look at you! What sort of fancy shindig is going on in Bronco tonight? Erica hasn't mentioned anything. And you're too dressed up for having a few beers at Doug's bar."

"No fancy shindig. And I'm not headed to Doug's." Dale self-consciously glanced down at his dark jeans and Western-cut leather jacket. "Do I look overly dressed?"

Morgan pushed the brim of his hat back just a fraction as he gave Dale a closer inspection. "You haven't told me where you're going yet."

"Do I have to?"

"No. You don't have to tell me anything." Grinning, he lifted a hand in a wave, then started walking in the direction of the house. "See you later."

Dale trotted after him. "Okay. I might as well tell you. Most likely you'll hear about it, anyway."

Morgan turned and arched his eyebrows. "You've got me curious now."

Dale tapped a finger against the brim of his black hat. It wasn't exactly a new one, but he only pulled it out for special occasions. Now, with Morgan raking him over with a keen eye, he was beginning to feel like a fool.

"You think the hat looks a bit too much for a casual date?" he asked.

"The hat looks like you've never done a day's work in your life. So who's the gal you're trying so hard to impress?"

Dale wanted to puff his chest out, but he didn't. "Kendra Humphrey. You remember, the baker I asked you about?"

Morgan was clearly surprised. "You asked *her* for a date and she accepted? Man, I never would've thought she'd agree to go out with you." He held up a hand before Dale could take offense. "Not that there's anything wrong with you. But she's a city girl. And—"

"Yeah. And I'm hayseed. But maybe she's getting into organic things," Dale joked. "Anyway, you have it all wrong, brother. Kendra is the one who asked me for a date. Not the other way around."

Morgan playfully swatted Dale's arm. "Since when have you started lying to your brother?"

Dale used his finger to make a cross over his heart. "If I'm lyin', I'm dyin'. But I'll tell you, Morgan, I nearly fell out of my chair when she asked me."

Morgan shrugged. "Well, if she's not concerned about dating a confirmed bachelor, then who am I to worry about either one of you. Go and have fun."

"Thanks, Morgan. And for what it's worth, I wouldn't ever want to do anything to hurt Kendra."

"I believe you," he said. "Now, I'd better go say good-night to Mom and Dad and head on home before Erica gets out of bed and tries to fix supper."

"I haven't had a chance to ask you today, but how is she?"

Morgan made an okay sign with his thumb and fore-finger. "So far, so good. Keep her and the baby in your prayers, will you?"

"Always, brother."

Minutes later, after Dale had climbed into his truck and headed to town, he wasn't just thinking about Morgan and his unborn child, he was also thinking about Kendra. If she was carrying Dale's child and the pregnancy was at risk, he'd be crazy with fear. He'd be worried about the wife he loved. He'd be frantic for the baby. A baby he would very much want to love and nurture and see grow into an adult.

But by the time he was entering Bronco city limits, he realized there wasn't any need for him to be mulling over such serious matters. Especially tonight. He and Kendra were simply going to enjoy each other's company. He'd leave the serious stuff to his married brothers.

Kendra gave her hair a final brush before she pinned one side back with a tortoiseshell barrette, then stepped back to carefully study her image in the dresser mirror.

Her dress was made of cotton material printed with tiny brown, gold and orange flowers. The bodice was fitted, while a full, tiered skirt floated over her brown suede boots. She'd fastened tiny silver-dove earrings to her ears, but that was the only jewelry she'd chosen to wear. After all, they were only going out for a burger or pizza. She didn't want Dale to think she was overdoing her appearance.

Satisfied that she looked decent, she walked over to the closet and pulled out a jean jacket when the doorbell rang.

Her heart thumping with eager excitement, she tossed the garment over her arm and hurried out to the living room to answer the ring.

After a quick peek through the peephole, she opened the door to find Dale standing on the small portico with his hat in his hand and a wide smile on his face.

"Hi, Dale. Please come in. I'm almost ready. Did you have any trouble finding the apartment complex?"

He stepped across the threshold and stood to one side while she closed the door behind him.

"No trouble at all," he told her. "The navigation system on my truck makes me feel like a genius."

He followed her out of the short foyer and into the living room, where Kendra turned a smile on him. "You should feel like a genius, Dale. I can't figure how to work the system in my vehicle. If I followed its directions, I'd end up in Wyoming or Idaho."

Her admission drew a chuckle out of him, but the amusement quickly fell from his face as his gaze swept over her.

"Wow, Kendra. You look too pretty tonight."

The compliment thrilled her and Kendra wondered if she'd reverted back to her teenage days, when the attention of a cool guy had left her sighing. She was being ridiculous. But just for tonight, it felt oh, so nice to feel young and desirable.

"You look pretty spiffy yourself," she told him.

On all the occasions Kendra had seen Dale, his

jeans had been extremely faded and work-worn with frayed hems. Tonight they were dark without any rips or strings, and his black hat, which was normally dusty and sweat-stained, looked so clean it could've been new.

"Thanks," he said. "Mom always told us boys that the best way to impress a girl is to show her you can clean up good. So I tried."

"You've done very well," she told him, then gestured around the living room that was simply furnished with a long burgundy-colored couch, two matching armchairs and a TV. "This is my little home. Would you care to see the rest of it?"

"Sure. From what I can see of this room you're a tidy housekeeper."

"I have you fooled," she said with a wry groan, then motioned for him to follow her through an open doorway. "Don't swipe your fingers over the coffee or end tables. They're probably dustier than one of your cattle pens."

They crossed a short empty space and through another doorway to the kitchen. The long, narrow room was outfitted with stainless-steel appliances and a work island in the middle. A large window over the sink revealed a view of the courtyard in back.

"This is where I do more baking. Whenever I'm not at the bakery." She gestured to their left, to the open space beyond a breakfast bar. "That's the dining room over there. But since it's just the two of us. Mila and I usually eat at the breakfast bar."

"This is cozy," he told her. "Mom would love this kitchen. She wouldn't have to walk her legs off to get from the stove to the fridge."

She said, "I've never seen Dalton's Grange, or your parents' ranch house, but compared to it, I imagine this apartment looks like a dollhouse."

"Originally, Dad built the ranch house on Dalton's Grange large enough to house his five sons, so, yeah, it's huge. But you have plenty of space for just you and Mila."

"Yes. But you're not counting the fact that it often feels as though Mila is the same as having three daughters."

He chuckled and she motioned for him to follow her out of the kitchen and into a hallway.

"Two bedrooms and two baths are down that way. I'd show them to you, but they're a bit messy. It's been a hectic week," she explained, then added, "Maybe the next time you're here I'll have them tidy enough for you to see. And when we have more time I'll show you out back. That is, if you—" She broke off as it suddenly dawned on her that she was chattering like a parakeet. She was also assuming that Dale would want a next time with her.

"If I what?" he prompted her to finish.

Her cheeks grew warm as she met his inquisitive gaze. "Sorry, Dale. I was getting a little ahead of myself. Are you ready to go?"

"Whenever you're ready," he replied.

He came to stand by her side and Kendra was reminded of the fact that they were completely alone, and he was looking at her the way a man looked at a woman he found attractive. Or was she imagining the faint glint in his blue eyes? Either way, he was shaking up her senses.

"Is Mila not here? I thought I'd say hello before we left."

"She's at the sitter's house. Which, lucky for me, is only four doors down from mine. I've been friends with Ada since we first moved here, so when Mila is with her, I don't worry."

"Oh, I assumed you probably had a sitter stay here with her." He leveled a rueful look at her. "But I guess it's probably best she isn't here. I don't imagine she was too happy about you going out with me tonight."

"Actually, Mila didn't put up a fuss at all. Probably because I promised her a trip to Happy Hearts in a week or two. Next to having a father in her life, the thing she wants the most is a dog or cat to call her own. And, anyway, she doesn't believe you're anything to worry about."

He let out a short laugh. "She knows how to make a guy feel really important."

They moved back into the living room where Kendra slipped on her jean jacket and picked up her purse from a console table.

As the two of them migrated to the front door, Kendra said, "You'll have to overlook her, Dale. She hasn't seen her father since a little before her fourth birthday and I think her memory of him is somewhat blurred. In her mind, she has the image of a perfect father. But you and I know there isn't such a thing. My father has been a wonderful parent, but even he makes mistakes."

He grimaced. "My dad has been far from perfect. But he tries. And he loves his family. In the end that's what matters the most, I think."

She stifled a snort. She could explain to Dale how Bryce hadn't even acknowledged his shortcomings, much less tried to make amends with his daughter. But this first date with him was hardly the time to spotlight her failed marriage.

Outside, Kendra locked the door to her apartment, and as they walked to his truck, he rested a hand against the small of her back. The night had turned chilly and a canopy of stars stretched above their heads.

She didn't know if it was walking so close to his side, or something about the velvety sky that was making her feel unusually romantic. But for one wild second, Kendra wished he would pull her into his arms and kiss her.

The urge was unlike anything she'd ever felt and caused her to wonder if she could restrain herself around this good-looking cowboy.

Why would you want to, Kendra? Don't you think you've gone long enough without a man's physical affection?

By the time he'd helped her into the truck and he'd driven out of the parking lot, she'd pushed the taunting voice out of her head. But not the desire to be close to him. She wasn't quite sure how she could get rid of that feeling.

After a short discussion about what they wanted to eat, Dale and Kendra ended up choosing Bronco Brick Oven Pizza, a small, family-owned pizza parlor located in Bronco Heights, not far from Kendra's Cupcakes.

After turning in their order, they took a seat at one of the small square tables.

When the owner, who also served as a waiter, arrived with their drinks, he placed a fat white candle in the middle of the table and stuck a burning match to the wick.

"There you go, Kendra. Candlelight for a lovely lady."

"How thoughtful of you, Mr. Leone. Thank you."

The older gentleman with curly salt-and-pepper hair smiled with approval as his gaze encompassed the two of them. "It's nice to see you with a companion, Kendra."

Dale noticed a blush bloom upon her cheeks and he couldn't help thinking how lovely she looked with a soft pink color on her lips and her hair curved gently upon her shoulders.

Smiling at the man, Kendra gestured to Dale. "Mr. Leone, I'd like for you to meet Dale Dalton. His family owns Dalton's Grange."

The barrel-chested man reached out and shook Dale's hand. "Oh, yes, I've heard of the ranch. Maybe you have a brother who comes in to eat quite often. His name is Shep."

Dale nodded. "Shep is my younger brother. In fact, he's the baby of the bunch."

Mr. Leone's tanned face spread into a clever grin. "He comes in with plenty of different ladies."

Dale let out a good-natured groan. "That's my little brother, all right."

The other man laughed knowingly. "Your pizza will be ready in just a few more minutes."

They both thanked Mr. Leone and once he moved away from their table, Dale looked at Kendra and said, "Nice guy. I take it you come here often."

"More often than I should. Mila loves the lasagna they make here." She picked up her drink and sipped through the straw. "Mr. Leone has told me some very interesting stories about his grandparents and some of the horrors and hardships they went through in Italy during World War Two. Sometimes when I'm thinking I've had a tough day, or life is hard, I think about his grandparents and realize my life is a romp through a flower garden."

"I do the same thing. Only I think of my parents," he admitted. "Things weren't always as good for them as they are now. Dad was— Well, he wasn't always the responsible sort of guy he should've been. And Mom didn't have it easy taking care of five boys on a shoe-string budget."

She cast him a curious look. "Clearly, he got things turned around. How did he do it?"

With a slight shake of his head, he said, "I guess you could say two things turned Dad around. Mom had a heart attack. And he won a huge pile of money in Vegas."

"Gambling?"

Nodding, Dale reached for his soda. "Yes. And thankfully he decided to use the money for a good cause—purchasing the property for Dalton's Grange."

"Hmm. Tell me if I'm being too nosy, but your mother's heart attack—was that before he won the jackpot?"

Other than his brothers, Dale didn't discuss his parents' past problems to anyone. But Kendra was different. Now that he was beginning to know her, he didn't think she was the sort to look down on anyone just because they'd made mistakes. Still, he didn't want Kendra thinking he'd ever follow his father's wandering footsteps.

"Yes, her heart attack was before. You see, Mom and Dad were having marital problems." He drew in a bracing breath. "Dad was a serial cheater, until Mom had a heart attack. The fear of losing her opened his eyes to the mistakes he'd made. So when the money came along, he wanted to use it to make a special home for her—for the both of them."

"I'm sorry your mother has gone through so much. But to me she sounds like a woman with a strong constitution. Otherwise, she wouldn't have survived the heart attack or her husband's betrayal."

He grimaced. "The whole thing is not something I

like repeating to anyone. But I, uh, thought you'd see it with an open mind."

A smile suddenly brightened her face. "That's a nice thing to say, Dale. And I do see your parents' problems with an open mind. And there's something else I see."

"What's that?"

"You shouldn't be trying to shoulder the blame of your dad's mistakes."

He stared at her, amazed that she'd so accurately picked up on his feelings. "Okay, I admit I'm guilty of thinking Dad's disreputable behavior puts a blot on me and my brothers."

"That's easy to understand. But it's not your fault. Just like it's not my fault that Mila's father has basically deserted her. I've learned you can't change a person for the better, Dale. He or she has to make the change on their own. Be thankful your father made that choice."

He grinned at her. "I'm glad you asked me out on this date, Kendra."

She laughed and the sound made his heart feel as if it just sprouted wings.

"I'm glad I asked you for a date too."

Kendra and Dale were both stuffed with pizza when they finally walked out of the restaurant and down the street to his parked truck.

"I've never eaten pizza that tasted so good. I made a hog of myself," Dale said as he helped her into the truck.

"That's because you were eating the real deal," she told him. "Not the fake stuff."

He climbed into the driver's seat, but didn't immediately start the engine. Instead, he looked over at her and Kendra was surprised to see a serious expression on his face.

"The real deal is always better than make-believe. But you know something, I'm not having to pretend I'm enjoying this evening with you. It all feels pretty darn nice."

Something inside Kendra melted like warm sugar, and without hesitation, she reached across the console and wrapped her fingers around his.

"I'm enjoying it too, Dale. Very much. It's a little crazy how easy it is for me to talk with you. I don't normally chatter this much to anyone. Not about personal things."

His blue gaze swept gently over her face. "Same thing with me. And according to Mila we're not even each other's type," he added with a wry grin.

Her spirits soared and for the first time since her divorce, Kendra saw a future full of blue skies and warm sunshine. Maybe Dale wouldn't turn out to be her special "forever" guy. But he was making her see that she could want again, that she could still hope and dream for the things she wanted in her future.

"I think we're proving my daughter wrong." She squeezed his hand, then eased back in her seat. "So where are we going now? I still have an hour and a half before I have to collect Mila from Ada's."

"What would you like to do? I'm here to serve."

She bestowed him with a warm smile. "Anything—as long as it doesn't involve a crowd of people. And don't get me wrong, I love people. They make my living. But when I'm away from work it's nice to have some quieter moments."

"Hmm. Well, we could drive to the outskirts of town and look at the mountains. There's a moon out tonight. I think we'll be able to see something."

"If nothing else, we can count a few stars," she told him. "Did you ever do that as a child?"

Chuckling, he started the engine and backed the truck onto the street, then headed in a northerly direction. "No. I was too busying seeing stars from being bucked off a horse or wrestling with my brothers. Did you count stars?"

"Whenever I was out of the city, where I could actually see them," she answered as she settled herself comfortably in the leather bucket seat. "The first time I ever visited a Western state, I was about ten. Dad took us to Arizona for a summer vacation and I was amazed at how the sky seemed to go on forever. And, yes, I had fun counting stars and daydreaming."

He grinned. "About baking cupcakes and running your own bakery?"

No, Kendra thought, her dreams had been about growing up and being a wife to a loving husband, and mother to a houseful of children. But sadly, by the time Mila was a few weeks old, she'd realized her dream of having a big family was not to be. Certainly not with Bryce.

"Well, not quite as early as ten," she said. "But by the time I entered my teens I'd been doing lots of baking. I learned everything I know about my profession from my mother, not from my college studies."

"You went to college?"

"I have a degree in business. Operating a bakery is more than just making sweet treats. In fact, there's a ton of office work that goes with it."

"Hmm. I imagine so. But I took it for granted that you had someone taking care of the business end of things for you," he said.

"So far I've been doing it all myself. But with the bakery getting busier and busier, I'm coming to the conclusion that I'm going to have to give in and hire a person to deal with all the purchasing orders, bills and that sort of thing. I'm also considering hiring another barista. The coffee part of Kendra's Cupcakes has really taken off in the past few months and with cold weather coming on, I expect it will pick up even more. Since Smitty is in college he can only work part-time. The same goes for Andrea."

He cast her a thoughtful glance as he braked the truck to a stop behind a line of vehicles at a red light. "You can't run the bakery all by yourself. But then you have to consider the extra salaries. Good thing you have a business head on your shoulders. I wouldn't know how to decide about such things."

"I'm hardly an expert, Dale. But operating my own bakery in South Beach taught me a lot about the business. And you're right, the extra salaries will cut into my profits. I'm hoping, however, that an increase in sales will make up for the loss." She glanced over at him. "What about you? Did you go to college?"

The light changed and he accelerated the truck as the traffic ahead of them moved forward. "Yes. For ranching and land development. I didn't necessarily like being housed up and taking classes, but in the end I thought it would help me be a better conservator of the land. And it has."

Her gaze traveled over his rugged profile. There was so much more about this man that she wanted to learn. Over dinner, he'd told her he was thirty-one. At that age, most men were usually married; some even had young children. Or they'd tried marriage and ended up divorced. But Dale hadn't experienced either and she wondered if he'd ever been in love and suffered a broken heart. Why else would he be avoiding commitment to a woman?

"So you've always planned on being in the ranching business?"

"Pretty much. Cowboy work is about all I've ever done. I don't think I'd be happy doing anything else."

At least he hadn't had any trouble dedicating himself to a vocation, she thought. "We're blessed to be doing what we like to do. Don't you think?"

"Very much so," he said, then inclined his head to her side of the street. "There's the headquarters of the Bronco Ghost Tours business. Ever go on one of Evan Cruise's spooky tours?"

She laughed lightly. "No. But I think it might be fun. What about you?"

"I haven't taken a tour. There's really no need. We have a real live ghost working on Dalton's Grange now."

Kendra sat straight up in the seat and stared at him. "A live ghost? There isn't such a thing," she argued.

He chuckled. "In this case, there is. You remember seeing all those flyers that Sullivan Grainger hung around town when he was searching for Bobby Stone?"

"Oh, when you said *ghost* I wasn't thinking about Bobby. So *he's* the phantom you have working on Dalton's Grange." She let out a good-natured groan. "Yes, I remember those flyers. They were fastened to every light pole and store window in town and folks were talking about seeing a ghost. Made me wonder what kind of town I'd moved into."

"Yeah, at that time no one in town knew that Sullivan was actually Bobby's twin and had come to Bronco searching for the brother he'd never known he had. So it's understandable why everyone believed a ghost was walking around town. The two men look practically identical," Dale said. "Did you ever hear Bobby's story? About his disappearance?"

"I hear all sorts of gossip through the bakery," she told him. "And the way I heard the story, everyone initially believed Bobby had died because he'd sat on the death seat in Doug's bar." Shaking her head with dismay, she said, "Why some people believe such folklore is beyond me."

Dale nodded. "Well, there are stories from local townsfolk, who insist the death seat has brought grief to more than one person who's dared to sit in it. And in a way, I suppose it did bring a bit of grief to Bobby. He ended up drinking way too much and then decided to go off mountain climbing. So when he disappeared, everyone naturally assumed he'd suffered a fatal fall. The death seat just happened to play into people's suspicions."

"I am acquainted with Bobby," she told him. "He and his fiancée, Tori Hawkins, frequently stop by the bakery. I've heard him mention working on Dalton's Grange."

"Yeah, Bobby's life has turned around and Tori is the main reason he's on a better track. Do you know the other Hawkins Sisters?"

"I do. They often come into the bakery. Back in November of last year, Mila and I went to the Mistletoe Rodeo here in Bronco. And last month we attended the Bronco Summer Family Rodeo. We thoroughly enjoyed both events.

"I'm a bit surprised that Mila liked the rodeo. She seems more like the ballerina sort. If I remember right, she was wearing a tutu when I first came into the bakery. That is what you call those frilly skirts, isn't it?"

She chuckled. "Yes. Mila loves her tutu. But dreaming about dancing in a ballet troupe is just a secondary interest with Mila. She went crazy for the rodeo and is totally starstruck by the Hawkins Sisters. She has a poster of Audrey and Jack Burris hanging on the wall in her bedroom. Now she's convinced she wants to grow up and be a rodeo star just like the Hawkins Sisters."

"Hmm. I wonder why—" He cast her a curious glance. "That evening in the bakery she talked about dancing on a stage, but she didn't mention anything to me about being a rodeo competitor."

Kendra shook her head. "She talks about plenty of things she shouldn't talk about. But I'm guessing she could see that you're a real-deal cowboy and she might have thought you'd laugh at her."

"I'd never laugh at any child's dream. In Mila's case, I would've encouraged her. The Hawkins Sisters are highly successful."

"True. But Mila has no background with horses and livestock and it's doubtful she ever will. But most children are fickle. In a few months she'll probably lose the idea of being a cowgirl."

"Possibly. But I wouldn't burst her bubble and discourage her cowgirl dreams. A person doesn't necessarily have to live on a ranch to be a rodeo competitor. For instance, Tori boards her horse on Dalton's Grange."

Kendra nodded while thinking how much Mila would enjoy seeing Tori's horse and meeting her rodeo idol. But she wasn't going to mention the idea to Dale. He'd think she was hinting for an invite to the ranch. And she didn't want to appear that forward.

Just like asking him for a date hadn't been forward? Who are you trying to fool, Kendra? You've been giving the cowboy all sorts of green lights.

As Dale maneuvered the truck through a few more blocks of town, the mocking voice lingered in her head. But thankfully, by the time he'd driven a few miles from town and parked on a wide pull-off, she'd pushed aside the thoughts.

"Would you like to get out for minute or two?" he asked. "It's a bit chilly tonight, but not exactly freezing."

"I'd love to stretch my legs and look around. I haven't been on this highway before."

"Shame on you," he gently scolded. "You need to get out more. The countryside around Bronco is especially beautiful."

Her soft laugh held a slight tremor, while every nerve in her body felt like she was humming with electrical current. What was this man doing to her?

"You're saying I need to see more than the inside of a bakery?"

"We all need a change of scenery from time to time," he answered.

After climbing out of the truck, he came around to her side of the cab to help her to the ground. His hand felt incredibly warm as it wrapped firmly around hers and once she was standing next to him, she realized she didn't want to let go of him.

"I have another jacket in the back seat if you think you'll be too cold," he told her.

His thoughtfulness touched her. "Thanks. I think I'll take you up on the offer. The wind is sharp tonight."

He fetched a denim jacket lined with sherpa wool from the back seat of the truck and draped it around her shoulders. She was instantly enveloped by his scent, which was a mixture of evergreen and sage, and something else that was undeniably masculine and sexy.

"Better?"

Not bothering to slide her arms into the sleeves, she pulled the front of the jacket together. "Yes. I'm toasty now."

With his arm curved against the back of her waist, they walked several yards away from the truck to where a guardrail separated the parking area from a steep drop-off. Beyond the gorge, the moonlight illuminated a pair of tall mountain peaks covered with dense forest.

"This is lovely," she said. "I imagine it won't be long before the mountains are snowcapped."

"Yes, and in a few short months Bronco will be decked out with holiday decorations. It's a fun time of the year. Has Mila already been talking about what she wants for Christmas?"

"You mean after she adopts a dog or cat?" she asked with a short laugh. "Mila starts her Christmas wish list early. This year she wants a barrel-racing saddle. One that's exactly her size."

"A saddle? Is she expecting Santa to give her a horse to go with it?"

Kendra groaned. "Thankfully, it hasn't occurred to her to ask for the horse yet."

"A horse and saddle. Well, lots of kids wish for those things at Christmas. It's not completely out of the realm of possibility."

Kendra looked up at his shadowed face. How would it be, she wondered, to have this strong man helping her raise Mila? How would it feel to have his love and support?

You need to slow down, Kendra. You're getting way ahead of yourself. Dale isn't in the market for a family.

Shaking away the warning voice in her head, she said, "Mila's wish list doesn't end there. The main thing she wants is a daddy. That will be at the top of the letter she sends to Santa. Just in case she can't find one on her own," she added wryly.

Dale let out a commiserative groan. "Mila's not asking for much, is she?"

"Believe me, I've tried to explain about how she can't go up to a group of men and pick one out. But she doesn't seem to listen." She let out a weary sigh. "We went to Audrey and Jack's wedding and I thought it would be a nice experience for Mila. I wanted her to see all the lovely flowers and dresses and the cake and hear the music. But the whole event has turned my daughter into a— Well, a little wedding monster."

He chuckled. "Wedding monster? I don't think I've heard that term before."

"Mila's probably the first," she said ruefully. "She's obsessed with getting me married. To the man of her choice, of course."

His arm gently squeezed the back of her waist. "I realize some of her talk embarrasses you, but don't let it get to you. People understand she's just a kid. As for her asking Santa for a daddy, you can remind her that Santa doesn't hand out every wish. When I was a little boy, I kept asking for a guitar. I never got it and Mom explained that whenever I was old enough to apply myself to lessons, Santa might deliver one."

"Did he?"

"No. And before long my heart's desire had already moved on to a pair of fringed chaps." Turning to face her, he clasped his hands around her upper arms. "I'm not trying to say Mila will grow out of her desire to have a father. And she shouldn't. Material things can't compare to a parent. But when the time is right, she'll get the father she wants. And not at the expense of your happiness."

She gave him a grateful smile. "Thanks, Dale, for helping me view the whole thing in a sensible way. Actually, Mila's wedding obsession isn't really what bothers me the most. It's feeling like a failure as a mother."

His hands tightened on her arms. "Kendra, you shouldn't be feeling that way. You're a wonderful mother."

The tenderness in his voice brought a mist of tears to her eyes and she bowed her head and swallowed hard. "Sorry, Dale," she said in a choked voice. "I didn't mean to get emotional. We're supposed to be enjoying ourselves."

"I am enjoying myself. Just being close to you like this, Kendra, is a pleasure."

Something in his voice drew her face up toward his and as she stared at him through watery eyes, her heart gave a hard lurch then jumped into a rapid thumping.

"It feels good to be close to you too."

She watched in fascination as his eyelids drooped and his head slowly descended toward hers until the only thing she could see was the hard line of his lips.

"It will feel even better when we get closer," he murmured.

She didn't try to utter a response. Instead, she closed her eyes and waited for his lips to settle over hers. A second later, his lips were lightly brushing against hers, teasing them with what was about to take place. Then, slowly and surely, his mouth took command of hers and a tiny moan vibrated in her throat as she surrendered to the pleasure.

His kiss swept her into a vortex where the two of them were whirling together through the darkness. To steady her dizzying senses, she planted her hands against his chest, and although the thickness of his shirt acted as a barrier between her fingers and his flesh, she could feel the heat of his body. She also felt a sweet hunger in his kiss, like a man supping at something he'd never tasted before.

Eventually, the headlights of a passing car caused them to instinctively step back from each other.

Dale was the first to speak. "Kendra, I should probably apologize for that, but that would make me a hypocrite. I wanted every second of that kiss."

Kendra realized she was breathing hard and her lips felt swollen. "No apologies needed," she said huskily. "The kiss was a nice…shared thing."

"A shared thing," he murmured. "Yes. It was."

The urge to step forward and wrap her arms around him was so great it left her trembling. Or was her shivering a result of the cold wind? No matter, she thought. This wasn't a time for her to be reckless.

As if he could read her thoughts, he said quietly, "We should probably be heading back to town."

Disappointment weighed on her, but only for a moment. Just because their evening together was coming to an end, it didn't mean their budding relationship was going to fade away. Not if she could help it.

"Right. I have to pick Mila up at Ada's in about a half hour," she told him.

Dale held her hand tightly as they walked back to the truck and just before he handed her up into the cab, Kendra's gaze caught and held his. The look in his blue eyes was both tender and promising, and suddenly she was so overcome with emotion, she found it impossible to speak.

Apparently, he must have felt the same way because he simply looked at her for long, silent moments before he handed her up and into the truck.

It wasn't until they'd reached town and he merged

into the traffic that he finally spoke. "I think it would be a shame if we don't go out again. Don't you?"

Her heart thumping a happy rhythm, she glanced over at him and smiled. "A huge shame," she agreed.

With his gaze remaining firmly on the busy street, he asked, "How about Tuesday? Can you get away from the bakery a little early?"

His question put a quizzical frown on her face. "Why Tuesday? Are you doing something special that evening?"

"Tomorrow is Sunday. Your bakery is closed and you need that day to rest. Mondays are usually too hectic as everyone gets back into the swing of their jobs. So Tuesday should be better for what I have in mind," he said and flashed her a clever grin. "If you agree, I thought I'd drive you and Mila out to Happy Hearts so that she could look at the cats and dogs up for adoption."

Kendra was so overwhelmed by his gesture she didn't know whether to laugh or cry. In the end, she swallowed hard and stared out the window at the passing shops and businesses.

"That's very thoughtful of you, Dale."

"I got you fooled. It's really selfish of me. I can spend time with you, while giving you the impression I'm a good guy."

His remark caused her gaze to swing back to him and she was totally surprised to see he wasn't teasing.

"You are a good guy, Dale."

He shrugged. "I try. But I don't want you to expect too much from me. I'm a cowboy. I don't have any experience dealing with kids or ladies like you, Kendra."

Was this a nice way of telling her he wanted to spend time with her, but she shouldn't expect more than a few pleasant kisses and some laughs in between? No. She wanted to believe he simply wanted her to understand him and not compare him to other men.

"For what it's worth, I don't have any experience dating a cowboy, either. So you'll have to overlook my ignorance about ranching."

Smiling now, he reached for her hand and Kendra was very glad he didn't let go until he walked her to the door of her apartment.

"I'd ask you to stay and say hello to Mila," she told him as they stood close together on the small concrete portico. "But it's already past her bedtime. And I think it might be better—"

"For her not to see me tonight," he said, finishing for her. "I imagine you're right. She probably needs a bit more time to process the idea of the two of us together."

She sighed with relief. "Yes. You took the words right out of my mouth. I'll tell her tomorrow about the three of us making a trip out to Happy Hearts. If I told her tonight, she probably wouldn't go to sleep until midnight."

He let out a wry chuckle. "I might not go to sleep until midnight, either."

Holding onto both his hands, she raised up on her toes and pressed a soft kiss to his lips. "Good night, Dale."

"That's not good enough," he whispered.

Before she guessed his intentions, his hands were on her shoulders, pulling her into his arms. And then he was kissing her, and just as before, the searching movement of his lips caused everything around them to fade away.

By the time he finally lifted his head, Kendra was far too dazed to utter a word, much less form a cohesive sentence.

"Good night, Kendra."

He walked off and as Kendra watched him climb

into his truck and drive away, she could only wonder if she was making a major mistake by letting herself get close to Dale. Or was she finally on a path to finding the real love she so desperately wanted?

Chapter Six

"Smitty, will you be able to handle the bakery plus the coffee tomorrow evening? Say from four o'clock through closing time? If not, I'll see if Andrea can come in and help you," Kendra asked the young man, who'd been serving endless cups of coffee ever since the bakery had opened early this morning. He had to be exhausted and she figured now was not a good time to ask him about working double duty for her tomorrow. Unfortunately, she didn't have any other options.

Smitty said, "Andrea can't come in. I heard her say she has a psychology test tomorrow afternoon. But no worries, Kendra. If you need time off I can handle things."

Kendra wearily pushed at the hair that continued to fall from her bun no matter how often she rearranged the clips. Dale was right when he'd said Mondays were usually hectic. This one had been exceptionally chaotic. She'd been serving her first customer this morning when Jackie had emerged from the kitchen with the frantic announcement that a water line had broken and was flooding the floor.

After shutting off the water supply, it had taken Kendra an hour to finally locate an available plumber willing to take on the job and then another hour for the man to finally show up. And the whole time the line of customers hadn't stopped.

"Thanks, Smitty. I'll tell Jackie to keep an eye out and if you get in a bind, she'll need to come out front and help you. I normally wouldn't ask, but this is sort of a special thing for Mila. She's going to Happy Hearts to pick out a dog or cat."

The young man grinned. "Now that is special. Steer her toward a dog, Kendra. A big one. Those little ones bark too much."

"Mila's babysitter has a dachshund and he rarely barks, but that might be because he's older," Kendra told him.

Jackie walked up to join their conversation. "It's too bad, Kendra, that I accidently let the stray orange cat out of the kitchen. He would've made Mila the perfect pet. Now the feline is probably caged up at the animal shelter and dreaming about his free roaming days."

Kendra shook her head. "Even if we had managed to keep the cat contained, I couldn't have kept him for myself. Morris belongs to someone. He must. Otherwise, why would a person be bothering to hunt him?"

Smitty said, "The way I heard it, the missing orange cat supposedly belonged to the young woman who was in that apartment fire a couple months ago."

"Yes and she died from her injuries," Jackie said sadly. "Morris must've used some of his nine lives to escape the fire."

The doorbell chimed and two middle-aged women entered the bakery and walked straight to the coffee counter. As they studied the menu displayed on the wall, Smitty said, "Duty calls. And I can already tell by looking at those two they're going to want extra caramel and whipped cream."

He moved away to tend to the customers and Jackie rolled her eyes. "Why is it that men seem to think they can read a woman's mind? But then they can't understand a word we actually say? It's infuriating."

Amused by Jackie's theory, Kendra asked, "Man trouble?"

"What man? I haven't been on a date in weeks. I must be doing something wrong. I'm beginning to think I need a complete makeover. Maybe turn my red hair into a cool blond. Or try for an exotic look and dye it black."

Kendra looked at her in horror. "Never! You need to stay just as you are. Sooner or later the perfect guy for you is going to come along."

"Easy for you to say. You have a hunky cowboy gaga over you."

This morning Jackie had overheard Kendra talking on the phone to Dale about their plans to go to Happy Hearts. Naturally, the young woman had leaped to the conclusion that Kendra and Dale were getting seriously chummy. And maybe they were, she thought. Those kisses he'd plastered on her lips had felt anything but casual. But would the attraction between them last?

"Jackie, there are no guarantees Dale will ever be more than just a cute guy who wants a date or two," Kendra told her. "Anyway, I've tried the serious thing before and it didn't work. If I'm meant to have something special with Dale, it will happen."

"It amazes me that you can be so nonchalant about

the whole thing, Kendra. I've heard the Daltons are rich. That the old man hit it big in Vegas. Just think. If you married Dale you wouldn't have to worry about money. And tell me, where could you find a cuter guy than Dale?"

Yes, Dale was nice-looking, sexy and not hurting for money. But none of those things was the reason Kendra was drawn to him. To be honest, she didn't know exactly why being with Dale made her happy. It just did.

"I hate to burst your bubble, Jackie, but when it comes to romance, money and looks really have no importance."

Jackie released a short, mocking laugh. "Who says? A girl can love a rich good-looking guy as easily as she can love a poor homely one."

Kendra walked over and pulled a nearly empty tray of pecan tarts from one of the display cases. "You're getting it all wrong. Sure, it's easy to fall in love with a handsome and successful man. My ex-husband was both. But he didn't love me back. And that's the important point. Love has to be a shared thing, or it isn't any good at all."

"I wouldn't mind giving handsome and successful a try." Jackie walked over and took the tray from Kendra's hands. "But in your case, Kendra, I wouldn't worry about Dale. There's more to him than looks and money. He's different."

Kendra leveled a droll look at the sassy redhead. "How did you reach that conclusion? Studying the dimples in his cheeks."

Chuckling, Jackie said, "No. Woman's intuition."

Kendra groaned. "And this from someone who said a man can't read a woman's mind? You're hilarious, Jackie."

"I know. It's a curse. I just can't help myself." She turned toward the kitchen. "You want more tarts on this tray or something different?"

"The pumpkin cupcakes are ready. Bring those out. The weather is full-blown autumn today—cool and foggy. They'll go quickly."

Jackie nodded. "Right. I'll be back in a jiffy."

Kendra followed the young woman into the kitchen, then entered another door that opened into her office. Every spare inch of the small room was crammed— there was a desk equipped with a computer, two chairs, a file cabinet and a couch piled with throw pillows. While the quiet room was meant for Kendra's office work, Mila often used the space to play with her toys. When she wasn't out front with the customers, cornering men who looked like potential marriage material for her mother.

After sinking into the chair at her desk, Kendra clicked the computer out of snooze mode and scrolled through the order form she'd been trying to finish for the past hour. So far today, each time she'd sat down at the computer something had interrupted her. Hopefully, with a break in the customers, she'd finally get the task completed before she was needed again.

Ten minutes later, Kendra had just finalized the supply order and was about to leave the office when the cell phone in her apron pocket rang. Since only her family and a few close friends, along with Mila's school, had her number, she couldn't ignore the call entirely.

Stifling a sigh, she pulled out the phone and was somewhat surprised to see the call was from her mother, Laura. Although Kendra was close to both parents, she didn't call them on a daily or even weekly basis. Her mother and dad both stayed very busy with their own successful businesses. Laura operated a combined hair salon and day spa, while her father, Weston, was a real-estate agent for the busy South Beach area and beyond. Once Kendra had become an adult, neither of her parents ever tried to run her life. But they'd always been there for her whenever she'd needed love and support. And when she'd decided to make the move to Montana, they'd encouraged her to follow her dreams to a new life.

"Hi, Mom. What's up?"

"Got a minute?" Laura asked. "Or have I caught you with a line of waiting customers?"

Kendra eased comfortably back in the leather swiveling chair. "Actually, I'm in my office right now. Smitty is handling things out front."

"Good. So how are you, honey? Sorry I haven't called sooner. But it's been a bit crazy here. End of summer haircuts and that sort of thing. And then we had a hurricane scare. Thankfully, the storm headed away from Florida."

"Yes, I was relieved when I saw that on the news." She smiled even though her mother couldn't see her. "It seems so crazy. You and Dad down there in the heat and the threat of a hurricane, and Mila and I up here wearing jackets and watching the leaves fall."

"Sounds lovely," Laura said wistfully. "Ready for some company?"

"Sure. Are you and Dad coming up soon? Maybe for Christmas?" Her parents hadn't yet made a trip to Montana, but they were planning to. To keep connected, Kendra was constantly sending them pics of Mila, the bakery and their home in the apartment complex.

"We're throwing around the idea of coming out to see you. Your father and I haven't seen snow in probably ten years and that was when we took the skiing trip to Vermont."

"I'd love for you to come for the holidays," Kendra said. "Then you could help me explain to Mila why she isn't getting a saddle for Christmas."

Laura chuckled. "Oh dear, she still wants to be a rodeo cowgirl?"

I wouldn't burst her bubble and discourage her cowgirl dreams.

Dale's comment suddenly drifted through Kendra's mind and she realized he was right. Mila needed her mother's encouragement, even if her dreams weren't feasible.

"Just as much as ever."

"And what about her quest for finding herself a father? I hope all of that has tapered off."

Kendra's thoughts instantly turned to Dale. He'd been the last man Mila had accosted with personal questions. And surprisingly, she had to admit her daughter had judged him correctly when she'd announced Dale wasn't the family type. He didn't consider himself daddy or husband material, but Kendra could see he had the makings of both.

"Not at all. Since I last talked with you, Mila has pulled some embarrassing capers. But I'm dealing with it."

Laura didn't immediately reply and Kendra was beginning to wonder if the call had dropped when her mother finally asked, "Honey, have you heard from Bryce lately?"

The unusual question had Kendra's spine straightening to a stiff line. "Bryce? No! Why would he be calling? He had no time for me and Mila while we were still living in Florida. Why would he suddenly want to talk now?"

"I don't know. But he called me yesterday and I'm not sure why. At first, I thought he might have misplaced your phone number and wanted to talk to Mila. But that wasn't the case."

Frowning, she said, "How strange. What did he say he wanted?"

"Nothing. He said he'd been wondering how you and Mila were doing and thought it best to ask me rather than call you directly."

Bitterness boiled on Kendra's tongue. "Naturally. He was probably afraid if he called me, Mila would want to speak with him. And that would've put too much stress on him—the phony creep."

"I got the impression something was on his mind. And when I asked him about Gillian, he muttered something like he didn't know or care. When I asked him to elaborate, he said they were no longer together."

Funny, Kendra thought, how little Bryce's marital status mattered to her. She didn't care how many women the man had in his life just as long as none of them were paraded in front of Mila. Which was another reason Kendra had decided to move so far away from Florida. She wanted her daughter to be shielded from her father's life in the fast lane.

"Somehow that doesn't surprise me, either," she said to her mother. "They were a mismatch from the very beginning. Gillian was hardly more than a teenager when they married."

"And she definitely acted her age," Laura replied. "But there's a good side to this news. The woman is no longer Mila's stepmother."

Kendra snorted. "She couldn't even be a bad stepmother. She wanted nothing to do with Mila and I suppose I should count myself lucky that she didn't."

"Well, I just thought I ought to give you a heads-up about Bryce. Just in case he starts ringing your phone," Laura replied. "So I'll say goodbye and let you get back to work."

Kendra swiped a hand across her furrowed brow. She couldn't allow this news about Bryce to worry her. She had too many important things to focus on besides her ex-husband.

"Wait, Mom. There's something else I'd like to tell you."

"Okay."

Since her divorce five years ago, she'd never once mentioned a man to her parents, or to her brother, Sterling. Mostly because there hadn't been a man worth mentioning. But now she felt a need to inform her mother about Dale.

"I've met a man," Kendra told her. "His name is Dale Dalton and he's a cowboy—a rancher. He lives on the family ranch called Dalton's Grange."

A short stretch of silence came back at her and Kendra figured her news had probably taken her mother by surprise.

"Honey, that's wonderful news. And you like this guy…in a special way, I mean?"

"I do. He's tall and dark and good-looking and comes from a big family. Counting him, there are five sons. They all work together on the ranch. I, uh, I don't know if things will actually go anywhere with him, but I— Oh, Mom's he's the first guy I've met in a long time that interests me."

"Then by all means you should see where this interest you have for the man takes you," she said.

"I've not known him long," Kendra told her. "Only a couple of weeks. But I would like to get to know him better. I just don't want to rush anything and make a mistake."

Laura laughed. "It took me about two hours to fall for your dad. One look at him and I was blind to any other man."

Kendra smiled to herself. "And what if Dad had run from you instead of to you?"

"Then he would've had a long, hard chase on his hands. I wasn't going to give up on catching him."

Obviously her mother had been certain about going after the man she loved. Yet Kendra wasn't even convinced she should be dating Dale, much less hoping he might become the love of her life.

Kendra sighed. "You clearly caught the right man. But, Mom, I've already made one terrible mistake with Bryce. I keep asking myself if I'm headed toward another mistake."

"Kendra, your father and I have told you this before—the biggest mistake you can make now is letting Bryce ruin the rest of your life."

Kendra was about to reply when the door to the office opened and Jackie jerked her thumb in the direction of the bakery front. Kendra acknowledged her with a nod and an okay sign formed with her thumb and forefinger.

"I will, Mom. Right now I have to go. I'm needed out front. I'll call you soon."

The two women exchanged goodbyes and Kendra slipped the phone back into the pocket on her apron, but as she made her way out of the office, unease rippled through her.

Since their divorce, Bryce had never called Kendra's parents and it had been over a year since he'd even bothered to call and check on his daughter. Something was off, she thought.

And suddenly she was very, very glad she was going to see Dale tomorrow. He made everything seem better.

Dale tamped down the last shovelful of dirt around the fat cedar post and leaned against the newly set post to catch his breath.

Shortly after daylight this morning, he and his brothers Morgan and Shep had started building cross fence in a back pasture of the ranch. Now that midafternoon had rolled around they were at least five hundred yards away from reaching their final destination. It would take two more days of steady work to finish this particular job.

Dale said, "Sorry, guys, but I have to head back to the house. I have an early date this evening."

Morgan and Shep looked at him as if he'd just spoken in a foreign language.

"Did I hear you right?" Morgan asked. "A date? We still have a few hours of daylight left to work on this fence. What are you doing? Planning on driving the woman to Great Falls or Missoula?"

Dale walked over to a work truck and picked up the denim jacket he'd thrown on the tailgate. "To make it up to you guys, I'll tamp all the dirt around the post tomorrow. And, no, I'm not planning on driving but a few miles out of town. I'm taking Kendra and her daughter to Happy Hearts. The kid wants a pet and that's the best place for her to get one."

"Heck, Dale, that doesn't sound like a date to me," Shep said. "Sounds more like a boring family outing."

Shep could label the outing any way he wanted, Dale thought. But he was the one who was going to be spending time with a beautiful blonde with lips that tasted sweeter than the cupcakes she baked.

"So what? What's wrong with me going on a family outing?" Dale quipped.

Shep's mouth gaped wide, while Morgan chuckled.

"Leave him alone, Shep. The man is falling in love. Can't you see it on his face?"

Dale scowled at the two of them, then, as if he needed to reassure himself, he walked up to the front of the truck and peered at himself in the side mirror. "There's nothing on my face except a day-old beard. Not a thing, except a handsome mug."

"Oh damn, do we have to hear this, Dale?" Shep asked with a good-natured groan.

Morgan leaned against one of the set posts. "Okay, since you're going to use the time off for a good cause, Dale, I say go enjoy your evening. Just be ready to stretch wire tomorrow."

"Don't worry. You guys are going to need extra vitamins to keep up with me," he joked, then walked over to his older brother. "Say, Morgan, before I head back to the ranch house, maybe you can give me a few pointers."

"About women? Bah!" Shep exclaimed with a grin. "I'm the guy you ought to be asking for advice."

Frowning at Shep, he said, "Not about women. About little girls." He turned a helpless look on Morgan. "How do you make JoJo like you?"

Morgan shook his head. "Like me? I'm her daddy. *Like* isn't exactly the thing I want from my daughter. Especially as she gets older. Respect, obedience, trust and admiration. Those are the things I want JoJo to have for me. Of course, I want her to love me too. Does that answer your question?"

Dale tried not to feel like an idiot in front of his brothers, but he did. It was stupid of him to allow a child of Mila's age to erode his self-confidence. But it would be even more foolish of him to dismiss Mila's part in his plans to date her mother. Kendra had told him she wasn't going to allow Mila to dictate her love life. But Dale could clearly see that Kendra would never deliberately do anything to make her daughter unhappy. If Mila started to sulk at having Dale around, he knew his time with Kendra would end quickly and permanently.

"Sort of. I'll try to keep everything you said in mind."

Dismayed, Shep shook his head. "Dale, why don't you wise up? Dating a woman with a kid is not what you need. Not unless you're looking for a major headache. And who wants one of those?"

Dale darted him an annoyed look. "You need a swift kick in the pants, little brother, but I don't have time to give you one right now. I'll see you two tomorrow."

As Dale's truck bounced over the rough pasture leading back to the ranch house, Shep's unsolicited advice continued to roll through his head. Yeah, Shep could be right, he thought ruefully. He could be setting himself up for a catastrophic heartache. But if a man was ever going to have anything worthwhile in his life, he had to take a risk, didn't he?

Hell, just look at his father, Dale thought. Look at Dalton's Grange. If Neal hadn't had the guts to gamble, none of them would even be on this ranch. No, the way Dale saw things, he had to take a chance on Kendra and her little strong-minded daughter.

After a hurried shower and slipping into clean clothes, he managed to arrive at Kendra's apartment at the same time she was driving up from collecting Mila from school.

Leaving his truck, he joined the two of them at the front of her SUV. "Hi, Kendra. Hi, Mila," he greeted.

Mila gave him a polite hello, while Kendra bestowed

a sunny smile in his direction. "Hello, Dale. Your timing is perfect. As soon as Mila changes her clothes, we'll be ready."

"Great. I'm ready whenever you two are." Dale looked at the girl and was relieved to see her expression had brightened somewhat. "Mila, are you excited about picking out a pet?"

She nodded emphatically. "Yes! I've been waiting a long time to get a dog or cat."

"Well, your wait is nearly over," Kendra told her, then with a hand on her shoulder urged her toward the door of the apartment. "Now hurry and get changed from your school clothes. I've laid your jeans and sweater on the bed."

As soon as Kendra opened the apartment door, Mila rushed inside. Glancing over her shoulder, she motioned for Dale to follow her.

"Come in and have a seat while Mila changes."

Inside the living room, he eased down on the end cushion of the couch, while Kendra sank onto the arm of one of the stuffed armchairs.

The room appeared just as clean and tidy as it had the evening he'd picked her up for their date. Dale was amazed how she found the time to take care of a child, their home and the bakery, which remained open until eight o'clock through the weekdays and five on Saturdays.

"Would you like something to drink before we go? Water? Soda?" she asked.

"No, thanks. I'm fine."

She said, "I was so glad the weather warmed today. Yesterday was so dreary, but the sun is shining beautifully now. Hopefully that's a good omen for Mila finding the right pet."

The other night when they'd gone out for pizza, Dale had been mesmerized by the image Kendra had made in her gypsy-style dress with her long hair loose upon her shoulders. He'd believed she couldn't possibly get any prettier than she'd been that evening. But now, in a pair of blue jeans and a black turtleneck sweater and her hair pulled into a ponytail, there was something about her that was simply beautiful and totally sexy. Maybe it was the happy light in her blue eyes, or the glow of her fair skin. He didn't know. He only knew he was struggling to keep from staring at her.

"I think Daphne and her staff at Happy Hearts are very good about matching people up with the right pet," he said.

One of her eyebrows lifted slightly. "Do you go out there often?" she asked.

"No. I haven't been out to the farm in quite a while. But I do try to donate regularly to their cause. I'm sure you've already guessed that when it comes to animals, I'm a chump," he added with a guilty grin.

She smiled back at him and Dale thought how looking at her was like gazing at a ray of sunshine. It filled him with hope and a joy he'd never quite felt before. The sensation was an effervescent thing, like bubbles popping and snapping inside him.

"That's a good kind of chump to be. Nowadays, there are so many orphaned animals that need our help. And someone is still hunting for Morris. I don't think he's been located yet."

"Morris?"

"Yes. The orange cat who's pictured on all the flyers around town," she explained. "Maybe you haven't seen any of the posters. There's one on a light pole not far from the entrance to the bakery."

He could explain that whenever he made a trip to the bakery, he had one thing on his mind and that was her. Everything else around him seemed insignificant.

"Sorry," he said with a wry chuckle. "I never was the most observant guy in the classroom."

"Well, I'll put it this way. Morris is sort of Bronco's feline version of Bobby Stone. At first, folks believed the cat perished in an apartment fire, but that theory was soon shot down when he was spotted in different places around town. Did I tell you he ran into the bakery not long ago? Actually, it was the same night you came in to pick up Erica's order."

"No. What happened?"

"It was almost closing time when one of my regular customers—she walks with a cane—was trying to get through the door and the cat dashed between her legs and into the bakery. Mila chased after him and he ended up hiding in the kitchen. I called animal rescue, but by the time they arrived, the cat was gone. Turns out Jackie inadvertently left the back door of the kitchen open and the cat slipped out."

"Aw, that's too bad. The cat needs a home."

"Yes. But I don't think he knows it quite yet. He's been on his own for so long now that he may be thinking being free is the way to go."

Kendra might have been talking about Morris, but it sure as heck came close to the feelings Dale had always held about being hemmed up by someone who professed to love him.

And how would you know the feeling, Dale? You've never had a woman really love you. The kind of love that flowed from her heart. The kind of love that bound you to her with unbreakable bonds.

He was so absorbed in his thoughts, he failed to notice he hadn't made a reply until she spoke again.

"But I have a feeling someone will latch on to Morris sooner or later. I only hope that happens before the really cold weather hits. I hate to think of him roaming the streets out in the ice and snow."

"Yes," Dale finally replied. "He needs to be rescued before that happens."

The sound of footsteps racing through the house had him glancing around to see Mila rushing into the room. She was dressed in jeans and a bright orange sweater with a jack-o'-lantern appliquéd on the front.

"I'm ready!" she announced.

Kendra glanced at Dale. "Give me a minute to get our coats. Just in case it gets cool before this outing is over."

As her mother left the living room, Mila walked over and sidled up to Dale's knee. He could say one thing about the girl—she was far from shy.

"Do you know all about cats and dogs?" she asked.

"A little," he said, while wondering if she was attempting to be friendly or planning to kick him in the shins.

"Do you have cats and dogs on the ranch where you live?"

He nodded. "We have several dogs and cats on Dalton's Grange."

Wide-eyed, she asked, "Do they live in the house with you?"

He smiled to himself as he took in her little features. How would it feel to have a child who resembled him? A son with the same dark hair and blue eyes? Or another daughter with a perky dimple...

Another daughter? What are you thinking, Dale?

Mila won't ever be your daughter. Your daydreams are starting to get dangerously foolish.

Blocking out the voice in his head, he answered Mila's question. "Only two of them stay in the house. A dog and a cat. They belong to my mom. The dog's name is Sam and the cat is Jewel."

He could see she was carefully digesting this information.

"Is your mommy pretty like mine?"

Thankfully, she was asking him easy questions, Dale thought. With any luck, Kendra would rejoin them before Mila could think up some hard ones for him to answer.

"She's very pretty. All mommies are, don't you think?"

She tilted her head to one side as she thoughtfully regarded him. "I guess so. Do you have a daddy?"

That one last word put Dale's attention on high alert. "Yes, I do. He's big and tall and rides horses."

A skeptical look crossed her face. "Your daddy rides horses? Isn't he too old?"

Dale held back a laugh as he imagined how Neal would react to Mila's question. "Neal—that's my daddy's name—isn't old. He rides almost every day. Ranchers ride horses to do their work," he explained. "So lots of times my brothers and I ride with him."

Dale could see wheels churning in her blue eyes, but he could only guess what she was thinking. Probably that she envied him. Not only because he had a father, but also having a father, plus a horse to ride, made Dale's life sound like heaven to her.

She asked, "Do you like your daddy?"

The simple question caused Dale to pause and ponder. Yes, he'd been angry and disappointed with Neal Dalton in the past, but on the other hand, he realized how blessed he and his brothers were to have a father who loved his sons and wanted them near him.

"Yes, I do. He's a pretty good dad."

She lifted her chin to a proud angle. "I have a daddy, but he doesn't live here. He lives in Florida."

Not knowing how to respond, Dale simply said, "I'm glad you have a daddy."

She swiped the heel of her palm against the end of her little nose, then folded her arms across her chest. "His name is Bryce and he's real smart. He works in an office and makes lots of money. Mommy says he can't come to Bronco to see me 'cause he's too busy with his work."

Dale glanced toward the doorway where Kendra had disappeared. She should be returning any minute now and if she walked in and overheard him saying the wrong thing to Mila about her father, it would make for a terribly bad start to their outing. On the other hand, he couldn't treat the whole subject like he was juggling raw eggs.

He said, "Well, adults get very busy with their jobs. And they don't get to do everything they'd like to do."

She nodded as though she understood. "Mommy stays busy all the time, but Smitty is taking her place today. I call him the coffee man because he makes all the coffee. Do you know him?"

"I've seen him at the bakery."

An impish grin turned up the corners of her mouth. "Smitty is cute. But he's too young to be a daddy."

Thank goodness this child didn't know everything about men.

Struggling to keep a straight face, Dale said, "I think you're probably right. Smitty needs to get a little older before he gets a wife and kids."

"Smitty has a girlfriend, though. Her name is Joni and she's kinda pretty, but he needs a different one."

"Why? What's wrong with his girlfriend?"

Mila's frown was full of disapproval. "Joni talks mean to him. That's not good."

Apparently, Mila kept her eye on more than her mother's romantic life, Dale thought. "No, talking mean is bad," he said, then pointed to the top of her head. "What happened to your tiara? Did you lose it? Or have you decided you don't want to be a princess anymore?"

Her features pinched together as she slapped a hand on top of her head. "No, I didn't lose it. And I don't want to be a princess. I want to be a queen. A rodeo queen with a crown and a banner across here." She swiped her finger in a slant across her chest. "And it's going to say Bronco Rodeo Queen."

"Wow! That will really be something to see. But what about dancing ballet on the stage? Remember you told me you were taking dancing lessons."

"I am," she said with another proud thrust of her chin. "I can dance and be a rodeo queen too. Mommy says a person that can do more than one thing is well-rounded."

"You know, Mila, I have a feeling you're going to be very well-rounded."

He'd just gotten the words out of his mouth when Kendra hurried into the room with two heavy garments thrown over her arm.

"I'm sorry it took me so long," she quickly apologized. "I couldn't find Mila's play coat. And I didn't want her to wear her school coat out to the farm."

Dale rose to his feet. "No problem. Mila and I were just having a nice chat."

Kendra's skeptical glance took in the both of them. "I won't ask," she said to Dale.

Chuckling, he slid a hand beneath her elbow. "Don't worry. I can use a few lessons in childcare."

"With Mila it's more like lessons in child psychiatry," Kendra joked.

Mila looked back and forth between Dale and her mother. "What does that mean, Mommy?"

Kendra rolled her eyes. "It means you're too smart. Now come along, or we're never going to get to Happy Hearts."

Out in the parking lot, they quickly transferred Mila's booster seat from Kendra's SUV over to the back seat of Dale's truck.

Once the child was safely buckled in and Kendra had climbed into the passenger seat, Dale set them on their way.

"It feels a bit odd to be out of the bakery at this time of day," Kendra said as she watched the residential area slip behind them. "It's not often I take off."

"I figured as much," he said, then chuckled. "I think my brothers wanted to wring my neck when I told them I was taking off the rest of the day. We're in the middle of building miles of new fence on the ranch. And we're doing it all ourselves—to save on cost."

Kendra looked at him. "Sounds like hard work. Will your brothers be speaking to you tomorrow?"

"Morgan will. Shep will probably be hissing at me instead of talking," he said, then added, "Only kidding. We all get along well. If one of us needs time away from the ranch, the others will step up. And Dad isn't the kind that stands right over us barking out orders."

Apparently listening in on their conversation, Mila

spoke up from the back seat. "Dale's daddy's name is Neal and he rides a horse," she told her mother.

Kendra glanced over at Dale and gave him a conspiring wink. "He does? That sounds interesting," she said to Mila. "Maybe one of these days we can go out to Dalton's Grange and see some of the horses. That is, if Dale wouldn't mind having company."

Dale could hardly believe what he was hearing and his first instinct was to lift her hand from the console and smack a happy kiss on the back of it. But with Mila watching the two of them like a hawk, he decided to express his joy by giving Kendra a wink.

"I wouldn't mind at all," he said as casually as he could. "Tori Hawkins boards her horse on our ranch. I imagine she'd be fine with you looking at her. Tori travels a lot, but she might even be there exercising her mare."

Glancing in the mirror, he could see Mila had gone wide-eyed and was leaning up in her seat as far as the safety belt would allow. "Tori Hawkins and her horse! Mommy, did you hear? Oh wow, that would be cool."

Lowering his voice, Dale said to Kendra, "Sorry. I just couldn't resist. After all, we were talking about horses."

Smiling, she reached over and gave his hand a brief squeeze. "It's okay. I think you've made a few points with her."

And maybe, just maybe, he'd made a few points with Kendra. How he'd managed to do it, Dale didn't know. But he was sure of one thing. She was making him a very happy man.

Chapter Seven

Kendra had almost forgotten what it was like to be strolling outdoors with sun shining on her face, autumn leaves drifting through the air and a man's arm snug around the back of her waist. Or maybe she'd never really known what the experience was like, she thought. Her ex had certainly never invited her on one of his many golfing excursions. And the one vacation they'd taken together had been spent gazing out a hotel window at a mountain full of skiers because Bryce had quickly decided he couldn't deal with getting cold and wet.

Sometimes she wondered how she could have been so blind to Bryce's faults. Or why it had taken her so long to finally see he was all about himself. Now that she was getting to know Dale better, she was beginning to see just how hollow her short marriage had been. Frankly, the more time she spent with Dale, the more she wondered if she'd ever truly been in love with her ex-husband, or if she'd simply married him because she'd thought it had been the right thing to do.

"I like this brown-and-white dog. She's pretty," Mila said as she gazed into the kennel at a collie mix. "And she's friendly too."

Mila's eager voice pulled Kendra from her somber musings and she focused on her daughter, who was giggling as the little dog licked the finger she stuck through the panels of the kennel.

"Yes, she's a beautiful dog," Kendra agreed.

The tall, blond young man who was touring them through the kennels spoke up. "Daisy is a collie mix and is very feisty. She needs lots of exercise and plenty of space to run. Most of the time we leave her out in the big yard so she's not confined. Also, another thing to consider is that she's long-haired dog. She'll require plenty of grooming."

Kendra turned a doubtful look on her daughter. "Mila, I don't think Daisy is the dog for you. Not while we're still living in the apartment. Maybe once we get a house of our own with a yard where the dog can run and play without needing to be on a leash." She glanced up at Dale for added support. "What do you think?"

Kendra watched him study Mila's wistful face, then turn his attention to Daisy. She understood she was putting him on the spot to ask for his opinion. Especially when she knew how hard he was trying to make friends with Mila.

He said, "I think Mila would be responsible enough to care for Daisy. And collies are smart and loyal. My brothers and I had one when we were growing up. He was a loving, family-type dog. But I think Daisy would be a little sad to be mostly cooped up indoors."

Mila looked up at Dale, then back to Daisy, and Kendra could see her daughter was carefully weighing everything he'd said.

While Mila continued to gaze lovingly at the dog, Kendra turned a grateful look on Dale. "Thanks for giving your honest opinion," she told him. "I appreciate it."

He shrugged. "As far as Mila is concerned I probably just drove the last nail in my coffin. But I want you both to be happy with whatever pet you choose. And right now I'm thinking we should go have a look at the cats. You know. Smaller, quieter, easier. At least, most of the time."

"I totally agree," Kendra told him. Then, she stepped closer to Mila and placed a comforting hand on her shoulder. "What do you think, Mila? Want to go look at the cats? We might see one that looks like Morris."

Mila gave the friendly dog one last wistful glance. "Dale says Daisy would be sad cooped up inside. I don't want her to be sad."

Kendra tenderly patted her cheek, while hoping Mila or the others couldn't spot the mist in her eyes. "I'm very proud of you, honey, for thinking of Daisy before yourself. We'll get a dog like her someday. I promise. And then the two of you can run everywhere together."

Dale must have recognized how much Kendra needed his support because he moved to her side and curled an arm around her shoulders.

A few steps away, the assistant quickly sized up the situation. "If you'll all follow me, I'll show you to the cats' housing. We have all colors and sizes. I'm sure you'll fall in love with one or two of them."

"Yes, we'd like to see the cats," Kendra told the young man.

The four of them started off in the direction of another building and when Mila skipped a few steps ahead of them, Dale lowered his head toward Kendra's ear.

"This is harder than you imagined it would be, right?"

"Very." She cast him a rueful smile. "I think I actually wanted Daisy as much as Mila did. But we can't always have what we want, can we?"

"Unfortunately, no. Sometimes we have to use common sense."

Kendra said, "I'm sorry I put you on the spot back there about the dog. But I'm grateful to you for helping Mila see what's best for her and Daisy. You know, Mila might not approve of you as my future husband, but she does respect your opinion. She understands you have experience with all sorts of animals."

"It's a good thing I don't have a kid of my own. I'd have a hard time telling him or her no. 'Cause it sure as heck wasn't easy discouraging Mila," he admitted. "She's a sweetheart and I want her to be happy. Let's just hope she finds a cat she falls in love with."

"You're a nice guy, Dale Dalton. Has anyone told you that lately?"

He chuckled. "I'm not sure anyone has ever associated me with the word *nice*. But I'm glad you think so. Now I have added pressure on me not to disappoint Mila—or you."

She cast him a clever glance. "Have you stopped to think I might worry about disappointing you?"

He chuckled again and this time Kendra spotted a twinkle in his blue eyes.

"Don't make my head any bigger than it already is," he said.

No. Dale was far from full of himself and Kendra liked that about him. To be honest, she was liking a whole lot of things about him. But where were these feelings going to lead her? Right now, with Dale by her side, his hand wrapped firmly around hers, she wanted to believe they were headed for something special. Yet she was afraid to allow her hopes to go that far.

They walked a few more yards up a gentle slope before they finally entered a building lined with numerous cages filled with cats of all colors and sizes. Along one side of the room, an open space had been fenced off to allow many of the animals to explore, play with their friends or toys, or simply snooze in a shaft of sunlight coming through a skylight in the roof.

"Those must be the lucky cats," Dale said, gesturing to the open space. "Wonder what a guy or gal has to do to get promoted to the playground?"

Hearing his comment, the assistant chuckled. "The cats are rotated twice a day, so they all get to have some freedom. Unless they have behavioral problems and pose a threat to the other cats. Fortunately, we don't have any troublemakers with us right now."

Mila hurried over to the nearest stack of cages and peered at the assortment of cats. Some of the animals ignored her, while others watched her with wide, curious eyes.

"Mommy, look! These cats are beautiful!"

"Yes, I see," Kendra told her. "You're going to have a hard task trying to find the one you like best."

For the next several minutes, Mila went from cage to cage studying each cat, then over to the play yard to study the lucky ones, as Dale had referred to them. But it wasn't until she spotted a pair of young kittens in a cage åt the end of the room that her face lit with joy. The two tabby cats, one orange and the other gray, were rolling and tumbling in a playful fight.

"Those are the ones I want," she said, pointing to the energetic kittens.

The assistant said, "Those are a brother and sister pair. They're four months old and Daphne doesn't want them to be separated. Not unless their adoption drags on for too long and they're forced to go to different homes."

Mila hurried over to their cage and poked a finger though the wire in an effort to gain the cats' attention. When the curious pair finally eased over to sniff at her finger, she laughed and looked over her shoulder at Dale and Kendra.

"They like me! See?"

"We see," Kendra told her, then turned a skeptical look on Dale. "All at once I go from having no animals in the apartment to two? What do you think?"

Dale chuckled. "Okay, this time I'm not trying to make points with Mila. Daphne is right about not wanting to split them up. At their age they need a feline buddy to be happy and content. While Mila is at school, they'll have each other to play with instead of shredding the furniture or the curtains."

"All right," Kendra told him. "You've convinced me. Besides, it's just one more little mouth to feed. And siblings shouldn't be separated. Right?"

The grin on his face said he was proud of her and Kendra basked in his approval.

"I have a feeling you're going to enjoy these kittens as much as Mila," he said.

She shot him a guilty look. "You're probably right."

When they joined Mila at the cage, she immediately turned a pleading look up at Kendra. "Can I have them, Mommy? They're cute and funny. And I'll take real good care of them, I promise!"

Kendra gave her daughter an indulgent pat on the top

of her head. "If Daphne okays the adoption, then you're going to have two kittens," she told her.

Squealing with joy, Mila hopped up and down before finally flinging her arms around Kendra's waist. "Thank you, Mommy!"

Kendra and Dale were exchanging knowing glances when Mila stepped back from her and looked up at Dale.

"And thank you too, Dale. For bringing us out here to Happy Hearts."

Wonder of wonders, Kendra thought. Was her daughter having a change of heart toward Dale? For everyone's sake, she could only hope.

"You're very welcome," he told Mila. "And you picked out the best kittens in the whole barn."

A beaming smile appeared on Mila's face and her daughter's reaction caused Kendra to recognize what a good father Dale would make. Only he didn't want to be a family man. At least, that was his feelings on the matter right now. But time had a way of changing a person, she thought. Eventually, he might decide he would like to be a daddy.

By the time they'd finished with the adoption process and loaded the pet carrier with the kittens in the back seat beside Mila, the afternoon was rapidly slipping into evening. As Dale drove them back to town, he stopped by Bronco Pets Emporium, and after purchasing food, bowls, a litter box and litter, and last but not least, an assortment of cat toys, drove the last few blocks to Kendra's apartment.

When he finally pulled into the parking slot, darkness had fallen and the streetlamps were creating an eerie glow over the sidewalk leading up to Kendra's front door.

"I'll help you carry everything in," he told Kendra. "And then I should be going."

Surprised, she looked at him. "Going? Why? Don't you want to stay and see how things go with those two little fur balls?"

He felt like Mila when Kendra had told her she could adopt the kittens. Like a kid wanting to jump up and down with joy. Controlling himself, he gave her a lop-sided grin instead. "Sure. But I don't want to wear out my welcome."

"Nonsense. I'll call in an order for lasagna from Mr. Leone and have it delivered. After all, this is a special evening for Mila. The kittens are the first pets she's ever had. She—" Her lips parted as though another thought struck her. "I wasn't thinking, Dale. You might have something else planned to do tonight. If you do, I'll understand."

"Unless you count going home and listening to Dad talk about cows and whether fall is a good time to buy or sell, I don't have a thing to do. I'd like to stay."

"Great." She glanced over the seat to see Mila was totally absorbed with the kittens before she turned her attention back to Dale. "I think she's a little preoccupied."

"Yeah. Just a little," he agreed. "It's good to see her so thrilled."

After hauling everything into the apartment, including the carrier with the kittens, Kendra called in the order for the lasagna. While they waited for it to arrive, they found an appropriate spot for the litter box in the laundry room and a place for the food bowls in the kitchen.

When Dale finally opened the carrier to let out the kittens, the two animals peered cautiously out at their surroundings, before the orange one stuck one paw outside the carrier and then another. Once she walked out, her gray brother followed, much to Mila's delight.

Dale asked, "What are you going to name them?"

"The boy cat is George and the girl is Gypsy."

"George and Gypsy. Those are good names."

The kittens suddenly realized they were free and began to explore the kitchen as fast as their little legs could trot across the tiled floor. While Mila took off after them, Dale walked over to where Kendra was getting plates out of a cabinet.

"Is there anything I can do?" he asked.

While he'd been helping Mila deal with the cats, Kendra had cut up a salad and made a pitcher of sweet tea. With those things already on the table, he figured setting the table was all that was left to do before the food arrived.

"You can dig out some silverware if you'd like." She pointed to a drawer to the right of the double sink. "It's in there."

He opened the drawer and as he began to pull out the utensils, she asked, "Do you ever help your mother in the kitchen?"

"Sometimes I help her with dish washing and cleaning up, but my cooking is limited. Us boys were usually out helping Dad, so we never got any cooking lessons. Now that Erica is on bed rest, Morgan wishes he'd learned how to fry bacon and eggs, at least."

"How is Erica doing? I miss having her and little JoJo stop by the bakery."

"From what Morgan tells me, she and the baby are still doing okay."

Dale glanced over his shoulder to see Mila was on the far side of the room, sitting cross-legged on the floor, while the kittens climbed all over her. He had to admit he'd surprised himself today during their trip to Happy Hearts. When he'd watched her looking at the collie with such longing, he'd wished he could give her everything her heart desired, just as any father wished to give his daughter. But being a father required far more from a man than giving his daughter material things. He'd have to know how to deal with tears, tantrums and tummy aches. He'd have to answer a thousand questions in just the right way. He clearly wasn't equipped for the job.

"That's good news. Still, I'm sure Morgan is stressed out with worry."

He glanced at Kendra. "I'll be happy whenever the baby does finally get here."

"So will I. They—" The remainder of her sentence was left hanging as the sound of the doorbell announced the arrival of their meal. "There's our dinner."

She started out of the room and Dale trailed directly after her.

"Wait, Kendra," he said to her. "I'll get the door."

"I have to pay," she explained.

By the time they entered the living room, Dale managed to catch her by the arm. "Forget it, Kendra. This will be my treat," he insisted.

With a hopeless roll of her eyes, she shook her head. "You are one stubborn man."

"But I'm a nice one. Remember?" he asked impishly.

Much later, after the lasagna had been consumed, along with a few treats Kendra had brought home from the bakery, she and Dale carried their coffee to the couch in the living room. Mila managed to coax the kittens into following her and now she was stretched out on the floor tossing a toy mouse back and forth to the kittens. The felines' silly antics had her giggling with delight.

"Normally at this time of the evening, Mila would be begging to watch TV or play a video game. I'd much rather see her playing with the kittens than staring at a screen." She looked at Dale, who was sitting close beside her on the couch. "I have to admit, you were absolutely right."

"I was? Which time?"

Chuckling, she said, "About having two cats instead of one."

His grin was nothing but humble. "Shoot, that was an easy deduction. Everything is better in pairs."

As though to prove his point, he reached over and clasped his hand around hers. The touch of his fingers only added to the warm vibes she'd been getting from having his long lanky body so close to her.

She said, "I, uh, used to think in those terms, Dale. I thought everyone and everything needed a companion. But that was before my marriage ended."

A moment of silence passed before he gave her hand a light squeeze. "I should have said everything is better with the *right* pair."

Her gaze was drawn back to his face, and the tender expression she found on his features melted a few more spots of her frozen heart. These past few days she'd felt herself growing closer and closer to him. Now, sharing things about her life with him felt right and even necessary. If she ever expected their relationship to grow into something meaningful, she had to be brave enough to expose her past mistakes. Otherwise, they'd only be two people spending time together.

She nodded, then glanced at Mila, who was too far away and too preoccupied to hear their conversation.

"Bryce and I were the wrong pair right from the start," she told him. "I just didn't realize that until it was too late."

His expression somber, he studied her face. "How long were you married?"

"Two years," she answered, then let out a rueful sigh. "I realize it sounds like I didn't give the marriage enough time. But in the end, it was too much time."

"I'm sorry it wasn't good," he said.

She lifted her gaze to his. "The problem was that I was expecting a traditional marriage like my parents have always had. You know, a typical home where spouses share everything. Before we were married, Bryce promised he would give me those things. But it didn't turn out that way."

His blue gaze continued to delve into hers. "I'm sure you believed he'd carry his promises through."

"I did believe him. He seemed eager for us to get married. Now, when I look back on things, it was his deception along with his indifference to Mila that hurt the most."

His eyes narrowed. "What do you mean?"

She grimaced. "The company he worked for wanted its executives to project the image of a settled family man. I didn't find this out until much later, after we were married, and then it became fairly clear that Bryce had considered his marriage to me as a stepping stone to becoming an executive—a cushy position with lots of perks. See, his main ambition in life was to travel, play golf and hang out with his buddies. That was how he spent his time while I was trying to build a bakery business in South Beach and raise our child."

"In other words he used you for his own gain," he said with disgust. "In my book, Kendra, that's evil."

Her snort was a mocking sound. "Of course, Bryce

would never admit such a thing. He'd swear he wanted the higher position to better 'our' lives. He was such a hypocrite. Unfortunately, I didn't really see the full picture until Mila was born."

A thoughtful frown creased his forehead. "Did he want a child?"

"While we were dating, he'd insisted he wanted me to have as many children as I wanted. Even after we were married and I unexpectedly got pregnant, he acted as though it was a good thing, especially for his image. But once she was born—" She glanced over to make sure Mila's attention was still on the kittens, before she turned back to Dale. "He took one look at the baby and that was it. He wouldn't have anything to do with her. To be frank, he considered being with me and Mila boring and a waste of his time."

"The man needed the hell kicked out of him." His thumb gently massaged the skin on the back of her hand as though he wanted to soothe away all the pain she'd ever suffered. "I'll tell you what else I think, Kendra. He didn't deserve the time of day from you. And he sure didn't deserve Mila."

She sighed. "He'd had the audacity to say if she'd been a boy, he might have been interested. As it was, he claimed he didn't have anything in common with a daughter. To hear him say such a thing about his own child was the final straw for me, Dale. I ended our marriage just as fast as the papers could be filed and finalized."

"And that's when you decided to move here to Montana?"

She shook her head. "No. I stayed on in South Beach for a couple of years. I was foolishly hoping if I stayed there Bryce might change and realize he wanted to be a part of his daughter's life. It never happened. He re-married a much younger woman with the maturity of a teenager. She certainly had no desire to be a stepmother. Not that she made any difference. By then it was clear that Mila didn't have a father. Not a real one."

Frowning thoughtfully, he said, "I'm hardly a guy to know what's best for a child. But I'm not so sure I'd want the man around Mila. What kind of influence would he have on her?"

Her sigh was full of regret. "I've always been careful not to say critical things about Bryce in front of Mila. She has this grand idea that he's a great guy and right now I think it's kinder to let her go on believing her father loves her. Later on, when she's older, she can decide for herself if he's someone she wants in her life."

Scooting closer to her side, he enveloped her hand between the two of his. Warmth flooded her and helped to ease the chill in her heart.

His voice low, he said, "Kendra, that first night I walked into the bakery and saw you, I felt certain you were married. But when Mila intercepted me and I figured out she was husband-shopping for you, I was bowled over. I couldn't believe that any man had been fool enough to let you go."

Tears stung her eyes and she desperately tried to blink them away before he could see them. But he did see them and when he groaned with misgivings, she felt like a maudlin fool.

"Aww, Kendra, don't be sorry you told me all of this. I'm glad you explained why your marriage ended and why Mila is so dead set on finding herself a father. I can understand it better now."

Even though her eyes were watery, Kendra could see his expression was full of tenderness. The notion that he cared about her and Mila's feelings caused her voice to turn husky. "I'm glad I could talk to you about this, Dale. And that you understand how things happened."

His expression suddenly turned awkward. "It's obvious I don't have any experience as a husband or father. Heck, I haven't even been serious with a woman. But in my thirty-one years I've learned enough about life to know you and Mila were given a raw deal."

Drawing up one knee, she squared around on the cushion in order to look at him head-on. "You've never been serious, but I'm curious to know—have you ever had your heart broken?"

His lips took on a wry slant. "I've had my pride broken a few times, but not my heart."

Which meant he'd never been in love. Not the deep kind that once it was lost left a wake of tremendous pain. A part of her was glad no woman had ever touched Dale's heart. But it also made Kendra wonder if he was incapable of feeling love to its deepest degree.

The thought had her gaze slipping over his profile and down to the middle of his chest, where diamond-shaped pearl snaps held his gray denim shirt together. She didn't have to touch him to know his chest would be padded with strong muscles- or that lower down, his stomach would be washboard hard. Everything about his lean body screamed masculinity and every part of it called to her. The only thing that was keeping her from wrapping her arms around him and inviting him to kiss her was Mila's presence.

Heaving out a heavy breath, she tried to push aside the erotic thoughts. "To be honest, Dale, I'm the guilty one for my failed marriage. Yes, Bryce was a hypocrite. But in a way I was worse—I was delusional about him, about love and what it really was. Now when I look back on that time when we were dating, I can see I was too young to know the difference between infatuation and love. He was good-looking, charming and already successful at a career in business. I fell for all of it. You know, like a girl goes gaga over the high-school quarterback. It's not real love. It's a euphoric fog and it takes a while for the mist to clear. But eventually it rolls away, and whenever that happens reality slaps you in the face. Believe me, Dale, I'm not going to let infatuation take hold of me again. Not ever."

He said, "I get what you're saying. But I don't believe you should take the majority of the blame for your marriage ending. You tried."

"Hmm. Yes. I tried. But sometimes trying isn't enough." She cast him a wan smile. "Now that you've listened to all my past troubles you're probably even more determined to remain a bachelor. I can't say that I blame you."

Shrugging, his gaze dropped to their entwined hands. "You might be surprised to know that when I was much younger I wanted all those things you talked about. The house and home. A wife to love me and children to carry on my name and eventually help me run a ranch of my own. But..."

More than curious now, she waited for him to continue. When he didn't, she asked, "What's the matter? Are you afraid I'll laugh at you or something?"

She softened her question with an impish smile and he squeezed her hand in a way that made it feel almost as intimate as a kiss.

"No. You're too sweet to poke fun at a person."

She purposely cleared her throat. "Uh, Dale, I should point out that just because I bake sweets, doesn't mean I am sweet."

He smiled at her, then glanced away. "You remember I told you about my dad's infidelity?"

"Sure. I could tell how deeply it affected you and your whole family."

"Well, when the truth exploded and Mom had the heart attack, something turned sick inside me. I saw all the pain she was going through because of Dad's betrayal. It took all the sunshine and happiness out of her life and for a long time she was just a shell of the mother we'd always known. My brothers and I hated Dad and for a while our whole family was split up."

"And your mother? Did she hate her husband?"

"No. I think Mom is incapable of hating anyone. But we all thought their marriage was going to end. That's when I decided I didn't want any part of love and marriage. To me, it wasn't worth the risk of the pain and suffering my parents were going through. And since then, I haven't met any woman who's changed my opinion on the matter. Until—"

His last word hung in the air and so did Kendra's breath as she waited for him to complete his thought. Was he going to say...*until I met you?* Yes, something in his voice made her think so.

Drawing her hand free from his grasp, she wrapped it over his forearm. "Dale?"

He lifted his gaze back to hers and from the dazed look on his face, she decided he must have surprised himself by even thinking the unspoken words.

"I'm sorry, Kendra. I shouldn't be saying this—not tonight. Not in the same room with Mila. But I'd be a liar if I didn't tell you how much I want you. How much you've come to mean to me."

Kendra silently groaned as she was overcome with the urge to fling her arms around his neck and press kisses all over his face. Instead, the most she could do was to glance over to make sure Mila hadn't moved within earshot. But to her amazement, her daughter appeared to be sound asleep with her head pillowed on her arm and the two kittens snuggled in sleeping balls against her chest.

"You don't have to worry about Mila overhearing you, Dale. Look over there. She and the kittens have played themselves to sleep."

He looked across the room to the spot where Mila and the kittens had been playing. "I feel awful now. I've interrupted her bedtime."

"No. The long day and all the excitement have caused her to fall asleep earlier than usual," she said in a hushed voice. Then, rising to her feet, she urged him up. "Come with me."

He followed her out of the living room and down the shadowy hallway. As soon as they reached a spot where they were safely out of sight, she turned and wrapped her arms around him. "Now I can tell you how much I want you too, Dale. So very much."

A look of amazement crossed his face and then a tiny groan sounded in his throat as he lowered his lips down to hers.

This time when he kissed her everything felt different. There was no hesitancy or set boundaries. There was only him and her giving and taking freely, hungrily.

If the kiss lasted for hours it wouldn't have been long enough. She wanted to keep holding the hard length of his body against hers, to keep the magical maneuvers of his mouth upon hers. But given the circumstances, they couldn't let themselves lose control.

Dale's thoughts must have been running along the same line as hers. After making a few more desperate plunders of her lips, he tore his mouth from hers and looked regrettably down at her.

"We, uh, can't do this now." His hands lingered on her shoulders as he drew in deep, ragged breaths.

Through drowsy eyes, she scanned his face. "No. You're right. We can't. But I'm happy, anyway. So very happy. Are you?"

Groaning, he pulled her head against his chest and stroked a hand over her hair. "Oh darlin', you have me walking on air. Tomorrow my brothers are going to have to tie a lariat around me to keep my feet on the ground."

Suddenly she wanted to laugh and sing. She wanted to dance him down the hallway and straight to her bed. She wanted him lying beside her, holding her, loving her. Not just for tonight. But other nights to come.

She clung to the front of his shirt. "So when are we going to be together again—alone? I'll need some time to figure this out."

His hands were caressing her face and shoulders and sliding down her arms as though he wanted to savor every second of touching her before he said good night.

"We're going to need more fencing supplies from town tomorrow. I'll volunteer for the chore and drop by the bakery," he suggested. "Maybe by then we can figure out something."

"Yes, that will give me a chance to plan." She smiled coyly up at him. "And see you again."

He chuckled knowingly. "Why do you think I'm going to do the volunteering?" he asked, then reluctantly set her back from him. "Now, I'd better get my hat and jacket and get out of here. Mila needs to be in bed."

"She's going to hate that she missed telling you good-bye," Kendra told him.

He cast her a doubtful glance as they headed back to the living room. "I seriously doubt it."

"Trust me. Every time she looks at George and Gypsy she's going to think of you."

"And everywhere I look I'm going to think of you," he murmured.

She reached for his hand and held it until they reached the short foyer leading to the front door, then released him so that he could slip on his jacket and tug his hat over his dark hair.

Once he was finished, she rested a hand on his arm. "Thank you for today, Dale," she whispered. "And tonight."

He pulled her close and placed one last kiss on her lips. "I'll see you tomorrow."

"Yes. Tomorrow."

He slipped out the door and once she'd locked it securely behind him, she leaned against the wooden panel and let out a dreamy sigh.

How much you've come to mean to me.

The moment he'd spoken those words to her everything in her heart had shifted like a dark cavern suddenly bursting open to the bright sunlight.

She might be taking things too quickly and she should probably think harder about getting seriously involved with Dale before she leaped into his arms. But for the past five years she'd been cautious and leery. She'd been skeptical of every man who'd taken a sidelong glance at her. Yes, she'd played it safe and kept her mind focused on raising her daughter and building her business. Yet, at the same time, she'd been very lonely. And now that Dale had walked into her life, she realized she didn't want to be lonely anymore.

Chapter Eight

The next afternoon as Dale drove into town for the fencing supplies, he hummed along to a song on the radio while his thoughts continued to whirl around Kendra and everything she'd said to him last night.

He'd not expected her to talk about her failed marriage or explain why Mila didn't have a father in her life. Each time he thought of the man shunning his newborn daughter, his stomach literally churned with loathing. And each time he imagined Kendra being emotionally hurt and humiliated, he wanted to go to Florida and hunt the man down. But Dale had to believe that hurtful part of her life was all in her past now. He had to believe she was ready to start a new life with him.

For how long, Dale? Have you finally decided one woman is all you'll want for the rest of your life? Do you honestly think you can be a father to Mila? And what if Kendra wants another child?

A few days ago, those questions would've shot arrows of icy fear shooting through him. But some sort of upheaval seemed to have taken place inside him. Ever since he'd taken Kendra into his arms and kissed her, his world had turned into a different place. She made everything in his life feel bright and special. He didn't want to give that up, even if it meant he might ultimately get hurt.

When Dale reached town, he went by Bronco Feed and Ranch Supply to pick up the post and wire. After the truck was loaded with the supplies, he drove deeper into the business section of Bronco Heights, where Kendra's Cupcakes was located.

Since it was midafternoon, he expected there to be a lull in business at the bakery, but he was wrong. The nearest parking slot he could find was a block away, and when he finally walked through the front entrance, he found the tables all taken and a line of customers waiting at the display counters. Presently, Andrea, the young brunette server, was taking care of those customers while Smitty was carrying a tray filled with fancy coffees over to the tables.

From the corner of his eye, he spotted a couple waving in his direction and he turned his head to see Tori Hawkins and Bobby Stone sitting at a table near the window. The couple had been gone to Australia on a rodeo tour and had just arrived back in Bronco only a few days ago.

As soon as Dale walked up to their table, Bobby held up both hands. "Okay, you caught me. I plead guilty. I'm eating Kendra's cupcakes instead of back on the ranch training horses."

"Don't worry. I won't tell anybody if you don't," he joked, then shook his head. "I imagine you came into town for a reason other than to see Tori and eat cupcakes."

Tori smiled lovingly at her fiancé. "Bobby tells me he showed up just to see me, of course."

"Of course," Dale said. "The man isn't dumb."

Bobby chuckled. "Actually, your dad wanted me to take Opal to the vet. She's limping again on her front left."

"I hope the vet gets Opal fixed," Dale said. "She's a special mare."

Bobby nodded. "Don't worry. She'll be okay. So what's your excuse for being here in Kendra's Cupcakes instead of building fence with your brothers?"

Dale playfully held a finger up to his lips. "Shhh. Somebody might hear you," he said, then grinned. "I came in for fencing supplies. But I didn't want to beat it right back to the ranch without a brownie."

"A brownie! So that's why you're here!" Kendra said in a teasing voice as she suddenly walked up by Dale's side and looped her arm around his. "And all along I thought it was me."

While Tori and Bobby laughed and exchanged knowing glances, Dale turned to Kendra. In spite of being in the busy bakery, he bent his head and placed a light kiss on her cheek.

"I didn't see you behind the counter so I came to say hello to Tori and Bobby," he told her.

The smile she gave him hit him smack in the middle of his chest. "While Andrea is on duty, I was taking advantage and doing some work in my office. Want to come back with me? You can take a brownie and some coffee with you. Since that's why you're here," she added teasingly.

Dale glanced over at Tori and Bobby. "See you two later. I have an offer I can't refuse."

"Sure, Dale. But I don't know why you're getting such special treatment."

Dale laughed and gave him a wink. "Frankly, I don't, either."

He followed her through the milling customers, then around the display cases and through a door to the kitchen. He barely caught the glimpse of a row of cabinets and several stainless-steel ovens before she opened another door to their right and they entered another small room, which appeared to be an office.

The second she shut the door behind them, he caught her by the shoulders and pulled her into his arms.

"Mmm," he murmured against her lips. "You taste better than anything I could get from one of your display cases."

"Oh, I don't know about that," she said with a provocative growl. "I'm a pretty good baker."

Chuckling under his breath, he moved his hands against her back and drew her even tighter against him. "You're pretty good at making me want you."

He pressed a light kiss on her lips, but before he could lift his head, her hand curled against the back of his neck and urged his mouth back to hers.

This time he knew she wasn't going to settle for a simple little kiss and he was only too eager to fill her request. With her soft body crushed against his and his lips feasting on hers, his senses began to spin and all he could think about was making love to her for hours on end. Nothing in his life would make sense until he could make her his woman.

When the burning in his lungs finally became too

much to bear, he lifted his head and stared into her blue eyes.

"I don't know what happens to me, Kendra, but each time I kiss you my mind goes a little haywire."

Smiling gently, she reached up and touched her fingertips to his cheek. "Mine goes a little haywire too. But that's the way it's supposed to be, isn't it? When two people have chemistry, the formula usually creates an explosion."

And he was on the verge of one now, Dale thought, as he eyed the couch pushed against one wall of the cozy room. With the door safely locked, he could make love to her right there, right now. No doubt, the experience would be fast and furious and mind-blowing. But Kendra deserved better than a quick romp on a couch with dozens of people in the next room. And so did he. Whenever he did finally have the chance to make love to her, he wanted their time together to be special.

He released a heavy breath and eased her out of his arms. "Yes, and at this moment my chemistry is boiling."

She chuckled knowingly, then turned her back to him and made a sweeping gesture with her hand. "In case you haven't noticed yet, this is my office. There's nothing fancy about it, but the space serves the purpose of what I need."

"You don't need fancy to do a good job. And you're definitely doing a superb job of running this bakery. It's the middle of the afternoon and it's jammed with customers. I'm amazed."

Facing him, she eased a hip onto the corner of the wide desk and Dale thought how perfectly cute she looked with a splotched apron tied over her jeans and long tendrils falling from her messy bun. At one point today she must have applied rosy color to her lips. Now, after their heated kisses, the color had faded to a pink that matched her cheeks.

"At this time of the day, the coffee items are what draws the customers in. People are wearing down and need something to perk them up. Poor Smitty is getting a workout."

He closed the short space between them and reached for her hand. "So far today I haven't been much help to my brothers. All I can think about is you and the two of us being together."

"Jackie asked me earlier if I'd taken some sort of sedative. She said I was out of it. Her way of telling me I haven't been making much sense. And I don't make much sense when I'm thinking of you."

He leaned forward and pressed a kiss on her forehead. She smelled like cinnamon and vanilla, and though he'd never considered those scents as being sexy, on her they were amazingly sultry.

"Have you figured out a plan for us to go out again? Alone?" he asked.

"On school nights Mila has to be in bed early. So the best I can do is make our date for Friday night. Mila has a good friend, Louisa, who lives a couple of blocks from us. She often stays overnight with her. And, in turn, Louisa, spends a night with us. I've already spoken to Louisa's mother and she's perfectly fine with having Mila over Friday night."

"Yes, but what about Mila? Does she know you're going on a date with me?"

Kendra nodded. "Yes, I told her."

"And? How did she react?"

Sighing, she pushed at the strands of hair on her forehead. "Well, she certainly didn't argue with me about it.

She knows better than to try to give her mother orders. But she did give me another reminder that you weren't my type."

Under different circumstances, Dale might have resented Mila's attitude. Particularly when he'd been nothing but kind to her. But he couldn't be angry at the girl. Especially now that he'd learned how her father had neglected her.

"Hmm. I guess her reaction could've been worse," Dale said with a good-natured shrug. "I'll just have to change her opinion by showing her I *am* your type."

Smiling, Kendra squeezed his hand. "You *are* my type, Dale. She'll eventually figure that out for herself."

"I hope you're right, Kendra. Because I don't want to just make you happy. I want Mila to be happy too."

She kissed his cheek. "Just be yourself and give her time."

He gave her a wry grin. "If you say so. Right now I'd better be heading back to the ranch. What time Friday evening do you want me to pick you up?"

"Six thirty, if you can make it."

"A major earthquake couldn't stop me," he promised. "And if you'd like, I can try to get reservations at DJ's Deluxe."

She thought for one quick moment before she said, "DJ's Deluxe is a lovely offer, Dale, but let's just have something simple—and closer to home."

He shot her a clever grin. "Something like *fast* food?"

Slipping off the corner of the desk, she rose on the tips of her toes and planted a promising kiss on his lips. "*Really fast* food," she whispered.

Dale cleared his throat and started to the door. "I'd better get out of here while I can."

Kendra followed behind him. "I'll get you a brownie and coffee for the ride back to Dalton's Grange."

"Mommy, why are you going out on another date with Dale tonight? You're only wasting your time. He won't ever get married to you. If you'd go out with Mr. Drake again, he'd probably ask you to marry him. And then we could have a big, beautiful wedding with lots of flowers and music. Just like Audrey Hawkins. And you'd have a giant diamond ring on your finger that sparkled when you turned your hand."

Kendra bit back an impatient sigh as she stood at the end of Mila's bed, watching the girl carefully pack her overnight bag. Although she hadn't put up a protest about going to Louisa's tonight for a sleepover, she was hardly exhibiting the excitement she normally displayed whenever she was going to stay with her friend. In fact, Mila had been whining for the past half hour and Kendra was on the verge of losing her patience.

"Listen, Mila, I'm not going to say this again. I am not romantically interested in Mr. Drake. I never will be. So don't mention him again. And just because I'm going out to dinner with Dale, doesn't mean I'm expecting him to marry me."

"You sound mean, Mommy."

Kendra picked up Mila's toothbrush holder and stuffed it into the overnight case. "I'm not trying to be mean, Mila. I want you to think about these things you're saying. Dale is a nice man and he cares about you. And deep down, I believe you know that."

Though she refused to look at her mother, Mila's lips spread into a smirk. "Yes. He's nice. But he won't ever be my daddy. My daddy is in Florida and one of these days he'll come to see me. I know he will!"

By the time Mila finished the last sentence, her lips were quivering and Kendra struggled not to break down in tears. She didn't want her daughter to hurt for any reason. On the other hand, she'd been looking forward to tonight and eagerly waiting to finally be with Dale again.

Sighing, she walked around the bed and gave Mila's shoulders an affectionate squeeze. "Maybe so. But for now you'll have to do with just a mommy."

Mila finished loading her overnight bag and didn't say any more on the subject. And during the short drive to Louisa's house, she remained quiet. Not a sulky quiet, but a thoughtful silence that told Kendra her daughter's mind was working overtime. Probably on how to turn her mother against Dale. The idea hurt Kendra. But she had to remember that Mila was also hurting because her friends had a daddy and she didn't.

An hour later, after she'd finished donning a short black sweater dress and a pair of brown suede fashion boots that reached her knees, her spirits begin to lift. And by the time she'd done her hair and added a bit of light makeup, she'd convinced herself that time would fix this obsession of Mila's to get her mother a husband. As for her daughter believing Bryce was going to show up in Bronco, she might as well believe she could catch a falling star. It simply wasn't going to happen.

When Dale arrived, Kendra was ready and waiting and the two of them wasted no time in driving to a fast-food restaurant that specialized in Mexican dishes.

"So how did things go with Mila this evening? Did she want to take the kittens with her when she went to stay with her friend?"

Smiling wanly, Kendra shook her head. "I convinced her the kittens would be traumatized to be moved again so soon after leaving Happy Hearts and she understood. But I— Well, I had to get a little stern with her earlier. She, uh, thinks I'm wasting my time dating you."

He lowered the tortilla chip he was about to put in his mouth and stared at her. "Is that what you're thinking?"

Kendra groaned. "Oh please, Dale. Not you too! Of course, I don't think I'm wasting my time! Would I be here with you if I did?"

He smiled sheepishly at her. "No. I guess not. It's just that I worry Mila will convince you to find a better man than me."

She reached across the table and touched her fingers to his. "Not a chance. I've found the man who makes me feel very special," she told him. "Eventually Mila will understand. I only wish she'd stop all this wedding nonsense. It's really beginning to wear on me."

"She's doing it all because she wants a daddy. Even I can see that. You know, she talked to me a bit about your ex-husband. She believes he's a wonderful man who is eventually going to come after her."

"Yes, well, it's like I told you. I've never bad-mouthed Bryce to her. Maybe it's wrong of me to deceive her. But she's just a little girl. And letting her believe her father is a great guy can't be as bad as her learning he'd turned his back on her."

"Yeah. I understand." He smiled at her. "And who knows, by the time Mila gets a little older she'll have the father she wants."

Was he implying he might take up the role of Mila's father? No. She wasn't going to let her thoughts go there. Not tonight. She needed more time with him and he needed more with her. Later, she could begin to ask questions.

"Yes, who knows," she repeated quietly, then, purposefully putting a cheery smile on her face, she deliberately changed the subject. "So how did the fence building go today? Are you getting close to being finished?"

"We are. About a mile more to go. After that we have a bunch of new calves to be branded. And with winter coming on, we're beginning to spread hay for the livestock. The hired hands usually take care of that chore, but that means us brothers have to deal with the other jobs they normally do around the ranch yard."

"In other words, the tasks and who does them depends on the weather and the time of the year," she said.

"Exactly."

"Do you like things that way?" she asked. "Or would you rather focus on one thing? Like Bobby does with the horses."

He grinned. "Variety is the spice of life. I enjoy doing different jobs on the ranch. Keeps things interesting." He leaned eagerly toward her. "I'd really love for you and Mila to come out to Dalton's Grange soon. I think you'll love it. And I believe you'll like my parents too."

Surprise widened her eyes. "You want me to meet your parents?"

A crease appeared between his dark eyebrows. "Well, sure. They'd think it mighty strange if you came out to the ranch and I didn't make a point to introduce you."

She forked a bite of burrito, while questions darted through her mind. "Oh, so they're used to you having a girlfriend visit you on the ranch."

He shot her a puzzled look, then let out a laugh loud enough to pull a few eyes in their direction.

"What's so funny?" she asked.

"These ideas you have about me. Like I'm a regular cowboy lothario or something. Kendra, I haven't had any girlfriend out to the ranch. There's not one I've wanted to show my home to—until you."

There it was again. *Until you.* Only two little words and yet to her it sounded so much like "I'm falling in love with you." But a woman could think most anything when she was gazing into the eyes of a man who made the rhythm of her heart change into a pagan drumbeat.

"I'd love to see your home and meet your parents, Dale. Mila hasn't forgotten your promise to show her the horses."

"And that's a promise I aim to keep."

A few minutes later, when they left the restaurant, the wind had grown cold and clouds were making a hasty trip south as they scudded across the night sky.

Dale flipped up the sherpa collar on his jacket and snuggled Kendra closer to his side. "This is hardly a night to take a stroll in the park," he said.

She slipped an arm across his back as they walked the last few steps to his truck. "Good thing. I wasn't wanting to stroll in the park tonight."

His knowing chuckle was swept away by the wind as he whirled her into his arms and lowered his mouth to hers. "All I want is you…close to me."

After a quick kiss on her lips, he helped her into the truck and drove the short distance back to her apartment without either of them saying a word.

She'd left a small lamp burning in the living room, and as they stood in the pool of light, Kendra quickly shed her coat and the white scarf she'd wrapped loosely around her neck, while Dale removed his coat and hat.

"Would you like for me to hang those up for you?" she asked.

"Don't bother. They'll be fine here."

He tossed the coat over the back of the nearest armchair and laid his hat in the seat. Kendra placed her coat and scarf alongside his.

"So will mine," she said, then rested a hand on his arm. "I'm not going to ask if you want anything else to eat or drink."

"You can ask me that later," he murmured. "Much later."

He pulled her into his arms and as she looked up at him, a clever smile tilted her lips. "Do you hear what I hear?"

"I don't hear a thing."

"Exactly. It's blessedly quiet. And other than two little kittens that must be asleep in their bed, we're completely alone."

His hand lifted to her face and the tip of his forefinger skimmed lightly over her cheekbone, across the bridge of her nose, then down to the hollow indention of her lips. "Alone. With you," he whispered. "This is all I've been thinking about, Kendra. You and me together."

With his hands cradling the sides of her face, his thumbs reached under her chin and lifted it upward. She could feel her lips trembling as they waited for his kiss. But the trembling didn't stop there. It was coursing its way up and down her body and turning her legs into two wobbly sticks.

"Dale. I never thought I'd ever want another man. But here I am, wanting you with every fiber in my body. And I'm not going to ask myself why. It doesn't matter. All that matters is that you want me too."

"Oh yes, darlin'. With everything inside of me."

He lowered his mouth to hers and for the next few moments they were lost in the erotic pleasure of their lips meshing and searching, their tongues curling and locking in a heated dance.

Desire plunged through her, washing her senses of

everything but him and the eager caress of his hands sweeping over her breasts, then cupping her bottom.

When he pulled her hips forward, she could feel his hard manhood bulged against the fly of his jeans and the notion that he was already that aroused filled her with a heady sense of power.

Groaning with pleasure, she clutched the front of his shirt, hoping against hope that her legs wouldn't collapse or she'd end up fainting at his feet.

But just as she thought she'd die from lack of oxygen, he pulled back from her. "I think you, uh, need to show me your bedroom."

Unable to do more than nod, she reached for his hand and led him down the dark hallway to her bedroom.

"I cleaned off the bed earlier this evening," she told him in a husky voice. "Otherwise, the room is cluttered so you might want to keep your eyes shut."

He chuckled under his breath. "Don't worry. My eyes are going to be on you and you alone."

Even in the semidarkness of the room she could see he was smiling at her, and suddenly all the emotions that had been building in her these past few days boiled to the surface and slipped from her eyes in a trail of salty tears.

Stepping forward, she wrapped her arms around his waist and rested her cheek against his chest. "Oh Dale. I haven't waited days to be in your arms. I've been waiting years for you—to find someone who makes me feel this much. Thank you for coming into my life."

His cheek rested against the top of her head as his arms circled tightly around her. "You want to know how I feel? I hate myself for not walking into your bakery three years ago. For wasting all that time we could've been together."

Her chin rested against his chest as she tilted her head back to look at him. "You think so? You think this would've happened back then?"

"You don't?"

"I'm not sure. I wasn't looking for a man."

Her logical reasoning put a smile on his face. "You weren't looking for one when you first saw me. But here we are."

"Yes, here we are. Enough said."

"Mmm. More than enough."

He placed another kiss on her lips, then, catching the folds of her dress with his hands, he began to tug it upward until the fabric bunched around her breasts. She lifted her arms straight up to allow him to slip the garment over her head.

Once he'd tossed it aside, she didn't have time to be embarrassed at standing in front of him with nothing on but a black satin bra and matching panties. He instantly swept her into his arms and began raining kisses over her neck, along the ridge of one shoulder, then down her chest until he reached the cleavage between her breasts. When that happened, he undid for the front clasp and let the garment fall around her waist, exposing her breasts. The exploration of his lips continued over the soft mounds until his mouth settled on one puckered nipple.

Fiery pleasure shot through her, rocking her balance and forcing her hands to find a steadying hold on his arms.

Groaning with need, she whispered his name and he lifted his head to meet her gaze. His eyes were half-closed and drowsy with desire and Kendra knew he was seeing the same sort of longing on her face. Strange, she thought, that for once in her life, it didn't bother her to let a man see her wanton needs. Moreover, she wanted Dale to see the feelings swirling through her and know how much these moments meant to her.

"Kendra. My Kendra."

He kissed his way back to her lips, and this time when his tongue plundered the inner cavity of her mouth, she was engulfed with the need to have his bare skin next to hers.

She lifted her hands to the front of his shirt and managed to pry two snaps apart before he broke the kiss and stepped back from her.

"I'll do this," he murmured. "It'll be faster that way."

While he dealt with removing his clothes, Kendra sat on the side of the bed and unzipped her tall boots. By the time she set them aside and stepped out of her panties, he'd shed all of his clothing, except for a pair of navy blue boxers.

Oh my. His body was a sight to behold and Kendra leaned back on one hand and took immense pleasure in gawking at him.

"You know, you really shouldn't wear clothes," she told him. "You're depriving the women of Bronco."

Chuckling, he joined her on the bed. "It's dark in here and you can't see all of me."

"Hmm. You're wrong. I'm getting a perfect view."

With his hands on her shoulders, he eased her downward until her back was flat against the mattress.

"So am I," he said. "And I don't want to close my eyes. I don't even want to blink. I'm afraid you might disappear."

Lying next to her, he rolled her into him, and as his arms came around her, she was enveloped by the hard heat of his body. As the heady warmth seeped through her, she slid her palms over his arms and shoulders, across his chest, then down to the hard flesh above the waistband of his shorts.

"I'm not going anywhere," she whispered as she pressed light kisses along the ridge of his collarbone. "We have all night."

All night. Dale should have been thrilled with her promise. Instead, he was thinking it wouldn't be enough time with her. Not even close to enough. He wanted days and months of making love to her. No. He wanted a lifetime of making love to her. And until he had her promise of forever, he wouldn't feel complete.

Making love to her for a lifetime. Do you know what that means, Dale? Are you ready to give your heart to this woman?

The voice of reason dashed through his mind as he pushed a curtain of hair away from the side of her neck and dropped his lips to the smooth, velvety skin. But he didn't allow the questions it presented to linger. No, he'd think of them later. When his senses were cleared of this enchantment of having her in his arms.

"Yes. All night," he whispered against her lips. "And we're not going to waste a second of it."

Her arm slipped around his neck and as he drew her even closer, her soft breasts flattened against his chest and her leg settled loosely over his. Instinctively, his hands slid down her back until he reached the flare of her hips, then with his hands on her buttocks, he pulled the lower half of her body next to his aching manhood.

She pressed the juncture of her thighs tight against his arousal, while at the same time her lips traveled across his face until her mouth was on his.

With a groan of surrender, he kissed her until the

room around them began to spin and the fire in his loins grew to unbearable proportions.

Beneath his hands, her hair felt like satin, her skin like warm velvet, and it was all surrounded by the sweet scent of exotic flowers. Touching her was like stepping into paradise. Tasting her was like lapping an endless bowl of sweet cream. And yet, none of the pleasures were enough to ease the ache that had been building in him from the first moment they'd kissed.

Breaking the contact between their lips, he was breathing hard as his gaze met hers. "I need to be inside you, darlin'," he said in a voice rough with desire. "Are you ready for this?"

Her eyelids drooped, while the corners of her mouth tilted up. "I'm more than ready for this—for you."

He didn't need to hear more. Quickly, he climbed off the bed, and after digging a condom from his wallet, he tossed away his shorts and rolled the protection over his hardened shaft. And all the while he could feel her watching him, and the knowledge that her eyes were feasting on his intimate parts aroused him even more.

When he rejoined her on the mattress, he positioned himself over her and she instantly parted her legs. He slipped one hand to the moist folds between her thighs and for a few incredible moments he touched her there. But soon, the unbearable need to connect their bodies overtook his desire to explore.

"I want to touch you everywhere, Kendra. I want to taste every part of you," he whispered. "But that's going to have to come later. Much later."

Planting his hands on either side of her head to support the upper part of his body, he lowered his hips and entered her with a slow, smooth thrust.

Somewhere beyond the roaring in his ears, he heard a

tiny moan in her throat and then, as he sunk deeper and deeper in her velvety body, he didn't hear anything. He couldn't think anything, except that he was drowning in a pleasure so intense it was nearly impossible to breathe.

"Dale. Oh Dale."

She whispered his name and then with her hands clamped onto his shoulders, she arched her hips up to meet his.

Hot, searing desire gripped his body as he began to thrust slowly, then faster. And all at once they settled into a perfect rhythm of give and take. Back and forth. Up and down. She was like a soft marshmallow in his arms and he wanted to fill himself with her and nothing but her.

"This is how it should be for us, darlin'. So good—so perfect."

"Yes. Perfect." Lifting her head off the mattress, she slid her open lips over his chest, around each nipple and on to the middle of his breastbone. "Don't stop loving me. Don't stop."

The raw desire in her voice acted on his senses as much as the hungry thrust of her hips, and the need to please her drove him onward. And just when he thought his heart was going to beat out of his chest, he felt her fingers digging into his back and her hips made one desperate arch against him.

He tried to hang on and extend their erotic trip a few more moments, but when a cry of release rushed out of her, the fragile thread holding the last of his control snapped. Suddenly he was flung into an empty space, where tiny pinpoints of lights were showering him, blinding him with their brilliance and pricking every nerve in his body with sizzling waves of ecstasy.

By the time his upper body collapsed over hers, he

wasn't sure he was still alive. His heartbeat was thrumming in his ears and his lungs were so starved for oxygen that he figured they were too damaged to work.

He gulped in several ragged breaths before he found enough strength to roll his weight to one side of her, and even then he was too drained to lift his head from the mattress.

When she finally rolled toward him and smoothed a hand over his damp chest, he groaned and opened his eyes to see her face was close to his and her eyes were soft and full of wonder.

"Are you okay?" she asked softly.

He wanted to laugh, but he didn't have the strength.

No. He wasn't okay. He was somebody else. Some guy he didn't know. What had happened to him? And why didn't he want to go back to the old Dale? The Dale that had always considered sex a purely physical thing?

He managed to grunt with amusement. "Shouldn't I be the one asking you that question instead of the other way around?"

"There's no need to ask me. You can see for yourself how wonderful I am."

Twisting his head in order to have a closer look at her face, he saw she was smiling at him as if she adored him. Could that be? Or was he only seeing something he wanted to see?

He grunted again. "Does that mean my condition looks questionable?"

Laughing softly, she scooted close enough to kiss his cheek. "No. I just want to know that you're happy."

Rolling onto his back, he pulled the top part of her body into his arms and nuzzled his nose in the curve of her neck. "Happy doesn't begin to describe how I feel right now. I'm pretty much on a cloud. And you know the best part about it? You're right here on the cloud with me."

"Together. Yes, that's the best part." Her fingers thrust into his hair and combed it back from his forehead. "Because I never thought—"

He eased his head back far enough to look at her. "You never thought what?"

The corners of her mouth dipped downward. "Oh, that I'd ever find a man that I would want to be this close to. I was actually afraid I had grown incapable of feeling anything for a man. And then you—" A sly grin suddenly replaced the dour expression on her lips. "Why the heck did you have to be so sexy? Before I even knew it, you'd turned my head."

"I find that hard to believe."

Her hand slid up and down his arm as though she was trying to memorize the shape of the flesh and bone. Or maybe she was trying to make sure the hot coals in his loins didn't cool anytime soon.

"Why?" she asked, then frowned. "Sometimes I get the feeling you thought I was too— Well, that maybe I'd be a snob."

He frowned. "I never thought you could be a snob to anyone. I just think—I'm just a simple cowboy. I'm not suave or sophisticated or comfortable at fancy events. Give me a horse and a saddle and a range to ride on and that's about all I want—along with you, that is."

Her chuckle was a sexy sound that slithered right down his spine and had his hands drawing her closer to him.

"I don't need or want suave or sophisticated. And I certainly don't need fancy. All I want is for you to be genuine and honest with me."

Pushing his fingers into her hair, he drew her face

close enough to place a long, lingering kiss on her lips. "I'll never make promises to you that I don't intend to keep, Kendra. That's not the way I work."

Her soft sigh brushed against his cheek. "I believe you. Otherwise, you wouldn't be here in my bed."

"Mmm. Speaking of being in bed, don't you think we need to make the most of our time here?"

Lifting her head, she gave him a coy grin. "I was just thinking I should go to the kitchen and make a pot of coffee? You need to replenish your strength."

Chuckling under his breath, he flipped her onto her back, then climbed over her. "I'll show you how much strength I have—without the coffee."

Snaking an arm around the back of his neck, she drew him downward until his chest was pressed close to hers. "Come here, cowboy."

With their lips bonded together and her hands making exploratory circles upon his back, the desire that had momentarily cooled was rapidly rising to a boiling point.

"I can't believe I already want to be inside of you again," he whispered. "I can't believe my body is telling me it has to have you."

With a needy sigh, she smoothed a hand against the side of his face. "And my body is telling me the same thing. I think you've cast a love spell on me."

"If it's a love spell, I don't want anything to break it."

He lowered his mouth to hers again and just as he was losing himself in her kiss, the phone on her nightstand rang.

The unexpected sound jarred the quietness of the room and he lifted his head to look at the offensive instrument.

"Are you expecting a call?"

"Not at all. I rarely get calls on the landline. I'll check the ID. It's probably a spam call."

She scooted out from beneath him and over to the edge of the bed. As soon as she spotted the identity of the caller, she quickly picked up the receiver.

"Hello, Bev. Is anything wrong?"

Sensing the call might be important, Dale sat up and waited uneasily for her to finish the conversation.

"Oh. That's not like her. No," Kendra continued. "Yes, and it's no problem. I'm just sorry to put you through this. I'll be there in just a few minutes."

She hung up the phone, then turned a look of utter disappointment on him.

"What's wrong?" he asked.

"That was Bev. Louisa's mother. She called to let me know Mila isn't feeling well and wants to come home."

The image of Mila sick and calling for her mother popped into his mind, and the anxious concern that followed it wasn't a typical boyfriend reaction. It was the sort of unease a parent would experience.

"Do you think it's anything serious?" Dale asked.

"Without seeing her, I honestly can't say. But I—"

When she didn't finish, Dale prompted her to explain. "But what? Is Mila throwing up? Running a fever or something?"

She shook her head. "Nothing so bad as that. Bev said Mila is complaining of a headache. She never has a headache. I can't say for certain, but I'm thinking my daughter is having an I-don't-want-Mommy-and-Dale-to-have-a nice-long-date-tonight kind of illness."

Only a few minutes ago, Dale's spirits couldn't have soared any higher. Now they were free-falling to rock bottom. If her suspicions were correct, then he'd have to fight extra hard for Kendra's love. And, yes, he did

Dear Reader,

Your opinions are important to us. So if you'll participate in our fast and free "One Minute" Survey, YOU can pick up to four wonderful books that WE pay for when you try the Harlequin Reader Service!

As a leading publisher of women's fiction, we'd love to hear from you. That's why we promise to reward you for completing our survey.

IMPORTANT: Please complete the survey and return it. We'll send your Free Books and a Free Mystery Gift right away. And we pay for shipping and handling too! ← *We pay for EVERYTHING!*

Try **Harlequin® Special Edition** and get 2 books featuring comfort and strength in the support of loved ones and enjoying the journey no matter what life throws your way.

Try **Harlequin® Heartwarming™ Larger-Print** and get 2 books featuring uplifting stories where the bonds of friendship, family and community unite.

Or TRY BOTH!

Thank you again for participating in our "One Minute" Survey. It really takes just a minute (or less) to complete the survey... and your free books and gift will be well worth it!

If you continue with your subscription, you can look forward to curated monthly shipments of brand-new books from your selected series, always at a discount off the cover price! Plus you can cancel any time. So don't miss out, return your One Minute Survey today to get your Free books.

Pam Powers

want that much from her. Tonight had opened his eyes to his feelings about her and the two of them being together. Not just for tonight, but for always.

"Damn, Kendra. Surely she wouldn't pull such a trick. Mila isn't a mean child. She wouldn't want to hurt you in such a manipulative way. Would she?"

Sighing heavily, she stood and gathered her underclothes from the floor. "In her mind, she doesn't think breaking up our night together is hurting me. She believes she's doing me a favor. According to her, you're all wrong for me. And she's trying to save me from making a mistake."

He stood and took her into his arms. "I think we just proved we aren't a mistake."

"No. We're not a mistake." She gave him a tight hug and then turned away to dress.

He raked a hand through his hair while his mind spun. What was he supposed to think? Do? Up until a couple of minutes ago, their night together had been perfect. Now he was torn with the notion of Mila actually being ill, or faking it in order to keep him separated from Kendra. Either was a miserable thought.

"I'd be glad to go with you to pick up Mila…if you'd like."

She stepped into her panties, then quickly donned her bra, and as Dale watched her hurried movements he wanted to circle his hands around her wrists and draw her back into his arms. A part of him wanted to tell her that if Mila was putting on an act, it would be a mistake to give in to her whims. But *if* was a mighty big word and he didn't have any right to interfere in her parenting decisions. Besides, he had to remember there was always a chance the child wasn't faking it and truly did need her mother's attention.

"Thank you, Dale. But I think it would be better if I handle this myself. Seeing you with me might make the situation worse."

She was trying to view the problem with rational reasoning. Even so, the fact that she didn't want the two of them to deal with Mila's problem together felt like a hard slap to his face.

"Okay."

He hadn't meant for the word to sound terse, but apparently she'd heard the disappointment in his voice.

Her dress bunched in her hands, she looked at him, her expression tinged with disbelief. "Are you angry with me?"

Groaning, he reached down and picked up his shirt. "No. I understand you didn't want this thing with Mila to happen any more than I did."

"So you're angry with Mila?"

Frowning now, he shoved his arms into the shirt and began to snap the front of it together. "Of course not. She's a young child. I'm not angry with either of you. I'm disappointed and worried, that's all."

She stepped closer and as she placed her hand on his forearm, Dale could see a torn look in her eyes.

"I'm sorry about this, Dale. Believe me, I'm just as disappointed as you are. And if you're thinking I'm trying to shut you out, I'm not. I just want to handle this with as little drama as possible."

He stifled a groan. "I get what you're saying, Kendra. And, yes, I'm sure you can handle this problem with Mila tonight, but I'm looking ahead to the future. What are you going to do the next time something like this happens?"

Her lips parted as though his question had caught her off guard. Surely, she wasn't thinking the issue with Mila would be resolved with a snap of her fingers.

"Honestly, Dale, I don't know. I'm not even sure how I'm going to handle the situation tonight. First, I want to make sure she isn't really sick. If she isn't, then I'm going to let her know that I'm not going to accept such behavior."

"Well, her health is the important thing," he said, then turned his back to her and quickly finished dressing.

A few short minutes later, they left the apartment together. Dale waited on the small porch, while she locked the door behind them.

When she turned to him, he gathered her into his arms and she tilted her face up to his. "This isn't the way I wanted our night to end. But the time we had together was pretty wonderful," she said.

She was using the word *wonderful*, yet her troubled face was a picture of sadness, he thought.

"Short or not, this night has been amazing for me, Kendra." He touched his fingertips to her cheek and did his best to ignore the desperate urge to make love to her again. "I'll call you tomorrow. And if you can, would you send me a text to let me know about Mila's headache?"

"I will."

He planted a swift kiss on her lips, then quickly walked to his truck before he could say or do something that might wreck their budding relationship. But why should he worry about making a misstep with Kendra? It looked as though Mila was in the driver's seat. And until he earned the child's approval, he didn't have a chance of winning Kendra's love.

Chapter Nine

Normally, Kendra spent her Saturdays working at the bakery, but this morning she'd asked Jackie to fill in for her. After Mila's unexpected complaint with a headache, she'd decided to stay home with her daughter just in case there was an ultra-slim chance that Mila had actually been sick.

Usually when Kendra took a day off, she used the spare time to do something special with Mila. More often than not, she'd take her daughter shopping, while making sure she kept the spending to a small amount. Sometimes, if there was a child-appropriate movie being shown, she'd take her to the theater, or there was always the park to enjoy the outdoors. But today Kendra was doing none of those things. Instead, she was using her time away from the bakery to clean house and catch up on her laundry.

This morning, when Kendra had informed Mila they wouldn't be going out for the day, the girl had been shocked and then she'd wanted to argue. But Kendra had quickly pointed out that a person with a bad headache needed to rest and get well. After that, Mila realized she didn't have leg to stand on, and thankfully, she'd been pleasant and obedient so far.

Perhaps she was being too hard on her daughter, Kendra thought, as she stuffed wet clothes into the dryer. But she couldn't let the stunt she'd pulled last night go unpunished. And it had been a stunt. As soon as Kendra had picked Mila up at Louisa's house and she'd learned that Dale had already gone home to Dalton's Grange, she'd been all cheerful smiles and insisted her headache had quit almost instantly.

Kendra had been so aggravated and disappointed, she'd come close to bursting into tears, but somehow she'd managed to clamp down on her emotions. Once they'd arrived back at the apartment, Kendra had decided to go along with Mila's fake illness and she'd made a big deal of checking her temperature and tucking her into bed. But she'd also decided her daughter had to learn there were consequences to telling fibs, especially when those fibs hurt other people.

With the clothes drying, she walked out to the kitchen and made herself a cup of coffee in a pod-cup machine. For the past hour, Mila had been perched on a seat at the table, entertaining herself with crayons and a coloring book. But now that the kittens had woken from a nap, she was sitting cross-legged on the floor, tempting them to chase a feather attached to the end of a plastic wand.

"Look, Mommy! Gypsy can go faster than George. She catches the feather first and then George takes it away from her. That's not fair."

"Gypsy doesn't care if her brother gets the feather.

They're having fun," Kendra said as she sat on one of the stools at the breakfast bar.

Mila glanced at her. "Did you have fun last night with Dale, Mommy?"

This was the first time her daughter had even mentioned Kendra's date with Dale and she wondered if the punishment of staying home today was causing her to think hard on the matter.

"Yes, we had fun," Kendra told her. "We ate Mexican food and enjoyed talking to each other."

As for the rest of the evening, Kendra was still walking on a cloud. Making love to Dale hadn't just been a pleasurable experience. Being intimately connected to him had affected her deeply and touched her heart in places she hadn't known existed. There had been moments she'd wanted to cry out as she'd suddenly and surely realized how much she loved him, how much she never wanted him to let her go. But she'd held back, afraid it would be too much, too soon, for him.

And maybe Dale would never want to hear those words from her, she thought ruefully. He'd not exactly been happy when he'd left her apartment. And she couldn't blame him. She'd promised him they'd have a whole night together and if the call about Mila hadn't interrupted them, they would have been well on their way to making love a second time.

Last night she'd sent him a brief text to let him know Mila was fine and he'd responded with one word—*good*. And today she'd foolishly carried her cell phone around in anticipation of his call. But now the afternoon was beginning to stretch into evening, and with no text or call from him, doubts were starting to creep into her thoughts. Had he decided dating a woman with a precocious child wasn't worth the headache?

"I'm glad you had fun, Mommy."

Was this Mila's way of apologizing? Kendra wondered.

"That's nice, honey. Thank you."

Mila climbed to her feet and walked over to Kendra.

"Mommy, do you think Dale is going to propose to you?"

Any other time, Kendra would have considered her daughter's question as just another one of her many wedding inquiries. But last night had Kendra wondering if Dale might change his mind about hanging on to his single status. She could easily imagine herself spending the rest of her life with him. But would he ever forget the marital struggles his parents had gone through? Would he ever put away the fears of heartbreak and divorce? Maybe, if he loved her. But so far, she'd not heard anything close to the word *love* pass his lips.

"I don't know, Mila. Dale and I need to know each other a lot longer before something like that happens. Why are you asking?"

She shrugged and glanced sheepishly to the opposite side of the room. "Because I can tell you really like him and he really likes you."

How had the child reached such a conclusion? Mila hadn't spent enough time with the two of them to know how they felt about each other. But sometimes it was easier for children to see things that adults could never see.

Kendra thoughtfully regarded her daughter. "Are you thinking Dale will propose to me?"

She shook her head. "Nope. He just wants to have fun."

Mila could be right. But last night, when Dale had made love to her, she'd seen more than fun in his eyes.

She'd seen something raw and real and tender. It might be a long leap from her bed to a marriage proposal, but it was a start.

Kendra was searching for the right words to counter Mila's emphatic statement when the phone lying a few inches from her coffee mug rang.

Seeing Dale's name light up on the screen, she eagerly snatched it up and swiped to answer.

"Hi, Dale!"

"Hello, Kendra. Did I catch you at a bad time?"

The sound of his voice was like a steadying hand against her back, and without even knowing it, her lips spread into a wide smile.

"No, you called at a perfect time. Actually, I just sat down with coffee," she said cheerfully, while from the corner of her eye, she could see Mila watching her like a hawk. "I've been house cleaning most of the day, so I'm taking a little break."

"Same thing here. We've been stretching the last of the barbed wire today and we decided to stop for a little break. Your text last night said Mila was fine, so I thought I'd call and check on her today. No more headaches?"

With Mila still standing nearby, Kendra was forced to carefully choose her next words. "Oh, that little problem quickly resolved itself last night. Everything is fine today."

He paused and she could easily picture the image of his strong face, his blue eyes. Now that she'd made love to him and discovered the wonder of touching him and holding his strong body next to hers, it was impossible to think of her future without him in it.

"I'm glad to hear it," he said, then added in a lowered voice, "After I got home to Dalton's Grange last night, all I could think about was you and the two of us together. I'm missing you."

Her sigh was laced with longing. "I'm missing you too. Will you be coming back to town anytime soon?"

"Uh, I'm not sure about that, but I thought— Well, the main reason I'm calling is to ask if you and Mila would like to come out and look at the horses tomorrow. With it being Sunday, we only take care of the essential chores and put off any major work until the weekend is over. So I'll have a bit of free time."

Even though the sky was gray with gloomy clouds, Kendra felt as if a bright ray of sunshine had just slanted through the kitchen window. "I'd love to, Dale." She looked at Mila and purposely raised her voice. "But give me just a minute to check with Mila. If her head is hurting there's no way she could walk around the ranch and look at horses."

Before Kendra could present the question to Mila, her daughter was jumping up and down. "Yes, Mommy! Yes! My head doesn't hurt at all!"

"Okay, Dale. Mila has made a miraculous recovery," she said shrewdly. "She can't wait to see the horses. What time should we be there?"

"Good to hear Mila is feeling well again. One or one thirty should be fine. Do you know where the ranch is located?"

"I've driven by the entrance before."

"The house isn't far from there. Just stay on that road and you'll find it."

"We'll be there," she told him. "Is there anything I need to bring with us?"

"No. I'll—" He broke off as a male voice yelled in the background. "Sorry, Kendra. My brothers are waiting for me. I'll be watching for you."

He ended the call and as Kendra placed her phone aside, Mila asked in a skeptical voice, "Are you sure Dale invited me to Dalton's Grange too?"

Kendra frowned. "Of course. He wants to show you the horses. Why are you asking?"

Her expression turned sheepish. "I thought he only wanted to be with you and not have me around."

Kendra studied Mila's glum face. Was this part of the reason she'd pulled the headache stunt last night? Because she thought Dale didn't want to include her in their plans?

Wrapping a hand around Mila's little chin, she tilted her face upward. "Mila, listen carefully to me. Dale isn't trying to take me away from you. And even if he was, I wouldn't allow that to happen. Not ever. Do you understand what I'm telling you?"

Mila flashed her a grin. "Yes! It means you'll always be my mommy. No matter what."

"You're right." She gave Mila's shoulders an affectionate squeeze. "Now, are you happy about going to Dalton's Grange?"

"Oh this is supercool! I'm going to go find my boots and hat so I'll be ready tomorrow!"

Kendra smiled as she watched her daughter race out of the kitchen. Tomorrow the three of them would be together, and hopefully Mila would begin to see Dale in a better light.

The next afternoon, when Dale spotted Kendra's SUV driving up the circular driveway that led to the front of the ranch house, he quickly strode out to greet them. After she'd parked the vehicle a respectable distance from the yard fence, he went to the driver's door to help her out.

"Hello, Kendra. I see you made the drive okay."

"No problems," she said as she stood beside him. "Mila sang to me most of the way."

Dale stuck his head into the open door to see the girl was in the process of unfastening her seat belt. A pink cowboy hat with white lacing around the brim was perched over her blond waves, while matching pink boots were on her feet. She looked far too adorable to be capable of using manipulative tactics on her mother, he thought.

"Hi, Mila. Need some help?"

"I can do it," she told him.

Dale gave Kendra a wink before he walked around the vehicle and opened the door where Mila was sitting.

"All cowgirls appreciate a helping hand," he told her. "And now that you're on Dalton's Grange, you're going to start turning into a cowgirl."

He helped her out of the vehicle and once she was standing on the ground, she stared at him in awe.

"I'm going to be a real cowgirl? Today? Really?"

"Well, sure. You're already looking like a cowgirl in your hat and boots. All you need now is a crown."

She shook her head at him. "I'm not old enough or big enough to be a rodeo queen yet. I have to grow before I can have a crown."

Dale shared a quick grin with Kendra before he turned back to Mila. "You don't have to grow that much. You can get in the Junior Queen contest."

Mila turned a doubtful look on her mother. "Is Dale telling me the truth?"

Kendra nodded. "I recall a rodeo queen contest for the younger girls going on back in the summer. When the time comes, we'll look into it. But like Dale says, first you have to learn to ride."

"And I'm going to give you your first lesson today," Dale told her. "What do you think?"

Mila clapped her hands and jumped up and down. "This is going to be fun, fun!"

Dale turned to Kendra. "One of the ranch hands is saddling a pair of horses for us now. But I'd like to take you both inside to meet my parents before we do any riding. Is that okay with you?"

"It's perfectly okay," she said, then motioned to Mila. "Get your coat from the car, honey. We're going into the house for a few minutes and then we'll go see the horses."

Once Mila had pulled on her coat, the three of them headed across the yard to the porch. As they walked, Dale could see Kendra looking around with interest.

"The ranch is beautiful, Dale. And I love the log exterior of the house. It fits in perfectly with the rugged landscape," she told him. "It's no wonder your dad fell in love with this place."

Her praise made him realize just how proud he was of Dalton's Grange and all the hard work that he and his family poured into the land.

"I'm glad you like it." He glanced over at Mila, who was busy gawking at everything. "What do you think about the place, Mila?"

"Everything is big! And it's pretty!"

Kendra chuckled. "Coming from my little critic, that means it *really* is pretty."

Dale pretended to wipe sweat from his brow. "Whew. At least Dalton's Grange has passed her test."

Inside the house, Dale led them to a large great room with a high ceiling built with exposed wood beams. A huge fireplace separated the comfortably furnished area from an equally large kitchen.

His parents were sitting on a couch, drinking coffee, but as soon as they spotted their son and visitors entering the room, the pair quickly put aside their cups and stood.

"Mom, Dad, I'd like you to meet Kendra and her daughter, Mila," he told them, then to Kendra and Mila, he said, "These are my parents, Deborah and Neal."

Kendra stepped forward and offered her hand to both of them. "It's very nice to meet both of you. Your ranch is magnificent."

Neal slanted a grin at Dale. "This young woman has good taste."

Dale chuckled. "That's why she's with me."

"Then you'd better hang on to her," Neal told him.

"Well, I want more than a handshake. I want a hug." Deborah gathered Kendra in a warm hug, then turned to Mila, who was watching her with wide eyes. "Can I have a hug from you too?"

Mila nodded and Dale was surprised to see the girl actually returned his mother's hug.

"You're just as pretty as your mother," Deborah told Mila. "Do lots of people tell you that?"

Mila nodded and grinned. "Lots of them."

Deborah laughed, then cast her husband an adoring look. "Why didn't we have a little girl before we stopped having babies?"

Neal cleared his throat. "Probably because we already had a house full of boys. She wouldn't have stood a chance."

"Not with you spoiling her rotten," Deborah joked.

"Kendra is the lady who baked all the cupcakes," Dale proudly informed his parents. "She owns and operates Kendra's Cupcakes."

Neal groaned and patted his midsection. "Now I

know who to blame for these extra two pounds I've put on. I like the vanilla ones with the sprinkles."

"Those are my favorites too," Kendra told him.

Neal looked at Dale and winked. "See, I told you. The girl has good taste."

"Where did you learn to make all those pastries? And the brownies! Oh, they were scrumptious!" Deborah exclaimed.

"Thank you," Kendra told her. "My mother taught me how to bake. And I've had years of practice."

Before Deborah could begin asking more baking questions, Neal spoke up. "Sorry, Kendra, we've forgotten our manners. You and your daughter have a seat and Dale can get you something to drink."

"It's nice of you to offer, Mr. Dalton, but we just finished lunch before we drove out. I think Mila is itching to go see the horses. But we might take you up on the drink later."

"We'd love that," Deborah told her.

"I'm going to give Mila a riding lesson," Dale told them. "She's going to be a first-rate cowgirl."

"Hey, that's good to know," Neal said and leveled a kindly smile at Mila. "We have too many cowboys around here. We need some cowgirls on the ranch. Especially one with a pink hat."

Mila giggled. "You're funnier than Dale," she told him.

Neal laughed. "That's only because I'm older, sweetie."

Dale reached for Kendra's arm. "I think we need to exit on that one." To his parents, he said, "We'll be back later."

Outside, as the three of them walked toward a huge barn located at the far end of the ranch yard, Kendra said, "I like your parents. They're down-to-earth and clearly crazy about each other."

"They are now," he replied.

After watching Deborah and Neal interact with each other, Kendra found it hard to imagine their marriage had ever been in jeopardy.

"I expect they always were, Dale. Things just happen."

"Yeah. Things just happen." He gave her a faint smile. "And today they're all going to be good."

Mila skipped slightly ahead of them and Kendra looped her arm through his.

"You're talking my language now," she told him.

They entered a long barn with horse stalls lining both sides and a dirt walkway running between. Skylights in the tin roof allowed shafts of golden light to slant in intervals down the length of the building.

As soon as they reached the first stall, where a gray horse was lying on a bed of clean wood shavings, Mila let out a happy squeal.

"Mommy, look how big he is! And how pretty!" She looked up at Dale. "Why is he lying down? Does he feel bad?"

Smiling, Dale patted the top of her head. "No. He's fine. He's just resting. Horses get sleepy just like you and me."

"Oh. But what if he got sleepy at the rodeo? That would be bad."

Mila's question had him casting a look of amusement over at Kendra. "There's too much excitement going on at a rodeo for a horse to get sleepy," he explained.

As they moved on to the next stall, Kendra couldn't help but notice the soft music coming from overhead speakers.

"Is the music for the benefit of the ranch hands? Or the horses?" Kendra asked.

Dale chuckled. "The horses. It helps keep them soothed and content."

"So that explains the classical music. The horses have highbrow taste," Kendra said as she recognized a familiar symphony. "I would've expected country or soft rock."

"The classical stuff is Shep's doing. He heard you were going to be visiting today and thought he'd impress you. Otherwise, we'd be hearing songs about truck driving and beer drinking. Whether the horses can tell the difference, I couldn't say."

She laughed. "Well, you'll have to thank him for me. I always did want to tour a horse barn with Chopin playing in the background."

"I'll be sure and let Shep know you liked his music loop," he said with a chuckle.

Standing between the two adults, Mila's attention was glued to a coal-black horse with a long wavy mane and tail. "Why do the horses have to be in the barn? I bet this one would like to be outside eating grass."

Kendra said, "I've been wondering the same thing. Why are these horses stalled? On our drive in to the ranch house, we saw several horses grazing in the pasture."

"Those horses are part of the ranch's working remuda. They're usually always outside. Unless there's a blizzard going on. Then we run all the horse stock into pens with loafing sheds for shelter. Most of the horses in here are in training. And a couple of them are being doctored for various issues."

"I see. Different horses for specific jobs," Kendra replied.

He flashed her a grin. "Right. Like the people who work for you in the bakery. Each one has a certain purpose."

His example pulled a laugh from her. "Most of the time we do. But when the bakery is overrun with customers we all end up doing a bit of everything."

Mila turned away from the stall and Kendra was somewhat surprised to see her reach for Dale's hand and give it a tug.

"When are we gonna see Tori's horse?" Mila asked. "Is he in the barn?"

Dale gave the girl an indulgent grin. "Tori's horse is a girl. In horse language that means she's a mare. And you're going to see her right now. Ready?"

"Yeah!"

Dale led the girl over to the next stall, where a brown-and-white quarter horse was chomping on alfalfa hay swinging in a net that hung from a rafter.

Mila tilted her head one way and then the other as she tried to peep through the stall gate. "I can't see all of her!"

"Here. I'll help you get a better look." Dale reached down and lifted her into his arms so she could peer directly into the stall. "Now you can get a full view of Bluebell. Pretty, isn't she?"

While Mila stared in fascination at the mare, Kendra's eyes misted over at the image of Dale carefully holding her daughter in the crook of one arm.

"Oh, Bluebell is really, really beautiful! And Tori makes her go really fast!" Mila exclaimed, then looked directly at Dale. "I want a mare just like Bluebell! And when I get old enough to work and make money, I'm going to get one!"

Smiling wryly, Dale glanced at Kendra. "Money,"

he repeated. "That one nasty issue has a habit of getting in the way of things."

"Unfortunately," Kendra replied, while thinking Bryce had made plenty of money, but it hadn't given them a solid, loving marriage. "But it can't buy the best of things, Dale. I learned that long ago."

He turned a thoughtful gaze on Mila. "No," he said gently. "The best things in life aren't for sale."

After allowing Mila a few more minutes to admire Bluebell, Dale set her back on her feet and announced it was time for her first riding lesson.

"What do you think, Mommy? Are you ready for a ride?" he asked Kendra.

Chuckling, she said, "I'm fairly sure you're going to need to give both of us a riding lesson. I haven't been on a horse in several years."

"Have you ridden much?" he asked.

"Only horses that you rent at a riding stable. You know. The kind that has one gait—super-slow."

He flashed her a grin. "I promise I have a nice quiet mount for you. And Mila is going to ride with me. Until she gets the feel of things. Don't worry—I'll take baby steps with her."

As usual, Mila had been carefully listening in on their conversation and she let out a loud protest. "I'm not a baby, Dale! I'm seven!"

He gave Kendra a subtle wink. "Seven! Gosh, I'd practically forgotten you were that old," he told the girl. "But when I said baby steps I was talking about my mare. She needs to stretch her legs slowly before she goes fast."

Somewhat mollified by his explanation, Mila asked, "Your horse is a girl too?"

"Sure. Her name is Moonpie. 'Cause she's sweet like your mommy's cupcakes."

Mila wrinkled her nose at him. "Do you give her kisses?"

Kendra could see his eyes covertly roll in her direction.

"Whenever I can," he answered.

Before they started the ride, Dale had feared he might have trouble with Mila being a little bossy and refusing to listen to his instructions. Instead, he'd been pleasantly surprised when the girl had carefully followed every command he'd given her. By the time the three of them had returned from a long ride in a nearby pasture, he felt comfortable enough to dismount and allow Mila to sit alone in the saddle.

When he'd led Moonpie at a slow walk around the ranch yard, Mila had been beaming from ear to ear and waving at the ranch hands.

"She's getting her queen wave mastered," Dale told Kendra, who was walking at his side.

Kendra laughed softly, something she'd done quite a bit this afternoon. The happy sound reassured him that she was enjoying her time here on the ranch.

"She'll be prepared when she wins Miss Junior Rodeo Queen of Bronco. I'm not sure there is such a thing, but she's having fun imagining herself in the role."

Lowering his head toward hers, he said, "Just between you and me, I'm not all that certain that Bronco has a junior queen contest, either. But like you said, it's something she can have fun dreaming about. Until she grows into big-queen age."

Touching her hand to his arm, she looked up at him.

"Dale, you've been so wonderful with Mila," she said gently. "You can't know how much that means to me. And to her."

Her praise poured into him like warm, sweet wine. "And you can't know how much it means to me to have the two of you here, enjoying my home."

Her gaze caught his and the dark smoky look in her eyes told him she was thinking about the two of them being alone and making love...again and again. The idea caused the pit of his belly to clench with longing.

"I haven't enjoyed anything so much. Not in a long, long time," she told him, then after a quick glance to make sure Mila couldn't overhear them, she added in a lower tone, "I only wish you and I could have a few minutes together—without an audience."

"I do too. But in the long run I think that the three of us being together like this will help matters. You know, maybe a change of opinion about my 'type,'" he added with quirky waggle of his eyebrows.

She squeezed his forearm. "Like I told you, you're definitely my type."

As it turned out, Dale and Kendra didn't get an opportunity to be alone together before she and Mila left the ranch much later that evening.

As soon as they'd finished riding the horses, the three of them had gone back into the house with the plan of having a brief visit with his parents. But the chat turned into a long conversation over cups of coffee for the adults and hot chocolate for Mila. Then Deborah had introduced Mila to her dog, Sam, and cat, Jewel. The girl had fallen instantly in love with the friendly pets, and by the time Kendra had managed to pry her away from the animals, the day was growing late and a purple twilight darkened the sky.

Dale had escorted the two of them to Kendra's SUV and after giving her a chaste peck on the cheek, he waved them off.

It wasn't until much later that night, when Dale was about to climb into bed, that his cell phone rang.

As soon as he spotted Kendra's name on the screen he snatched the phone off the nightstand and hurriedly punched the accept button.

"Kendra, I wasn't expecting to hear from you again tonight."

He picked up her soft sigh before she spoke. "I apologize for calling so late. Were you about to go to bed?"

"Not yet," he said. "I still need to jump in the shower. Is anything wrong?"

"Not a thing. I've been waiting for Mila to go to sleep and she was so wired from all the excitement of the day that it took her a while to settle down. I wanted to be able to talk with you and not have to worry about her walking in and overhearing part of our conversation."

Her voice was low and husky and the sound of it had him closing his eyes and remembering the taste of her lips, the way her soft, naked body had yielded to his.

"I'm glad you called. We didn't have much of an opportunity today to talk about me and you. Mila and my parents kept us occupied."

"Yes, but I adore your parents and enjoyed talking with them. And Mila— Well, it's like you said, we needed to share the day with her. I think you really made an impression on her today. After we got home, she made some positive remarks about you. I didn't make a big deal out of it. I want her to realize for herself what a great guy you are."

He smiled even though she couldn't see him. "I don't know about the *great* part. But I hope she can see I'm going to do my best to make her mother happy. At least, I'm going to try."

She sighed. "I've been trying to think of a way we can be alone together and all I can come up with is taking Mila to the sitter. We couldn't make it a whole night, but at least we could be together."

Dale was yearning to make love to Kendra and yet the instant she'd said the word *sitter* he was put off. "As much as I want to be with you, darlin', I don't think that would be a good idea."

"Why? What else am I supposed to do? I don't have relatives around here to watch her. And now that I've found you, I deserve to have a social life, don't I?"

"Sure you deserve it. But I don't want her to resent me."

"So you think we should just cater to her wishes?"

Frustration laced her voice and Dale could've told her that he was feeling just as vexed. "No. I think we just need to have a bit more patience and give her time to get used to the two of us being a couple."

There was a long stretch of silence and then she said, "Dale, for such a diehard bachelor, you have all the makings of a wonderful father."

Diehard bachelor. He wasn't one of those men. The kind that wanted to flit from one woman to the next for the rest of his life. No. Since Kendra and Mila had come into his life, he was thinking in totally different terms. He was beginning to imagine himself as a husband and father. Whether he'd be wonderful in those roles, he couldn't say. But he knew he'd be a damn sight better than Kendra's ex.

"It would be nice if Mila saw me as you do. But for now, what about us getting together for dinner in a day or two? We could grab some fast food and Mila could bring a friend. That way the two of us might have a chance to be together without her hanging on to our every word."

There was a slight pause and then she said, "Sounds good to me. I'll tell Mila to invite Louisa. I'm sure her mother will agree to let her join us. Let's make it Wednesday night. Tomorrow and Tuesday I'm going to be working later than usual. Some extra cleaning on the ovens."

Wednesday sounded like an eon away, but he'd settle for whatever time he could get with her.

"Sounds good. If I happen to come to town before then, I'll stop by the bakery. To say hello," he added in a low, suggestive voice.

A soft chuckle sounded in his ear. "To say hello. Of course," she said, then her voice dropped to a murmur. "Dale, I want you to know how wonderful today was for me. And for Mila. She'll never forget it. Neither will I."

He breathed deeply as the ache to hold her practically overwhelmed him. "It was special to me too, Kendra. I'll show you just how special whenever I see you again."

"I can't wait. Good night, Dale."

She ended the call and in spite of his dusty clothes, Dale lied back on the bed and stared thoughtfully up at the ceiling.

When he'd walked into Kendra's Cupcakes for the first time and spotted Kendra behind the counter, he'd dreamed about having a date with the beautiful blonde. Now, a few weeks later, he was imagining himself as a family man.

Had he lost his senses? Or had Kendra opened his eyes to the fact that love and marriage didn't necessarily mean suffering and loss? Was he finally beginning to believe he could have the same sort of happiness his brothers enjoyed now that they were married?

Dale couldn't answer the self-imposed questions, much less understand the rapid changes he'd undergone. He only knew that common sense couldn't compete with the feelings in his heart.

Chapter Ten

By Tuesday, Kendra was so desperate to be with Dale again that she could hardly serve her customers for watching the door and hoping to see his tall, rugged figure step into the bakery.

When she glanced up and spotted him walking down the sidewalk, she quickly informed Jackie she needed to leave for a half hour and to cover the front for her, then hurried to intercept him before he could enter the bakery.

"Well, when did you start greeting your customers on the outside?" he teased.

Grinning slyly, she grabbed his hand and hustled him back down the sidewalk. "Are you in a hurry?"

"No."

"Good. I am. I have thirty…forty minutes at the most. Would you like to drive us to my apartment?"

He looked at her as though she'd just handed him a pot of gold coins. "Seriously?"

"Yes, seriously. Why do you think I'm herding you to your truck?"

"Because for some reason today, you want to keep me out of the bakery?"

She laughed. "Exactly. Because I'd much rather have you in my bedroom."

Less than five minutes later, she was opening the door of her apartment with a key she kept hidden beneath a holly shrub.

"Are you sure this isn't going to cause problems back at the bakery?" he asked as they stepped into the house and she carefully locked the door behind them.

"Jackie is watching the front for me. She can handle things. Sometimes it's necessary to have a few minutes leave of absence, and you are a *very* necessary reason."

She turned away from the door and he quickly snatched her into his arms. "I don't know why or how this idea entered your mind, but I like it—a whole lot."

"It entered my mind because I couldn't keep waiting, hoping for a time to make love to you again. I know we don't have much time, but—"

"Who's worried about time?" he interrupted. "We're not going to waste one second, my darlin'."

He fastened his mouth over hers and they kissed deeply and hungrily for long moments until the need for air forced them apart.

Still gasping for air, she grabbed his hand and led him down the hallway to her bedroom. She said, "I left for work in a rush this morning and didn't straighten the bedclothes."

He took off his hat and tossed it toward a dressing bench at the foot of her bed, then popped the snaps down the front of his shirt. "The only clothes I care about are yours and mine and how fast we can get out of them."

Desperately eager to be in his arms, Kendra pulled the sashes on her apron, then quickly shed her jeans and sweater. By the time she'd removed her undergarments, he was stripped down to nothing, and judging from the sight of his hard erection, there wouldn't be much time for foreplay.

She reached for him at the same time his hands wrapped around her waist. Locked in each other's arms, they fell sideways onto the bed. His lips fastened over hers once again, while his hands began a wild exploration of her body.

"Kendra, Kendra. I've been aching for you. For this. We were meant to be together."

The passionate words were spoken against her lips and she wanted to swallow them up and store them for later—whenever it would be impossible to touch him like this.

"Yes, Dale. Together."

He used another minute to kiss her and then he eased to a sitting position. "I need to find a condom," he said hoarsely.

Reaching for his arm, she tugged him back down on the mattress. "I didn't explain the other night that I'm on the pill. I thought you might not trust just one type of birth control."

His eyebrows arched. "Are you trying to tell me that I don't need a condom?"

She nodded. "Not unless you're worried."

"Worried? Hell, I'm ecstatic!" Laughing and groaning at the same time, he rolled her onto her back, then poised himself above her. "Do we have much time left?"

She smiled up at him. "We have enough."

* * *

When Kendra arrived back at the bakery, she was relieved to see the few customers standing in line were waiting for coffee, a job that Smitty handled by himself.

Tightening the sashes on her apron, she walked behind the counter and waited for Jackie to check out a customer.

"Did you have any problems while I was gone?" Kendra asked.

Jackie's expression was sly as she studied Kendra's swollen lips and messier-than-usual bun. "No. Did you?"

Kendra rolled her eyes. "No. And since you're dying to ask, yes, that was Dale that I left with. We had a few things to talk over."

Jackie chuckled knowingly. "Talk? With a guy like Dale I'd be doing more than talking, Kendra! Are you thirty or eighty?"

Turning her back to Jackie, she pulled a tray of half-empty cupcakes from one of the display shelves and hoped her assistant didn't see the blush on her cheeks. Her time with Dale might have been short, but the passion between them had been hot and incredible, and just as earth-shaking as the first time they'd made love.

"Don't worry, Jackie. I'm aware of my age."

"I hope so. Because you need to latch on to Dale," Jackie said, then reached to take the tray from her. "I'll take care of this. Why don't you go sit down and collect yourself?"

Kendra smirked at the redhead. "Collect myself? I've never felt better."

"I'll bet you do." Laughing, Jackie started toward the kitchen, then suddenly turned back to Kendra. "Oh, I almost forgot. There was guy in here earlier who was looking for you. I'd never seen him before."

"Hmm. What did he want? To sell us some new coffee or frozen desserts? Which I'd never serve my customers."

Jackie shook her head. "If he was trying to sell something, he didn't mention it. He was only interested in talking with you."

Kendra frowned. "That's odd. Did he leave a message or his name?"

"No. But I got the impression he'll be back," Jackie said.

Puzzled now, Kendra asked, "What did he look like?"

"Thirtyish. Blond. Kind of good-looking, but a little too smooth for my taste. You know the sort. Soft hands, creased slacks and Italian loafers. Give me a guy with boots and manure splattered on his jeans. Then you know he's not lazy."

Oh God, could it be? No! Surely Bryce wouldn't come all the way to Montana! Especially when he hadn't bothered to come around when Kendra and Mila had lived in Florida, only a few miles away from him.

Pressing a hand to her forehead, she tried not to panic. But she couldn't help but wonder if her past had come to Bronco to mess up her future.

"Kendra, what's wrong? Are you getting sick?"

Drawing in a bracing breath, she did her best to smile at Jackie. "I'm okay. It's just that I have a lot of things on my mind and a bunch of work in my office to finish."

"You go on," Jackie told her. "I'll take care of things here in the front for you."

Yes, but who was going to take care of her ex-husband if he showed up and tried to mess with her and Mila's lives?

You, Kendra. You're a strong, successful woman now. You're not going to make the same mistakes you made years ago.

The next day Dale and his brothers were finishing up a job in the branding pen, when his cell phone buzzed. Stepping over to the corral fence, he pulled the phone from his shirt pocket and glanced at the ID.

Smiling at the sight of Kendra's name, he said, "Hello, beautiful."

"Dale," she said in a rush. "Do you have a minute to talk?"

The quiver in her voice instantly set off alarm bells in Dale's head. "Sure, I have time. We just finished branding a pen of calves."

A moment of silence passed and then she asked, "Do you have manure splattered on your jeans?"

Frowning quizzically, he glanced down at his nasty jeans. "I do."

He heard a short breath ease out of her, while at the same time he noticed there were no sounds of the busy bakery in the background. Instead, he could hear the wind and the rumble of traffic. Which told him she must be standing outside on the sidewalk.

"I'm glad," she said. "That means you're my kind of guy."

Had she been drinking something stronger than the bakery's coffee? Her voice sounded odd and she wasn't making a whole lot of sense, but for the moment he decided to go along with her.

"Oh. I thought you might've been afraid I'd show up at your apartment this evening wearing my dirty work clothes."

"No. I— Oh Dale, I don't know what to do! I'm scared!"

She was crying now and his first instinct was to jump in the truck and get to her as fast as possible.

"Sweetheart, what's happened? Is Mila okay?"

"She's at school. She's fine. But I don't know— Dale, I'm sorry, but we're going to have to postpone our little dinner this evening."

Confused, Dale stared across the ranch yard to where Bobby was working with a red roan yearling. Only a few weeks ago, Dale had told his friend not to feel pressured into getting married just because others expected him to be a family man. Now, here he was hanging anxiously on a woman's every word.

"What's wrong?" he asked. "I can hear you're upset."

She didn't answer immediately and Dale got the impression she was trying to compose herself.

Finally, she said, "I'm trying not to cry. It's just that I don't need this happening in my life right now. But Mila does and—"

When she didn't continue, he asked, "So this is about Mila?"

"Mostly." She drew in a deep breath. "Bryce has come to Bronco. He showed up here at the bakery yesterday and again today, right in the middle of the morning rush."

Dale went stock-still as he struggled to absorb what she was saying. "Bryce? Your ex?"

"Yes. I was knocked sideways, Dale. We've been living here in Montana for more than three years and other than a card on Mila's birthday, he hasn't bothered to contact us. Now he's suddenly decided he wants to be a father."

The bastard. Where did he come off playing with

other people's lives? "Uh, what about his wife? Was she with him?" Dale asked.

She snorted. "They've divorced."

The cogs in Dale's head began to spin faster. How was this going to affect their budding romance? These past several days they'd both been so happy. And yesterday, after their brief, but incredible session of lovemaking, they'd clung to each other, hating to part, even for one evening. Now…

"What a jerk," he muttered.

Her groan was a sound of frustration. "Bryce wants to see his daughter this evening and I'm afraid if I try to put him off, he'll just pester me more. And— Well, I don't have to tell you how she's longed for her father to be in her life. She's talked to you about him and how much she wants a daddy."

Oh yes, she'd made it very clear how much she wants a father and how she definitely didn't want Dale in the role, he thought.

"Does Mila know her father is in town?"

"No. I plan to tell her when she gets out of school this afternoon."

A sick feeling hit the pit of his stomach. "She's going to be very excited."

His voice must have sounded hollow because she let out another exasperated groan.

"I understand this is hard for you."

Hard? That didn't begin to describe what this news was doing to him. "Don't worry about me. Just take care of Mila. She doesn't deserve to be hurt a second time," he said crisply, then, closing his eyes, he wearily pinched the bridge of his nose. "What about the little dinner we'd planned? Are you canceling it completely?"

There was long pause and then… "Of course, I'm

not canceling it, Dale. I thought— If you can, that is, we'd get together tomorrow night. By then maybe I'll know what Bryce's intentions are."

"So you don't know how long he's planning to hang around?"

"No. And whatever he tells me I'm not going to put much stock in. He's good at telling people what they want to hear. Not necessarily the truth."

"All right. Unless something comes up, I'll be at your apartment about six thirty tomorrow evening."

Her sigh of relief caused the frown on his face to deepen. What had she been thinking? That he'd turned his back on her now that Bryce had shown up in her life? Or was she simply worried about the whole situation?

"Okay. I'll see you then. And, Dale, thank you for understanding."

He didn't understand. Not completely. She was postponing their date because her ex-husband was in town. That didn't make a heck of a lot of sense to him. But she was already distraught enough without him adding to the problem.

"We'll talk when I see you." He told her goodbye, then hung up before something rolled out of his mouth that would do more harm than good.

He was slipping the phone back into his pocket when Shep walked up to him.

"What's wrong? You look like you could eat a handful of nails."

Dale grimaced at his brother. "Just a handful? I could eat a bucketful and not even flinch."

Shep chuckled. "Feeling tough today, are we?"

"No! I'm feeling like a fool."

"You mean, more so than usual?" Shep teased.

Dale's frown turned into an outright glare. "Kendra just broke our date for tonight. Her ex-husband is in town. How would you handle that kind of news?"

Shep let out a short laugh. "I'd probably hunt the guy up and give him a not-so-gentle persuasion to leave town."

Oh sure, Dale thought miserably. Mila would really love him if he beat up her father. "Shep, violence is not the solution."

"Then I'd say you'd better step back and take a deeper look at the whole situation. This setup with Kendra sounds pretty sticky to me." He slapped a hand on Dale's shoulder. "Come on, forget about it for now. Let's go to the house and have a beer before we have to jump on the rest of that fence."

Sounds pretty sticky. Yeah, Shep was sure right when he'd spoken those words. It was going to be as awkward as hell if the man came around while Dale was with Kendra. But there was no use in him worrying about that possibility…until it happened.

By the next afternoon, Dale was so anxious to see Kendra and hear about Mila's meeting with her father, he decided to drive into Bronco early and stop by the bakery. If the place wasn't overrun with customers, they might be able to talk a few minutes without Mila around to overhear their conversation.

He had just parked his truck and was walking down the sidewalk to the bakery when he saw a sleek black car pull into a nearby parking slot. His steps slowed as he watched a tall blond man dressed in slacks and a pale blue shirt emerge from the driver's side and walk around to the back door of the luxury sedan.

Dale wasn't surprised when he lifted Mila out to the ground. Something about the vehicle and the man had told Dale he wasn't a native of Bronco and he'd been right.

Trying not to stare at the man who'd caused Kendra and her daughter so much anguish, Dale walked on toward the bakery. He'd made it almost to the door, when Mila spotted him and called out.

"Dale! Dale!"

Turning slightly, he saw she'd left Bryce and was tearing down the sidewalk to intercept him. Dale stopped and gave her the cheeriest smile he could manage.

"Hi, Mila. Did you just get out of school?"

Her face beaming, she grabbed his hand. "Yes! My daddy came to pick me up! Remember, I told you he'd come to see me!" She turned and proudly pointed at Bryce, who was slowly walking toward them. "That's him! I want you to say hello, Dale. Will you?"

How could he resist the child? He couldn't. It was no fault of Mila's that the man had ignored the fact that he had a child…until now. Now that Dale had fallen in love with both mother and daughter, he thought miserably.

"Hello," Bryce said. "I hope my daughter isn't pestering you."

My daughter. Just hearing the man say the words made Dale physically ill.

"No. Mila is, uh, we're buddies."

The man's eyes narrowed as they scanned Dale's face. "I see. Well, I'm Bryce Humphrey—Mila's father."

Like hell you are. "I'm Dale Dalton. Kendra's boyfriend," he added with a meaningful look.

Mila tugged on Bryce's sleeve and Dale could see he wasn't enjoying having the child's hand touching his clothing.

"Dale is a cowboy, Daddy. He rides horses and ropes

cows. And he makes Mommy laugh a lot," Mila explained.

Bryce glanced down at her. "That's nice, honey. But now I think we should let Mr. Dalton be on his way. And I need to let Kendra know you're here."

Dale considered turning around and heading back to his truck, but why should he give this guy a break? Dale had more business here at the bakery than this phony.

"'Bye, Dale. See ya later."

Mila and Bryce entered the bakery and Dale waited until they were well inside the bakery before he followed.

Kendra was behind the counter tending to a customer, but she looked up when the door chime sounded and immediately spotted him. She looked utterly frazzled and Dale desperately wished he could sweep her out of here and away from all the customers and work and, most of all, her ex-husband.

As he stood to one side and waited for Kendra to have a pause in customers, he glanced to his left and saw that Bryce and Mila had taken a seat at one of the tables. Seeing the girl with her biological father should be making him happy, Dale thought. But it didn't. Mila needed a real father, not one who was trying to fake the role of a parent.

Don't you think you're doing a bit of faking yourself, Dale? Since when have you become such an expert at child-rearing and what a seven-year-old girl needs?

The goading voice in his head had Dale turning away from the pair and he edged a few steps closer toward the counter, where Kendra was counting change back to a young woman.

As soon as she finished the transaction, she skirted around the counter and wrapped her hand lightly over his forearm. "Come on," she said. "Let's go back to the office. I'll get Jackie to watch the front."

Dale gladly followed her into the private room and as soon as she shut the door behind them, she practically fell into his arms and buried her face against his chest.

"Oh, Dale, I'm so glad you here. Hold me. Just hold me."

Her words were muffled against his shirt, but he could hear the angst in her voice and he instantly wrapped his arms around her and held her tightly.

"Has that jerk been giving you trouble?"

"Not exactly. It's just a strain having him around. I saw the three of you out on the sidewalk and I could only imagine what Mila must have been saying to him and you."

"Don't worry. She didn't say anything out of line. I told Bryce that I was your boyfriend. He didn't look too pleased with the information."

Her hands clutched his back. "Too bad. Our relationship has nothing to do with him."

"Do you mean that, Kendra? Truly?"

Tilting her head back from his chest, she looked up at him, and the wounded shadows he saw in her eyes made him feel like a heel for asking the question. But damn it, he had a right to know where they stood.

"Do you have to ask, Dale? You are the guy in my life now. Not him."

"Yes, but he's Mila's father. And he's divorced."

"I can't change either of those facts. I want to think you care enough about me to handle this awkward situation until he goes back to Florida."

"And when will that be? Has he mentioned how long he plans to stay?"

"He hasn't and I haven't asked. I didn't want to give him the impression I was interested."

"You think that's why he's really here in Bronco? Because he's interested in you? And using Mila as an excuse?"

She shook her head. "I honestly don't know, Dale. But whatever his motive, I can't trust him."

His gaze probed hers. "You're worried about Mila, aren't you?"

Her nod was stiff. "Dale, I wasted years staying in South Beach and hoping Bryce would decide to be a father. At that time I believed it would be a good thing for Mila to have him in her life. Now, I'm far from sure. He puts on a sincere front, but I have a feeling the facade will eventually drop. Mila isn't a baby anymore. She isn't fooled. Once she figures him out, she'll be hurt. Not to mention disillusioned."

The thought sickened Dale and yet he felt like an outsider looking in. He had no right to interfere. A fact that left him feeling more helpless than he could ever remember.

"Maybe it's best that Mila figures out now that he's a phony," he said. "At least, she'd be saved a worse heartache later on. However, there's one thing you haven't considered, Kendra."

Her eyes widened. "What's that?"

"The possibility that the guy has changed."

After all, Dale had gone through an inner transformation since he'd met Kendra. No one else might have noticed the change in him, but he was becoming a different man. Whether this new side of him was good or bad, he couldn't yet decide.

Groaning, she pulled out of his arms and walked over to her desk. With her back to Dale, she absently drummed her fingers on the desktop. "The fact that he's here in Bronco proves his life has taken a different turn, but as for his character…that's questionable."

Walking over to her, he gave her shoulders a gentle squeeze. "I'm going to get out of here and let you finish work. I'll be at your apartment at six thirty. That is, if you still want us to have a date," he added.

Her lips formed a perfect *O* as she whirled around to face him. "Of course, I want to keep our date! Why wouldn't I?"

He shrugged. "You're stressing over all of this. Later on might be better for you."

Grabbing both his hands, she held them tightly as though he was a lifeline, and Dale could only wonder if she thought of him more as her protector than as her lover.

"I need you, Dale. And whether you realize it or not, Mila needs you too."

Bending his head, he placed a soft kiss on her lips. "I'll see you at the apartment."

With time on his hands, Dale's first instinct when he left the bakery was to drive straight to Doug's bar and down several beers, but numbing his senses with alcohol wasn't the answer. Besides, he wasn't about to drink and then drive across town to Kendra's apartment.

Eventually, he decided to use the remainder of the afternoon to pick up a few items he needed from Bronco Feed and Ranch Supply. While he was there, he ran into a couple of cowboys who worked on a ranch that bordered Dalton's Grange, and by the time he'd shaken loose of their company and driven to Kendra's apartment, he was only a few minutes early.

Mila answered the door and on their way to the living room, she informed Dale that her mother was running late and was still getting ready.

"She had some extra stuff to do at the bakery," Mila explained as she watched Dale take a seat on the couch. "Jackie got sick and was throwing up so she had to go home."

From what Dale had gathered from Kendra, Jackie was her extra right hand. No doubt, the woman leaving work early put an even bigger strain on Kendra's day.

"That's too bad," Dale told the girl.

Mila was wearing jeans with a blue tutu fluffed over the hips and the rhinestone tiara on her head. She looked almost as she had that first night he'd walked into the bakery. So much had happened since then, he thought. The mother and daughter had become an integral part of his life.

She twirled her way across the living room until she was standing in front of Dale. "Mommy says it was just something she ate and not the flu."

"That's good to know," he said, while thinking what he really wanted from this child was her thoughts about her father. Had she found him as wonderful as she'd professed him to be? But Dale wasn't about to pump her for such information. On the other hand, if she offered it freely, he wasn't about to shut his ears.

As though she could read his thoughts, she plopped down on the cushion next to him and said, "I was super-duper happy when I saw my daddy yesterday. And he was happy to see me too."

Mila was smiling from ear to ear and the expression revealed more than any words she could have told him.

"I'm glad you were happy. Were you surprised to see him?"

"No. I've been thinking he was going to come soon and he did. Now I can see him all the time. 'Cause he won't be in Florida."

Her remark sent a sense of dread spiraling through him. "He's not going to be living in Florida?"

Grinning, she lifted her chin. "No. He's gonna stay here in Bronco—so he can see me."

Dale wondered if Bryce had actually told Mila such a thing or if this was the girl's wishful thinking. Either way, the idea left him uneasy. "Uh, that will be nice for you."

"Oh yes! And it will be nice for Mommy too. 'Cause him and her are going to get back together and we're going to be a whole big family again!" She let out a sigh of contentment. "But first they'll have a big wedding with flowers and music and all that fancy stuff. And I'll get to be the flower girl and wear a wreath of roses in my hair."

"You already know the wreath will be made of roses?" he asked cautiously.

"Sure I do. Because I'm going to tell Mommy to have roses for her flowers. They're the prettiest and they smell the best."

And that was the most important thing when a woman was remarrying her ex, Dale thought sourly, then silently muttered a few curse words.

Actually none of what Mila was saying sounded like Kendra, but he wasn't about to point this out to the child. Her mother would have to set her straight. Unless Kendra did decide she wanted to give Bryce one more try.

Oh God, he wasn't going to think about that possibility tonight.

The sound of footsteps caught his attention and he

turned his head to see Kendra entering the room. She was wearing another flounced dress that was cinched in at the waist with a silver concho belt and a pair of tall black cowboy boots. And although there were faint shadows of fatigue beneath her eyes, the warm smile on her lips made her face glow. She looked so lovely it made him ache with longing.

Rising quickly, he walked over and kissed her cheek. "You look far too beautiful tonight to be eating fast food," he told her. "I think we should go to a nice restaurant—wherever you'd like."

"Sounds good. But it's not really necessary. We can eat whatever."

Dale glanced over at Mila. He'd been so busy listening to the girl talk about her father, he'd not thought to inquire about her little friend.

"What about Louisa?" he asked. "Is she still planning to go with us?"

"Yes. I told her we'd pick her up on the way." To Mila, she said, "Go get your coat, honey. It's going to be chilly tonight."

Mila skipped out of the room and once she was out of sight, Kendra raised up on tiptoes and placed a hurried kiss on his lips.

Smiling slyly, he asked in a low voice, "Was that kiss a teaser of better things to come?"

"That was a promise for better things to come," she whispered. "As soon as I can make arrangements."

She handed him her coat and as he helped her into the sleeves and smoothed the fabric across her shoulders, he tried to reassure himself that he had nothing to worry about. Kendra might not love him yet, but she wanted him and that had to be enough for now.

As for her ex-husband, Dale could only hope that whenever Kendra was around him, she would only remember the suffering and heartache the man had caused her.

Chapter Eleven

That night on their way home from dinner, while Mila and Louisa had been chattering nonstop in the back seat, Kendra had made plans with Dale to meet again on Friday night. Mila could have another sleepover with Louisa and hopefully she and Dale would have an uninterrupted night together.

However, by the time Friday rolled around, their carefully made plans were foiled when Bryce called and invited Mila to a children's animated movie showing at a theater in Bronco Heights. Once the girl was given a choice between a sleepover with Louisa or going to the movies with her father, she'd not hesitated to choose the outing with Bryce.

Kendra had been devastated, but when she'd called Dale to give him the disappointing news, she'd insisted they could still salvage a big part of the evening.

"Bryce and Mila shouldn't be home from the movies before nine thirty or ten. That would give us two or three hours together," she told him.

"I don't mind telling you, Kendra, this whole setup is making me feel cheap."

She gripped the phone as she stared at the wall of her office. "It didn't make you feel cheap before. If it did, you didn't mention feeling that way."

"Before was different. Bryce wasn't in the picture," he said.

He sounded more than perturbed and Kendra could understand up to a point. But she was dealing with the situation as best as she could.

"He isn't in the picture now!" she said, unable to stop her voice from rising. "He has nothing to do with you and I being together."

"The hell he doesn't! He's the reason our plans have blown up in our faces."

"Is that my fault?" She shot the question back at him. "Am I supposed to keep Mila away from her father just so you won't be offended?"

The line went deathly quiet and then he said in a tight voice, "No. Heaven forbid that I should ever come between Mila and her real father. She and Bryce should go to the movie. In fact, now that I think about it, you should probably go with them. The three of you together—a family back together. Mila would love it. As far as that goes, Bryce would probably love it too."

Kendra's back teeth snapped together as anger poured over her. "You're sounding like a jealous idiot! And frankly, I don't have the time or desire to listen to such crap."

Her hand shaking, she punched the end-call button on the face of her phone, then dropped it onto the mouse pad on her desk.

Dropping her head into her hands, she closed her eyes and tried to calm her breathing when a knock sounded on the door. She looked up just in time to see Jackie stepping into the office.

"Am I needed out front?" she asked.

"At the moment, the only customers out there are coffee drinkers, and Smitty is handling those." Her eyes narrowed as she walked over to Kendra's desk. "Why are your cheeks fire-engine red? Let me guess, your ex is causing problems."

Kendra rolled her eyes toward the ceiling. "It's probably awful of me to say, but I'll be shouting hallelujah whenever he leaves."

Jackie perched a hip on the corner of the desk. "You used to tell me how much you wished he would come to see Mila. Now he's here and you're already wanting him to leave. You've made a quick turnaround."

She sighed. "Yes, I guess I have. Because deep down, I'm not sure he's sincere about being a father. Not for the long haul. Besides, I'm getting vibes from Bryce that he'd like to strike things up with me again. And that just isn't going to happen. Not ever."

"It's none of my business, Kendra, but was that Bryce on the phone just now?"

Kendra ran a hand over her burning eyes. She'd slept very little last night and this morning she'd had to hurry around in a groggy daze to get ready for work. Unfortunately, her day wasn't getting any better.

"No. It was Dale."

Jackie's mouth gaped open. "You were angry at Dale? Why?"

Good question, Kendra thought. Why was she angry? Because he resented the constant interruptions of their plans? Because he wanted her to consider his feelings as important as Mila's?

Groaning, she shook her head. "Everything is closing in on me, Jackie. Trying to deal with Mila, Dale and Bryce all at the same time. Trying to make them all happy. It's becoming too much for me. But me getting angry with Dale— I was wrong and I feel terrible about it."

Jackie shook her head. "Kendra, when are you ever going to try to make yourself happy?"

The question caused Kendra to pause. *Make herself happy?* The night she and Dale had made love for the first time, she'd actually believed she was on her way to a life of contentment. Now, the days ahead of her looked shaky at best.

She said, "Jackie, a woman can't just *make* herself happy. It's something that has to occur naturally."

Jackie lifted her arms in a gesture of frustration. "You're hopeless, Kendra. You can't sit around and wait and hope. You got to go after whatever you want—and that means Dale!"

Kendra was trying to decide how to counter her assistant's advice, when the door suddenly cracked open and Andrea peeped inside.

"Sorry to interrupt, but I need help," she said. "Customers are backed up to the door."

Jackie hurried out of the office and Kendra rose to go join them.

Halfway across the room, her cell phone rang and she paused to check the ID. If it wasn't important, she'd let voice mail pick up the call.

Dale!

Her hands trembling, she punched the accept button. "Dale, are you—"

"Don't say anything," he interrupted. "I need to apologize, Kendra. I was out of line and I'm sorry. The things I said— I was frustrated. I want to be with you and—"

"I want to be with you," she said, finishing his sentence before he could say more. "And I'm sorry too, Dale, for losing my cool and practically shouting at you. This is all just as frustrating for me. I want us to be together. Terribly so."

He released a long sigh of resignation and the sound sent a chill rushing through her. Clearly the strength of their bond was being stretched to the limit and Kendra wasn't sure how much longer he was going to hang on.

"I feel the same way. So I—I'll be there tonight. As long as I'm still invited, that is."

She fell back against the closed door and realized she was close to bursting into tears. "You're still *very* invited, Dale. I'll be waiting for you."

"'Bye, Kendra."

He ended the call without giving her a chance to say goodbye, but Kendra wasn't going to worry about that trivial detail. She'd be in his arms tonight and that was all that mattered.

Saturday night, Dale was in the tack room, going through the motions of oiling a saddle he'd cleaned only two days ago, when from the corner of his eye he saw Shep walk by the open doorway, then slowly back up.

"Hey, brother, what are you doing in there?" he called to Dale. "It's Saturday night. Aren't you going into town?"

Dale glanced in his direction. "Aren't you?"

"Sure. I have a hot date with a cute little nurse. Black hair and caramel-brown eyes and a little turned-up nose. Mmm. She says she wants to check my temperature."

Dale shot him a droll look. "Where did you meet her? Doug's?"

Shep chuckled. "No. At the gas pumps. She needed fuel and so did I. Our eyes met and— Well, you know how it is."

Yeah, Dale knew exactly. The moment his eyes had met Kendra's something inside him had clicked. Like a button being pushed or a light switching on. Now he was paying the price.

"Yeah, brother, gasoline fumes have a way of sparking a romance. Lucky for you. I'm not so sure about the nurse."

Chuckling again, Shep stepped into the tack room and walked over to where Dale was sitting on an overturned feed bucket. "After tonight, she'll count herself lucky," he joked, then asked in a more serious tone, "So why are you out here instead of getting ready to go see Kendra?"

"I saw her last night."

Shep's expression was one of disbelief. "And that's enough? Man, I thought you were gaga over the woman."

Grimacing, Dale began to rub a spot on the saddle he'd already polished a dozen times. "I am gaga over the woman," Dale admitted. "But I'm beginning to see my feelings for Kendra don't really matter."

Last night, Dale and Kendra had spent a whole two and a half hours in her bed. After that he'd hurriedly dressed and left the apartment before Mila and Bryce returned from the movie. Kendra had practically begged him to stay. As long as the two of them weren't in bed, there was nothing wrong with Bryce and Mila finding him there, she'd argued. But Dale had felt awkward about the whole setup and left, anyway.

To be honest, he'd not wanted to have another face-to-face with Bryce again. The urge to punch the guy was so intense he could hardly control himself. But there had been more pushing him to grab his hat and jacket and walking out the door. It was a feeling that he was falling into a hopeless pit. They'd made sweet, passionate love last night and yet she'd not spoken one word to him about the future or how he'd become a permanent fixture in her heart. Maybe she didn't understand that he wanted more from her than sex. He wanted her love.

Shep had remained silent while Dale's dour thoughts had been circling his brain, but now his younger brother snorted.

"Dale, that has to be one of the stupidest remarks I've ever heard you make. Why wouldn't your feelings about Kendra matter?"

A ball of raw emotion was suddenly clogging his throat. "Because with her and Mila I'm standing on the outside looking in." His eyes narrowed as he turned his gaze on his brother. "You know, if I remember right, I think you warned me about dating a woman with a child. But I didn't pay you much mind. I thought I could deal with Kendra having a daughter, but it's not— Well, things haven't turned out like I thought they could. How I wanted them to."

Shep frowned. "I thought you loved Mila. The three of you certainly seemed happy together when they visited the ranch."

"I do love Mila. That's not the problem." Dale tossed aside the cloth he'd been using on the saddle. "The problem is her real father has shown up in Bronco. She and Kendra haven't seen him in more than three years. Mila is over the moon with having her dad show her attention. And Kendra is—"

When he broke off, Shep cursed. "Hell, Dale, now—

adays a man is fortunate if a woman gives him one chance in life to make her happy. She damned well isn't going to give a loser a second chance. Kendra doesn't want him, if that's what you're thinking."

Ever since he'd driven away from Kendra's apartment last night, he'd been swimming in the miserable thoughts of Bryce worming his way back into Kendra's life. Maybe he was a fool for thinking in those terms, but he couldn't help himself.

When Dale failed to say anything, Shep went on, "I'll tell you one thing, brother. If I loved Kendra, I wouldn't sit around and give her ex the chance to win her back. And, anyway, who says the guy is going to stay around Bronco?"

"Mila. She says her dad is going to buy a place in town. But Kendra hasn't mentioned the possibility. She says she doesn't know anything about his plans."

"If the guy is planning to hang around, Dale, that's all the more reason you need to get a firm hold on Kendra's affections. And you can't do that by polishing a saddle until you wear a hole in the leather." Shep started toward the door, then glanced over his shoulder at Dale. "If you're not going to go see Kendra tonight, just make sure you stay away from Doug's."

"Why? A miserable man isn't supposed to drink beer?"

Shep grinned. "Sure, you can drink beer. But if you're at Doug's you might unintentionally end up sitting in the death seat and I don't want you ending up like Bobby Stone."

On that last bit of advice, his brother disappeared through the door and Dale thoughtfully screwed the cap back on the jug of neat's-foot oil sitting between his feet.

Why should he mind ending up like Bobby? Yeah,

the guy had gone through some misery. But his life had taken a turn for the better. He had a good woman's love now and that was a hell of a lot more than Dale had.

Something was wrong with Dale. Kendra hadn't seen him in several days. Not since the night Mila had gone to the movies with Bryce. Her calls to him had ended up in his voice-mail box and her text messages hadn't fared much better.

Been very busy on the ranch.

Those were the only words she'd received from him and with each passing day, she was growing more hurt and perplexed. Sure, a rancher's work was never done. But this wasn't about work monopolizing his time.

No, she thought, as she pulled a tray of peanut-butter cupcakes from the hot oven. Dale was obviously avoiding her. Oh yes, the last time he'd been at the apartment, he'd made love to her. But even as he'd held her close, she'd sensed his thoughts were far away. Since then, she'd been trying to tell herself he'd soon get back to the sweet understanding Dale she'd fallen in love with. But now she was beginning to doubt she'd ever see that Dale again.

"Kendra, the timer hasn't gone off yet, but these cinnamon rolls look ready to come out. You should probably have a look."

Kendra glanced over to Andrea, who was peeping into an industrial-size oven. "If they're brown, pull them. Do you have the glaze mixed?"

"It's ready. I'll take care of the rolls. You go ahead and finish the cupcakes."

Andrea had only started helping Kendra with the

actual baking about six weeks ago, but thankfully, the young woman was catching on very quickly.

Glancing at her watch, Kendra saw she had an hour to go before she dropped Mila off at Ada's and unlocked the door at five thirty, but there was still much to do in the kitchen before opening the front to the public.

"You have enough time, Kendra. But do you have enough energy?" Jackie asked as she paused at Kendra's side. "You look awful."

Kendra walked over to a worktable, where two dozen cupcakes were waiting to be frosted. Jackie followed on her heels.

"Thanks, Jackie. I always look forward to your cheery words to start the day," Kendra said dryly. "And I have a good excuse for looking awful. I got about three hours of sleep last night."

Bending her head close to Kendra's, Jackie whispered, "I hope it was Dale keeping you awake."

"Not in the way you're thinking," she snapped, then grabbed up an icing gun and began to squeeze white buttercream on the cupcakes. "Dale has been missing in action. He doesn't come around to see me. He won't answer my calls. Any sensible woman would tell him to go jump in the lake. But I—"

"Care too much to do that," Jackie said, finishing for her.

Kendra nodded miserably. "I swore I'd never make a fool of myself over a man again. But I have."

Jackie picked up a second icing gun and went to work helping Kendra top the cupcakes. "Look, Kendra. You don't actually know what's going on with Dale. You need to find out before you start making assumptions," she said. "And here's something else you might need to know. Maryann, the real-estate agent who works down the street, was in the bakery yesterday and she told me that Bryce had been in her office inquiring about houses for sale."

Kendra frowned as her cloudy day was already growing cloudier. "How would Maryann know Bryce?"

"She ran into Mila at the bakery and your chatty daughter introduced him to her," Jackie explained.

"Mila's proud to finally have a father to introduce."

"Yeah, but is he a real father?" Jackie shook her head. "Don't bother answering that. Just tell me you're going to drive out to Dalton's Grange and have it out with Dale face-to-face."

Kendra glanced at her assistant. Jackie might be flighty at times, but right now she was making sense.

"If you can take over for me here, I'll drive out to the ranch this afternoon. Ada is picking up Mila at school and keeping her until I finish work tonight, so it's a good time for me to go."

Forgetting the icing for a moment, Jackie slung an arm around Kendra's shoulders and squeezed. "I'll take care of everything here. You take care of Dale," she said.

If Kendra hadn't alerted Dale with a text message that she was coming to the ranch, he would've already ridden out with his brothers to round up a herd of heifers. Now, as he waited for her to arrive, he wished he'd left with his brothers, anyway.

These past few days he'd been trying to forget her face, the touch of her hand, her soft sighs and gentle smiles. He'd been trying to convince himself that stepping out of her life would be better for everyone. Now he had to convince her.

The sound of an approaching vehicle had him glancing toward the road leading into the ranch yard. When Kendra's white SUV came into view, he left the porch and walked out to meet her.

This time when she climbed out of the vehicle, Dale didn't greet her with a kiss. Those days were over with, he thought sickly. But, oh, she looked so lovely in a long black skirt and her blond hair flowing loosely over a white sweater. And how could she even smile at him after the way he'd been ignoring her?

A lump suddenly formed in his throat, making it painful to speak. "Hello, Kendra."

"Hi, Dale. I apologize for interrupting your work. I, uh, needed to take advantage of Mila being with the sitter. Otherwise, she would've had a fit to come with me."

He slanted her a skeptical glance. "I'm sure you could've gotten Bryce to watch her. Mila would choose him over Dalton's Grange any day."

The corners of her lips turned downward, but she didn't bother contradicting his remark. Probably because she knew he was speaking the truth.

What the hell is wrong with you, Dale? You're behaving like a child and sounding like a brat.

"Sorry, Kendra. That was a cheap shot. I want Mila to be happy. And she deserves to have her father in her life."

"Does she? I'm glad you're sure about that," Kendra said. "I'm still trying to make up my mind about the situation."

What did she mean by that? he wondered, then quickly doused his curiosity. Kendra and Mila were no longer his business.

Slipping a hand under her elbow, he said, "Let's go in. The house is quiet right now. Mom and Dad have gone to town and my brothers are out on the range."

She nodded and the two of them didn't speak until they were in the great room and he suggested she take a seat.

"I don't think I should bother sitting down."

"Why?" he asked.

Her features crumpled and it was all Dale could do not to sweep her into his arms and smother her with kisses. Had he gone crazy? He wanted this woman more than he'd ever wanted anything in his life. But sometime in these past few days, he'd come to the conclusion that it was time for him to be generous, to consider the needs of others before himself.

"I can see that you—" Turning her back to him, she bowed her head. "I came out here, Dale, to find out what has happened with you—why you haven't called or come to see me. I didn't understand. But now I can see for myself that you've quit caring."

Quit caring. Oh God, help him get through this, he prayed.

"Kendra, I think you're a wonderful person and Mila is a sweetheart. But since— Well, I've been doing a lot of thinking and I can see that I'm just not the settling down kind."

She turned to face him and her eyes were brimming with tears. "In other words, you've decided dealing with me, a child and an ex-husband is too much for you."

"If you want to put it that way, yes. I'll admit that once your ex showed up, it opened my eyes to what being married and having a child is all about. And I—I'm just not cracked up for that kind of life." He'd never been much of a liar, but he was doing a bang-up job of it now, he realized.

"I haven't tried to rope you into anything," she said.

"Be honest, Kendra—you want a husband, a family.

And that's what you need to focus on, instead of wasting your time on me."

Her blue eyes clouded with confusion as she stepped close enough to place her hand on his forearm. "Then those times we, uh, were together was just sex for you?"

Was it possible for a man's heart to burst into a thousand pieces, Dale wondered. Because his felt on the verge of exploding with pain.

"I— Yeah, I guess it was."

He couldn't look her in the eye, not while every word coming out of his mouth was a lie. But he was doing this for her sake and Mila's, he told himself. One day she'd be glad and thank him for it.

A breath shuddered out of her and she quickly turned her head away. "Well, there's not much use in me saying anything else, is there?"

"No. No use at all."

She started toward the door and somehow he managed to follow, even though the walls and the floor seemed to be tilting to a drunken degree. Maybe he was about to pass out, he thought, and when he woke up he'd find out this was all just a nightmare.

"Goodbye, Dale. I hope you won't avoid the bakery just because there is no *us* anymore. I'll still be glad to see you."

"That's nice of you, Kendra."

Dale, can you be any more of a bastard? She ought to be slapping your face and calling you what you really are.

"Please tell your parents hello for me."

"Sure."

He walked with her as far as the steps of the porch, but that was as far as he could go. Otherwise, she was going to see what a cowboy looked like when he cried.

* * *

With only a week of September left on the calendar, the hours of sunlight were growing shorter, forcing Dale and his brothers to begin and end their workdays in the dark. However, this morning as Dale and Morgan finished saddling their horses, the sun was already peeping over the ridge of the mountains, but the weak rays were hardly enough to counter the cold wind blasting them in the face.

"This weather is miserable," Dale muttered as he buttoned his sherpa-lined jacket tightly at his throat. "I should have pulled on my duster. It cuts the wind better."

"Go to the house and fetch it," Morgan told him. "We have plenty of time to make the ride out to check the bulls and get back by midafternoon."

Dale tugged the brim of his hat farther down on his forehead. "I don't want to bother. I'll be warm enough when the sun gets a little higher."

"Suit yourself." He nodded his head in the direction of the door directly behind them. "Let's go in the barn and drink a little coffee before we go."

Shrugging, Dale said, "Let's go."

Inside the barn, Morgan filled two foam cups from a thermos and the brothers sat down together on a wooden bench. An overhead heater was blowing air in their direction, but Dale felt little warmth.

It's not the weather making you feel cold and empty inside, Dale. You'll never feel warm again. Not without Kendra.

Dale couldn't deny the mocking voice in his head. A little over a week had passed since he'd told Kendra they were finished and he was just as crushed now as he'd been when she'd driven away.

"This isn't like you to dawdle around when we have work to do," Dale said. "Taking care of Erica must be wearing you out."

"No way. She's carrying my baby. It's an honor to do things for her," Morgan told him. "I only wish I could do more to make this time easier for her."

Dale studied his brother's profile. "You love her very much, don't you?"

"This will probably sound corny to you, Dale, but sometimes I feel like I'm full up to here with love for her." Smiling, he used a finger to measure a spot at the base of his throat.

Dale's gaze drifted down the barn to where a ranch hand was already busy mucking out one of the horse stalls. But he didn't really see the cowboy. All Dale could see was the crushed look on Kendra's face when they'd parted.

"Must be nice to feel that way about a woman and have her feel that way about you."

"You ought to know."

Grimacing, Dale said, "If you're talking about Kendra, then you're barking up the wrong tree. I'm not seeing her anymore."

Morgan muttered a curse. "You think that's news? The whole family can see you've been moping around like a calf with shipping fever."

"I don't need your sarcasm, Morgan. Not today or any day."

"Right. You need help and in the worst kind of way." He took a sip of coffee, then said, "Tell me why she broke up with you."

Dale stared into his cup. "She didn't. I'm the one who ended things."

Morgan's expression turned to disbelief. "I thought

you were smarter than that, Dale. I thought you realized that Kendra was the kind of woman who wanted
a family. Not an affair. What happened? You started
getting cold feet?"

"Not exactly. I realized I was fighting a losing battle.
Her ex-husband is in Bronco now."

Morgan didn't so much as flinch. "And that made
you tuck your tail and run? When have you ever backed
away from a fight? When has any Dalton held up a flag
of surrender?"

Dale said, "Believe me, it was all I could do not to
tell him exactly what I thought of him and then show
him a one-way road out of town. But that would've only
made matters worse. You see, Mila is crazy about the
guy. He's never been a part of her life before now. He
never bothered to be a father. But that makes no difference to her."

"So you think the man is unworthy of Mila's ado-
ration?"

Dale tried to wash the bitterness from his mouth
with a swig of coffee. "Morgan, you and I both know
we weren't raised to serve judgment on another person."

Morgan studied him for a long, thoughtful moment.
"So you're trying to be fair and noble about this whole
situation. Is that it?"

The pain in Dale's chest was rapidly spreading to his
stomach and beyond. "Isn't that what a decent man is
supposed to do? I figure in the end Mila needs her two
parents together again. Families are better off together,
not apart. Just look at us, Morgan. Think how awful it
would be if Mom and Dad were divorced."

"Mom has always loved Dad unconditionally. That
kind of love doesn't end. You think that's how Kendra
feels about her ex?" Morgan snorted. "I doubt it. And

who gave you the right to decide she should be back with a man who'd obviously wronged her? Are you trying to sentence her to a life of unhappiness? Or are you just afraid of love and marriage and being a father?"

Without him even knowing it, Dale's spine stiffened. "I'm not afraid! I mean, once I might've been afraid, but not anymore. And Kendra—I want her to be happy."

"Don't you believe you can make her happy?"

Groaning, Dale's gaze dropped to the toes of his boots. "At first I'd hoped I could. But now... I don't know if she loves me, Morgan. She's never spoken the words to me."

"Have you spoken them to her? Did you ever think she might be waiting on you? You need to remember she's been hurt by a man before. It's only natural she'd be cautious about handing out those words to another fellow...unless she knew for certain that he really cared."

Dale looked at him and as his brother's words of advice slowly sunk into his breaking heart, he felt a spark of hope try to flicker beneath the pain.

"You really think she might be waiting on me?" he asked in wonder. "If she knew how much I loved her, do you think she might forgive me?"

Grinning now, Morgan clamped a hand on his shoulder and gave it an affectionate shake. "You'll never find out until you try, little brother."

Later that night, Kendra was curled up on the end of the couch, trying to reassure her mother that she was surviving, in spite of her breakup with Dale, but Laura wasn't buying in to her daughter's phony cheerfulness.

"If this was a FaceTime call, I know I'd see tears in your eyes," she told Kendra. "So drop the pretense.

What you need to be doing is figuring out what went wrong with you and Dale and try to fix it."

Kendra pressed fingertips against her furrowed forehead. For the past week and a half she'd been walking around like a zombie, so numb with pain that getting through each hour was a struggle.

"It's an unfixable problem. Dale wants to keep his freedom. He's decided there's too much drama in dating a woman with a child and an ex-husband."

Kendra's reply was met with a long stretch of silence, then her mother said, "From everything you've told me about the man, none of that sounds like it fits his character."

I can see that I'm just not the settling-down kind.

When Kendra had first met Dale, he'd told her he wasn't looking to get married. Even Mila had warned her over and over that Dale wasn't her type, or the marrying kind. It was humiliating to discover a seven-year-old girl had a better judgment of men than Kendra.

"Dale explained it in a different way, but the end results are the same. Let's face it, Mom. It's not meant for me to have a real family."

"You're talking nonsense, honey. If you love him—"

"There's no *if* about it, Mom," she interrupted. "In spite of him treating me like a disposable dishcloth, I still love him deeply. I realize there's no logic to my feelings, but that's the way it is for me."

"Darling daughter, there is no logic to love. And all I was going to say is don't count everything over yet. Not until you've explained to Dale how you really feel about him."

Kendra frowned. "You think he doesn't know? How—" The chime of the doorbell caused her to pause.

"Someone is at the door, Mom. I'll have to call you back."

Glancing at her watch, she decided it was a bit early for Mila to return from her playdate with Louisa. Besides, Mila knew where the outside key was hidden. And she didn't think the caller was Bryce. Several days ago, she'd made it brutally clear to him that she had zero interest in getting romantically involved with him again. Since their frank conversation, he'd kept a cool distance, only coming around whenever he had plans to see Mila.

When Kendra reached the door and peeked through the peephole, she was stunned to see Dale standing on her porch. What was he doing here?

Her hands trembling, she quickly unlocked the door and swung it wide.

"Hello, Kendra. May I come in?"

Realizing her mouth was gaped, she quickly snapped it shut and gestured for him to enter. "Certainly."

Cold wind followed him over the threshold and Kendra wasted no time in shutting the door and fastening the lock.

"I should've called," he said as she moved alongside him. "But I was afraid you, uh, would refuse to see me."

She couldn't refuse this man anything. At least, not while he was standing this close and she was aching to throw herself into his arms.

What a little fool you are, Kendra.

Ignoring the taunt in her head, she said, "Whatever you might think, I'm not a vengeful person, Dale."

"I'm relieved to hear it."

Gesturing ahead of her, she said, "Let's go to the living room. It's much warmer in there."

Once there, he pulled off his hat and, holding it with both hands, he looked at her with an expression she could only describe as humble. Which didn't make much sense. But his being here didn't make sense, either.

"You might as well sit down, Dale."

"Am I interrupting anything?"

"No. I was just talking with my mother." She walked over to the couch and sat down. Otherwise, her legs were likely to betray her and she'd end up collapsing right in front of him. "Mom is already thinking ahead to December. She and Dad are considering flying out for the Christmas holidays. But you're not here to talk about my parents or Christmas."

He pulled off his denim ranch jacket and placed it and his hat on an armchair, then walked over and took a seat on the cushion next to hers.

"I'm here to talk about you and me," he said frankly.

Everything inside Kendra began to tremble. "I don't understand. You made it clear we were no longer a couple."

He closed his eyes and drew in a sharp breath. "I know. I said a lot of damned stupid things to you that day on Dalton's Grange. I didn't mean any of them. I—I was— Well, in the words of my brother Morgan, I was trying to be fair and noble."

The pain she'd been going through these past several days had done something to her brain. It didn't seem to be able to process what he was saying.

Frowning, she asked, "What do you mean 'fair and noble'? All I heard was that you're not a settling-down man and everything between us was just sex."

Grimacing, he reached for her hands. "I'll never forgive myself for saying those things to you, Kendra. But I thought— I believed in the long run I was doing the right thing."

"For yourself? Because you don't want a wife and

child hanging around your neck?" she asked, unable to stop bitterness from tinging her voice.

"No! Because I thought Mila has needed her father for so long and she'd be much better off if she had her parents back together—the three of you as a family again. I was in the way of that, Kendra. I guess I still am."

Disbelief furrowed her brow. "Dale, how could you think I'd ever want such a thing? Bryce is no good. Not for me. And whether he ends up being a good father to Mila is something he has yet to prove. But I've already made it very clear to him that I want nothing to do with him romantically or any other way."

He let out a sigh of relief. "I'm glad to hear it, Kendra, because I've decided I'm not so noble after all. I love you too much to let Bryce have you."

Kendra stared at him in wonder. "You…love me? Is that what you said?"

His expression sheepish, he nodded. "I thought you knew how I felt. But I thought— Well, that you didn't feel the same way. So I kept my feelings to myself. But now I have to know, Kendra. Do you care enough for me to give us another chance?"

Like a thousand exploding stars, joy flashed through her and she flung her arms around him and smacked hurried kisses all over his face. "Oh, Dale, you darling fool! I've been in love with you ever since that night Mila had her headache! Even when you said all those things to me at Dalton's Grange I still loved you. I'll never stop loving you."

His arms came around her and as his face buried in the curve of her neck, she thought the sound he made was something like a sob.

"Kendra, sweetheart, I've never been good at expressing my feelings. And I'm probably not saying anything right tonight. But I want you to know I'll always love you too. I want you to be my wife. I want us to have children and a home and be a real family. I desperately hope you want the same thing."

She eased his head up far enough from her shoulder to look into his deep blue eyes. "Yes, Dale! Yes, I want to be your wife. I want us to have children and a home and all the things that go with it." Pressing her cheek to his, she whispered, "Good or bad, we'll deal with all of it together."

His arms tightened around her. "I don't expect the idea of you marrying me instead of Bryce is going to go over very well with Mila. I figure I've got a lot of work ahead of me to try to win her approval."

Leaning her head back, Kendra gave him a clever smile. "Oh, I wouldn't say that. This will probably surprise you, but Mila has been missing you. She told me so herself. I guess you'd started to grow on her. And I also think that she's beginning to figure out for herself that Bryce isn't turning out to be the perfect father she imagined him to be. This past week, on two different occasions, he found excuses not to see her as he'd promised. I could tell she didn't believe him."

"She's a smart girl. She's going to figure out a lot of things. Especially how much I love her mother."

Kendra moved her lips to his and he captured them in a long, promising kiss that was still going on when Mila's voice suddenly shattered the silence.

"Yay! Looks like we're finally going to have a wedding!"

Laughing, Dale held his arm out to Mila and as the three of them hugged, Dale said, "That's right, sweetie. A big wedding with a pretty little flower girl with a rose wreath in her hair and sparkly cowgirl boots on her feet. How does that sound?"

Tears of joy misted Kendra's eyes as she watched Mila circle her arms around Dale's neck and kiss his cheek.

"It sounds like we're going to have the best wedding ever!" Mila happily exclaimed.

Kendra squeezed Dale's hand and as he looked at her, she could see forever in his eyes.

Epilogue

Two weeks later, on the front porch of the Dalton's Grange ranch house, Kendra held out her left hand to allow Tori Hawkins, and her two cousins, Audrey Hawkins, who was married to Jack Burris and Corinne Hawkins, to get a closer look at the engagement ring Dale had slipped on her finger a few days earlier. The autumn afternoon sun glinted on the large square diamond flanked on both sides by a row of smaller round diamonds.

"Kendra, this is exquisite!" Tori exclaimed, then smiled suggestively at Dale, who was sitting close to his fiancée's side. "Looks like you mean to have Kendra for keeps."

Smiling smugly, Dale slipped his arm around Kendra's shoulders. "She's stuck with me from now on."

Audrey spoke up in a teasing voice. "It looks to me like Kendra is enjoying being stuck."

The three cowgirls had agreed to come out to the ranch this Sunday in order for Mila to meet her rodeo idols, and so far, the child had been happily monopolizing their attention. As for Dale, he didn't know the first thing about weddings or anything they entailed, but as long as he was sitting close to Kendra, feeling the warmth of her side pressed to his and seeing her smiles, he was a contented man. Later tonight, when they were alone in bed, he'd get her complete attention.

Besides, this afternoon get-together was mostly for Mila and worth it to Dale to see the girl thoroughly enjoying herself. The past two weeks, she'd gone through some major changes in her life. Her mother had gotten engaged and she'd had to say goodbye to her father, who'd gone back to Florida only a few days ago.

For a while Bryce had implied he might remain in Bronco permanently and Mila had even been telling everyone her daddy was here to stay. But shortly after Dale and Kendra had become engaged, the man had admitted that Montana just wasn't his style and he was going back to Florida. Even so, he'd insisted that he'd learned his lesson and vowed to be a father to Mila on a more regular basis. So he and Kendra had been talking to their former divorce attorney about renegotiating their custody agreement, to create a new visitation schedule. And Kendra had agreed to allow Mila to visit her father on designated dates in Florida, and Dale could only hope Bryce kept his promises.

Well, he thought to himself, at least he'd get some Florida sunshine himself out of the bargain, since he and Kendra planned to take Mila back and forth on her visits. He'd grudgingly talked to Bryce about a family trip to Disney, too, perhaps next summer—if things worked out.

"I already have a dress picked out for Mommy's wedding. It's in the Ever After wedding boutique in town,"

Mila declared as she carried a stack of magazines and wedding brochures over to where the Hawkins women were seated in cushioned lawn chairs.

After opening one of the brochures, Mila held the page up for the women to view. "This will be her dress. See, it has lots of lace and tiny pearls and a veil with a train that goes a long way behind her. So long that someone will have to carry it."

Tori winked at Kendra and Dale. "You mean, someone like you?" she asked Mila.

Mila's blond ponytail swished back and forth as she shook her head. "Oh no! I can't carry the bridal train. I'm going to be the flower girl. I have to toss out the rose petals."

Audrey exchanged an amused glance with Corinne, before posing another question to Mila. "You already know your mommy is going to have roses as her wedding flowers?"

Mila glanced at her mother. "Well, sure. 'Cause she loves roses. They're her favorite flower. And mine too."

"Roses. Hmm. I'll have to remember that," Dale whispered in Kendra's ear. "Maybe by the time we get married, I'll have memorized a few more of your favorite things."

She smiled dreamily at him. "My favorite thing is you, darling. We're going to have a wonderful life together. You, me and our children living here on the ranch. I never thought I could be this happy."

Dale leaned over and pressed a kiss to her forehead. "And I'm going to do my best to make sure you stay that way."

"So have you two fixed a wedding date yet?" Tori asked Dale and Kendra.

Dale looked questioningly at Kendra and she smiled

coyly at Tori. "Not yet. But we're thinking about when we might like to have the ceremony. Right now we're just celebrating being engaged, aren't we?"

Dale's smile for his fiancée was full of love and promise. "We're thrilled, and so are our families."

Still clutching her armload of wedding magazines, Mila sidled up to Corinne's chair. "When are you and cowboy Mike going to get married, Corinne? I bet you want a big fancy wedding like my mommy is going to have. Would you like to look at my books for a dress?"

Hearing Mila's question, Dale glanced over at Corinne just in time to see a tight grimace pass over her face. Mike Burris was a brother to Jack and brother-in-law to Audrey. Like his famous brothers and the Hawkins Sisters, he was a rodeo cowboy, too, and for a while now he'd had an on-again, off-again relationship with Corinne. Judging by the agitated expression on her face, she wasn't exactly happy with Mike at the present.

Smiling wanly at Mila, Corinne said, "I'm not planning a wedding, sweetie. Mike and I are just friends."

Mila looked disappointed, while Dale gave Kendra a conspiring wink and murmured close to her ear, "I have a feeling that relationship might soon change."

With a knowing smile, Kendra squeezed his hand and whispered back to him. "No doubt about it. Cowboys are hard to resist."

* * * * *

SPECIAL EXCERPT FROM

The baby was only the first surprise...

Retired rodeo cowboy Dean Hunter has escaped
to Charming, Texas, for some solitude, some surf
and a new start. But his plans are interrupted
by his stunning—and sparring—neighbor next
door...and the baby he discovers on Maribel's
doorstep!

Read on for a sneak preview of

A Charming Doorstep Baby
by Heatherly Bell.

Chapter One

"Another drink for Maribel."

Maribel Del Toro held up her palm. "No, *thanks*. I might not be driving, but I have to worry about walking while under the influence."

For an establishment that was a historical landmark, the Salty Dog Bar & Grill had mastered the art of a modern twist. The ambience fell somewhere between contemporary and classic, with a long bar of gleaming dark wood, one redbrick wall and exposed ceiling beams. Separate and on the opposite side of the bar the restaurant section was filled with booths. To top it all off, a quaint sense of small coastal town community infused the bar. Maribel loved it here.

Her brother, Max, was the occasional bartender and full-time owner. Situated on the boardwalk in the quiet town of Charming, Texas, it was the kind of place where everybody knew your name.

Especially if you were the younger sister of one of

the three former Navy SEALs who owned and operated the establishment.

"You had one beer. Even I think you're skilled enough to make it to the cottages without falling." Max grinned and wiped the bar.

"Ha ha. My brother, the comedian. I'll have a soda, please and thank you."

Afterward, she'd take a leisurely walk down to her beach rental a short mile from the boardwalk. Lately, she'd been digging her toes in the sand and simply staring off into the large gulf. Her father had once said if she ever got too big for her britches, she should consider the vastness of the ocean. She often had from her childhood home in Watsonville, California. The Pacific Ocean was an entirely different feel from the Gulf Coast, but both reminded her of how small her own problems were in comparison.

The doors to the restaurant swung open and some of the customers called out.

"Val! Hey, girl."

"When are you gettin' yourself back to work?"

"Soon as my husband lets me! Believe me, I miss y'all, especially your tips." Valerie Kinsella stopped to chat with customers and let a few of them check out the bundle in her front-loaded baby carrier.

She sidled up to the bar, her hand protectively cradled on her son's head of espresso brown curls that matched his mother's. "Hey, y'all. How's it goin'?"

"Hey there." Max hooked his thumb in the direction of the back office. "If you want Cole, he's in the back checking the books. We want to give the staff a nice bonus around the holidays."

"Well, dang it, I'm going to miss out on that, too. But I didn't just come by to see Cole. I sleep next to him every night." Valerie elbowed Maribel. "How are you enjoying your vacation?"

"Loving it. The beach rental unit is just perfect."

"And even if it is hurricane season, the weather seems to be cooperating."

Oh yeah. By the way, somebody should have told Maribel. When she'd eagerly booked this vacation for November, everyone forgot to mention the tail end of hurricane season. But this part of the Gulf Coast hadn't been hit in many years, so it was considered safe. Or as safe as Mother Nature could be. In any case, the lovely row of cottages near the beach were being sold to an investor, according to her sister-in-law, Ava, and this might be Maribel's last chance to stay there.

She nodded to Valerie's baby. "What a cutie. Congratulations again."

"Wade is such a sweet baby. We're lucky." Valerie kissed the top of his head.

He was a healthy-looking kid, too, with bright blue curious eyes the same intense shade as his father's. Maribel didn't have any children of her own, but she had plenty of experience. Loads. More than she'd ever wanted, thank you. In a way, that was why she was here in Charming, taking a sabbatical from all the suffering and gnashing of teeth. It went along with her profession like the ocean to the grains of sand.

"When do you go back to teaching?" Maribel gently touched Wade's little pert nose.

"Not until after the holidays. I've had a nice maternity leave, but it's time to get back to my other kids. The students claim to miss me. I have enough cards and drawings to make me almost believe it."

Maribel spent a few more minutes being treated to Valerie's "warrior story," i.e., her labor and delivery.

She was a champ, according to Cole. Valerie claimed not to remember much, which to Maribel sounded like a blessing in disguise. Mucus plug. Episiotomy. Yikes. Maribel had reached her TMI limit when Cole, the former SEAL turned golden surfer boy, came blustering out of the back office looking every bit the harried father of one.

"Hey, baby." He slid his arm around Valerie, circling it around mother and child.

Maribel had known Cole for years since he'd been a part of the brotherhood who for so long had ruled Max's life. She imagined Max and his wife would be headed to Baby Town soon, as well. And though it was information still being held private, Jordan and Rafe were newly pregnant. Maribel had been given the news by a thrilled Jordan just last week.

Maribel slid off the stool. "Well, folks, I'm going to head on back to my little beach shack now."

Shack wasn't quite the right word. She'd been pleasantly surprised to find a suite similar to resort hotel villas. It contained a separate seating area and flat-screen, attached kitchenette and separate bedroom with a second flat-screen and a king-size bed. The bedroom had sliders opening up to a small patio that led to the private beach.

"Need a ride?" Cole asked.

"Nah. Part of the ambience of Charming can only be enjoyed by strolling."

Max gave a quick wave. "Don't forget, Ava wants you over for dinner soon."

"I'm here two weeks. Plenty of time." She slid a pleading look Valerie's way. "I'm hopeful for another invite to the lighthouse, too."

"Anytime!" Cole and Valerie both said at once, making everyone laugh.

Max rolled his eyes, but he should talk. He and Ava often finished each other's sentences.

Outside, the early November evening greeted her with a mild and light wind. Summers in the gulf had resembled a sauna in every way, but autumn had so far turned out to be picture perfect. Except for the whole hurricane season thing. Still, it was warm enough during the day for trips to the beach. When she dipped her toes in, the gulf waters were less like a hot tub and more like a warm bath. Maribel ambled along the seawall, away from the boardwalk side filled with carnival-style rides for children. The succulent scent of freshly popped kettle corn and waffle cones hung thickly in the air. She passed by shops, both the Lazy Mazy kettle corn and the saltwater taffy store. The wheels of an old-fashioned machine in front of the shop's window rolled and pulled the taffy and entertained passersby. In the distance, Maribel spotted a group of surfers.

The views were everything one would expect from a bucolic beach town with a converted lighthouse, piers, docks and sea jetties. The first time she'd been here was for Max and Ava's wedding six months ago, and she'd fallen in love with the area. It was the only place she'd considered escaping when she'd decided to resign from her position as a social worker. The offer from a multi-author doctor corporation was one she'd consider while here. They wanted a psychologist on board to assist with their heavy caseload, and that meant Maribel would put her hard-earned PhD to use. Although she wasn't excited by the prospect. Maybe after this vacation, she'd be able to clear the decks and finally make a firm decision. The offer was attractive, but it would be a huge change for her. She wasn't sure she'd be able to do much good and felt at a crossroads in her life. And this was the perfect location to decide what she'd do for the rest of her professional life.

The small row of beachfront cottages were rented year-round by both residents and tourists. Maribel had lucked into a rental during the off-season, meaning she had the peace and quiet she craved. As far as she could tell so far, she had only one neighbor, immediately next door. He was the most irritating male she'd ever had the misfortune of meeting. Sort of. There was, in fact, quite a list. He was, at the moment, in the top five.

On the day she'd arrived, she'd been to the store to stock up on groceries for all the cooking she'd planned to do. Hauling no less than four paper bags inside, she'd set one down just outside the heavy front door, propping it open.

When she'd returned for it, a huge cowboy stood outside her door holding it.

"Forgot something." He'd brushed by her, striding inside like he owned the place.

"Hey," she muttered, following him.

The man spoke in a thick Texan drawl, and he hadn't said the words in a helpful way. More like an accusatory tone, as in "You dingbat, here's your bag. If you need any other help getting through life, let me know."

She'd caught him looking around the inside of her rental as if apprising its contents. But he didn't *look* like a burglar.

"I didn't forget." Maribel snatched the shopping bag from him, deciding in that moment he'd made it to the top five. Of all the nerve. She hadn't been gone a full minute.

"You might not want to just leave anything out here unattended. Unless you want someone to steal it."

Steal? Here in the small town of Charming, Texas?

She flushed at the remark. "I don't think anyone is going to steal my box of cereal or fresh fruit."

"Regardless, you should care for your property. Don't invite trouble."

Okay, so he'd figured out she was a single woman and wanted to look out for her.

"Great. If you're done with your mansplaining, I'm going to cook dinner."

"Are you liking this unit well enough? Everything in working condition?"

Now, he sounded like the landlord. *Good grief.* Top three most irritating men, easily.

"Yes, thank you, I have located everything I need." She rolled her eyes.

"I'm next door if you need anything else."

"I won't."

He'd tipped his hat, but she'd shut the door on him before he could say another word.

Since that day, she saw little of him, and that was fine with her.

Twenty minutes of an invigorating walk later, she arrived at her cottage. There was her neighbor again, the surly surfing cowboy, coming up from their lane to the beach carrying a surfboard under his arm. He might be irritating as hell, but he looked like he'd emerged from the sea shirtless, ready to sell viewers the latest popular male cologne.

She wondered whether he was attempting to cover two hero stereotypes at once. He wore a straw cowboy hat, and though this was Texas, after all, the hat didn't *quite* match with the bare chest and wet board shorts he wore low on his hips. A towel slung around his neck completed the outfit of the salty guy who once more simply nodded in her direction. Before she could say, "Howdy, neighbor," he stared straight ahead like she no longer existed.

No worries. She hadn't come here to make friends. Even if he resembled a Greek god. Thor, to be more specific—who wasn't actually from Greek mythology. This demigod had taut golden skin, a square jaw and a sensual mouth. His abs, legs and arms were chiseled to near perfection. But she was going to ignore all this because it didn't fit into her plans.

Focus. Men were not part of the plan. Even sexy irritating males, her weakness. She was here to unplug and had turned off her cell, giving her family the landline for emergencies. In her plan for mindfulness and peace, she was practicing yoga every morning before sunrise. And reading. Not from her e-reader but actual print she had to hold in her hands.

Rather than dwelling on her problems, Maribel would set them aside for now. Since months of dwelling on her problems hadn't given any answers, she was trying this new approach.

Once she'd spent enough time away from her situation, her mind would produce fresh results and ideas.

Because she had to decide soon how she would spend the rest of her life.

Dean Hunter hopped out of the shower and wrapped a towel around himself. Another day completed in his attempts to hit the waves and master the fine art of surfing. All he had to show for it? Two more fresh cuts, five new bruises and a sore knee. He had to face facts: he was a disaster on the water, having spent most of his life on a working cattle ranch. He'd been bucked off many a horse, and how interesting to find it wasn't any less pleasant to slam into the water than the ground. Seemed like water should give a little, and of course it did, more than the ground ever would. Still hurt, though, equal to the velocity with which a person slammed into a wave.

Why am I here?

A question he asked himself twice a day.

He should have simply backed out of this vacation and lost his deposit. This time was to have been a getaway with Amanda, where he'd get down on bended knee and pop the question. The cottages were going to be a surprise wedding gift to her. A way to show her all he'd accomplished. They'd have a vacation home every summer, a whole row of them. He was a damn idiot thinking that maybe he'd finally found the right woman. He and Amanda were both part of the circuit and had been for years. They had a great deal in common, and eventually they'd decided moving out of the friend zone made sense.

Then, six months ago, he'd walked in on Amanda showing Anton "The Kid" Robbins the ropes. And by "the ropes," he meant he'd walked in on her and the twenty-six-year-old, Amanda straddling him like a bucking horse. No way a man could ever unsee that. He'd walked out of his own house and moved into a hotel room. One more race to win, he'd told himself, and maybe then he'd go out on top. But that hadn't happened.

To think that Anton had been his protégé. Dean hadn't been ready to retire, but he saw the sense in training the new kids, giving them a hand up. Someone had done this for him, and he would return the favor. He couldn't ride forever, but he'd thought he would have had a little more time. Now Dean was the old guard and Anton the new. He didn't have as many injuries (yet) as Dean and was also ten years younger.

Dean still had no idea how he'd gotten it all so wrong. He hadn't been able to clearly see what had been in front of him all along. His manager had warned him about Amanda, who was beautiful but calculating. Dean had wanted to believe he'd finally found someone who would stick by him when he quit the rodeo. He'd had about six months with her, during which time she convinced him he'd found the right woman. *Yeah, not so much.*

Their breakup happened right before his last ride. He'd already been reeling when he'd taken the last blow, this one to his career. In some ways, he was still trying to get up from the last kick to his ego. At thirty-six, battered and bruised, he'd been turned in for a newer model. Anton still had plenty of mileage left on him, time to make his millions before a body part gave out on him.

So Dean should have let the opportunity to buy this investment property go. There were ten cottages, and in anticipation of his stay here to check them out thoroughly, they'd kept them vacant for him. All except Cute Stuck-up Girl next door. The moment he'd noticed he wasn't here alone as expected, he'd phoned the real estate agent.

"Thought I was going to be here by myself."

"You were, but Maribel Del Toro apparently has some influential friends in this town, friends who know the current owner and have some pull. We thought it best not to reschedule her reservation like we did the others."

"How am I supposed to inspect her unit?"

He'd already found an excuse by hurrying to help

bring in a grocery bag in before she had a chance to say anything. You would have thought he'd wrecked the place instead of tried to help. He'd obviously insulted her in the process, but how else was he supposed to check inside? He never bought a dang thing before he inspected every nook and cranny, and that included a horse.

"We will give you a clause to back out if something is wrong in that unit. These deals fall apart all the time."

"And why is she right *next* to my unit?"

The real estate agent sighed. "Remember, you asked for new storm windows if you were even to consider buying. Progress on the others was not complete, and hers was the only unit available when she arrived."

By nature, Dean was a suspicious sort, and he couldn't help but wonder why these units were going far too cheaply for ocean-front property. But as a kid who'd grown up in Corpus Christi to a single mother who never had much, it would be a nice "full circle" gesture to buy this. And after years of punishing his body and garnering one buckle after another, he was a wealthy man. Still, he didn't like anyone to know it, least of all women. So he dressed like a cowboy even if he was technically a multimillionaire. At his core, he was a cowboy and always would be.

While the injury was said to be career ending, he could have gone through rehab and come back stronger than ever. Having come from nothing, he'd been wise about his investments, and while others enjoyed buckle bunnies, gambling and drinking, Dean had socked away every nickel. He had investments all over Texas, including his ranch in Hill Country.

In the end, he'd forced himself to walk away from the rodeo before he didn't have a body left to enjoy the other pleasantries in life. Oh yeah. That was why he was here in Charming trying his hand at surfing in the Gulf of Mexico during hurricane season. It was just the shot of adrenaline a junkie like him needed.

He would find his footing in his new world with zero illusions he'd find a second career as a competitive surfer. Instead, it was time for the second part of his life to begin, the part that was supposed to matter.

Life *after* the rodeo. Life after poverty.

He'd already been coming here for a short time every summer just to remember his roots. He'd drive from Corpus Christi to Charming, counting his blessings. Enjoying the coastal weather.

Remembering his mother.

Once, he could recall having ambitions that went beyond the rodeo. An idea and a plan to fix for others what had been broken in his own life. Somewhere along the line, he'd forgotten every last one of those dreams. He was here to hopefully remember some of them in the peace and quiet of this small town. Here, no one would disturb him. No one except his feisty neighbor, that is, who behaved as if he'd deeply insulted her by carrying in her groceries. She'd immediately put him on the defensive, seeing as it had merely been an excuse to get inside her unit. It was as if she could read his mind. He didn't like it.

He often watched Cute Stuck-up Girl from a distance as she sank her feet in the sand and read a book. Two days ago, he'd seen her fighting the beach umbrella she'd been setting up for shade. It was almost bigger than her, which was part of the problem. She'd cursed and carried on until Dean was two seconds away from offering his help. He'd walk over there and issue instructions on how to put the umbrella up until she got all red in the face again with outrage. The thought made him chuckle. He'd put the umbrella up *for* her if she'd let him. Not likely.

Finally, she got it to stay up and did a little victory dance when she must have assumed no one was watching.

And he'd found a laugh for the first time in months.

After changing clothes and towel-drying his hair, Dean plopped on his favorite black Stetson and headed to the local watering hole. A little place along the boardwalk that he'd discovered a few years ago sandwiched between other storefronts and gift shops. At the Salty Dog Bar & Grill, the occasional bartender and owner there was a surfer who'd given Dean plenty of tips. Cole Kinsella had even offered Dean one of his older boards, since as a new father, he wasn't taking to the water as often.

Safe to say, Dean liked the bar and the people in it from the moment he'd strode inside and momentarily indulged in one of his favorite fantasies: buying a sports bar. It was one of the few investments he didn't have because he'd been talked out of it too many times to count. This place resembled a sports bar, but was more of a family place that also happened to have a bar. The restaurant section sat next to the bar separated only by the booths. Instead of huge flat-screens on every spare amount of space, there were chalkboards with the specials written out in fancy white cursive.

Everyone was friendly and welcoming. The first night Dean had come in, he'd met a group of senior citizens who were having some kind of a poetry meeting.

The only gentleman in the group, Roy Finch, had offered to buy Dean a beer.

"Don't mind if I do." Dean nodded. "Thank you, sir."

"You're a cowboy?"

"Yes, sir. Born and bred." Dean tipped his hat.

"Don't usually see that many of you here on the gulf."

"Our profession usually keeps us far from the coast."

"What you doin' in these parts?'

"Good question." Dean took a pull of the beer the bartender had set in front of him. "I guess I'm lookin' for another profession."

"All washed out?"

"That obvious?" Dean snorted. "I was part of the rodeo circuit longer than I care to say."

"Thought I recognized you. Tough life."

They'd discussed the rodeo and the current front runners, which unfortunately included Anton. The man thought he was God's gift to women, overindulging in buckle bunnies and earning himself quite a reputation both on and off the circuit.

Dean had gone over a few of his injuries with Roy, but held back on the worst ones. Mr. Finch had introduced him to his fiancée, Lois, and some other women who were with him and were all part of a group calling themselves the Almost Dead Poets Society. Every night since then, Dean met someone new.

Now, he sidled up to the bar, but the surfer dude wasn't behind it. A dark-haired guy named Max, going by what everyone called him, was taking orders.

"What can I get you?" he asked Dean in an almost-menacing tone.

"Cold beer."

"We have several IPAs, domestic and imported." He rattled off names, sounding more like a sommelier than a bartender.

"Domestic, thanks."

"Here you go," he said a moment later, uncapping a bottle and taking Dean's cash.

This guy wasn't quite as chatty and friendly as Cole had been. He was also busy as the night wore on and, after a while, got grumpy.

"Max," someone called out. "C'mon! I ordered a mojito about an *hour* ago."

This was a great exaggeration, as Dean had listened to the man order it no more than fifteen minutes ago.

"And if you ask me again, you're not getting it *tonight*."

Dean would go out on a limb and guess this man was one of the owners of the bar. Cole had explained they were three former Navy SEALs who had retired and saved the floundering bar from foreclosure.

Turning his back to the bar, Dean spread his arms out and took in the sights. A busy place, the waitresses in the adjacent dining area flitted from one table to the next. He saw couples, families and a group of younger women taking up an entire table.

"Hey there, cowboy," a soft sweet voice to his right said. "I'm Twyla."

Dean immediately zeroed in on the source, a beautiful brunette who looked to be quite a bit younger than him. He shouldn't let that bother him, but for reasons he didn't understand, only younger women hit on him. He guessed it to be the fascination with the cowboy archetype, which usually happened when traveling in urban cities or coastal areas. He happened to know men who'd had nothing to do with ranches or rodeos who wore Western boots, a straw hat and ambled into a bar. They never left alone.

But a beautiful woman would only take time and attention away from Dean's surfing. Besides, were he to take up with any woman, it would be with the girl next door. Literally. She was as gorgeous a woman as he'd ever laid eyes on. Dark hair that fell in waves around her shoulders, chocolate brown eyes that made a man feel...seen.

"Dean. It's a pleasure." He nodded, failing to give her a last name. She didn't seem like the type to follow the rodeo, but one never knew.

He intended to remain anonymous while in Charming, though a few had already recognized him. The night before, he'd given out his autograph and taken a few photos with a family visiting from Hill Country. He ought to ditch the hat and shoot for a little less obvious.

"You're on vacation?" Twyla asked.

"How did you guess?"

"Not many cowboy types around here."

"Actually, I'm a surfer."

Speaking of exaggerations...

"You're kidding. Well, you're in the right place. Pretty soon the waves are going to kick up, depending on whether a system hits us. But don't worry, we haven't had a direct hit in decades." She offered her hand. "I own the bookstore in town, Once Upon a Book."

Her hand was soft and sweet, making Dean recall just how long it had been since he'd been with a woman. *Too* long. And even though it seemed like bookstores had become as out-of-date and useless as broken-down cowboys like him, he didn't feel a need to connect with this woman.

She had a look about her he recognized too well: she had a *thing* about cowboys. He wasn't interested in indulging in those fantasies. Been there, done that, bought the saddle. He was done with women who were interested in the part of him he was leaving behind. Rodeo had been fun, his entire life for two decades.

And now it was over.

They chatted a few more minutes about nothing in particular, and then Dean set his bottle down on the bar, deciding to call it an early night.

"Nice meeting ya."

"I'll see you around?" she asked.

"You will." He waved and strode outside.

The sun was nearing the end of its slow slide down the horizon, sinking into the sea, assuring him the sky would be dark by the time he drove to his rental. He looked forward to another night of peace and quiet, retiring to bed alone and hogging the damn covers. There were good parts of being alone, few that they were, and he needed to remember them lest he be tempted to remedy the situation.

He arrived to find a basket in front of Cute Stuckup Girl's house she'd obviously forgotten to bring inside, again, and Dean figured he'd knock on the door and finally introduce himself. This time, he wouldn't be as irritated and try on a smile or two. Maybe even apologize for their rough beginning.

Just a quick hello, and he'd be home lickety-split. He stepped over the crushed shell walkway between them, heading toward the front door.

Then the basket made a tiny mewing sound.

What the hell?

Dean approached and bent low to view, with utter horror, that his neighbor had left her baby on the doorstep.

Chapter Two

Maribel was in the middle of chopping onions for her mother's arroz con pollo recipe when she heard a loud pounding on the front door. This was odd, because everyone she knew in Charming would call or text first. But she'd told Ava to drop by anytime. Maribel dried her hands on a dish towel, then walked toward the door. The pounding had become so fierce it could not possibly be her sweet sister-in-law. This was more like a man's fist. Or a hammer.

There was urgency in the knocking. She could feel it, like a pounding deep in her gut. With an all too familiar deep sense of flight-or-fight syndrome coursing through her, she swung the door open.

There stood her neighbor, holding a large basket.

His expression was positively murderous. "Forget something?"

Wondering why he was still so concerned about her

forgetting stuff and ready to tell him off, she peered inside the basket. "Oh, you have a baby."

"Your baby." He snarled, then pushed his way inside, setting the basket down.

"*Excuse* me?"

"It was right on your doorstep. This is dangerous. How absent-minded are you, exactly? Are you going to tell me you didn't even realize?"

Her hackles went up immediately at even the suggestion that she, of all people, would forget a *baby*. He didn't know her or her history. He quickly went from top five to number one most irritating male she'd ever met.

"Number one!" she shouted.

"*Excuse* me?"

"I don't have a baby, *sir*!"

"Well, it's not *my* baby!"

They stared daggers at each other for several long beats. His eyes were an interesting shade of amber, and at the moment, they were dark with hostility. Aimed at her, of all people. Because he didn't know her and that she'd sooner be roasted over hot coals than put a child at risk.

Her mind raced. In the past few days, she'd never seen him with a baby. No sign of a woman or child next door, so her instinct was to believe him. It probably wasn't his baby. And either he was certifiably insane, or he really was indignant that she would have forgotten her baby.

Which meant... Realization dawned on Maribel and appeared to simultaneously hit him.

They both rushed out the front door, him slightly ahead of her. Maribel ran to the edge of the short path in one direction, and Cowboy went in the other.

"Hey!" he shouted after whoever would have done this terrible thing. "Hey! Get back here!"

"Do you see anyone?"

"You go back inside with the baby. I'll go see if I can find any sign of who did this." He took off at a run, jogging down the lane leading to the beach.

Her breaths were coming sharp and ragged. Maybe this was a joke. Yes, a big practical joke on Maribel Del Toro, the burned-out former social worker. But she didn't know of anyone who'd leave a baby unattended outside as a joke. It wasn't funny. Who would be this stupid and careless?

Inside, the baby lay quietly in the basket, kicking at the blanket, completely unaware of the trauma he or she had caused. Why *Maribel's* door? And who was this desperate? Almost every fire department in the country had a safe haven for dropping a baby off, no questions asked. Of course, Charming *was* small enough to only have a volunteer fire department, and she wasn't sure they even had a station in town. But Houston was only thirty minutes away and had a large hospital and fire department.

Dressed in pink and surrounded by pink and white blankets, a small stack of diapers was shoved to one side of the basket. The baby looked to be well cared for. Two cans of formula and a bottle were on the other side. Obviously, a very deliberate, premeditated attempt to get rid of a baby. Maribel unwrapped the child from the soft blanket and unbuttoned the sleeper. As she'd suspected, due to the baby's size, she found no signs of a healing umbilical cord. Not a newborn. The belly button had completely healed. Maribel's educated guess would make the infant around two to three months old.

Someone had lovingly cared for this baby for months and then given up. Why?

The question should be: Why this time?

Drugs? Alcohol? Homelessness? An abusive home? For years, Maribel had witnessed situations in which both children and infants had to be removed from a home. Usually, the need became apparent at first sight. Garbage inside the home, including drug paraphernalia. Empty alcohol bottles. Both kids and babies in dirty clothes and overflowing diapers. No proper bed for the child or food.

But she'd never seen a baby this well cared for left behind.

"Where's your mommy?" Maribel mused as she checked the baby out from head to toe.

A few minutes later, Cowboy came bursting through Maribel's front door slightly out of breath.

"I couldn't find anyone."

"I don't understand this. Why leave the baby at *my* front door?" Then a thought occurred out of the blue, and she pointed to him. "Hang on. What if they meant to leave the baby at *your* front door but got the wrong house?"

"Mine?" He tapped his chest. "Why *my* house?"

"Let's see. What are the odds somewhere along the line you impregnated a woman? Maybe she's tired and wants *you* to take a turn with your child."

Even as she said the words, Maribel recognized the unfairness behind them. She'd made a rash conclusion someone this attractive had to be a player with a ton of women in his past. And also, apparently, someone who didn't practice safe sex.

And from the narrowed eyes and tight jawline, he'd taken this as a dig.

"That's insulting. I don't have any children. If I had a baby, believe me, I'd *know* about it."

"It doesn't always work that way, Cowboy." She picked

up the baby and held her close, rubbing her back in slow and even strokes.

"My name's *Dean*, not Cowboy." He pointed to the diapers. "What's that?"

"Diapers," Maribel deadpanned. "Are you not acquainted with them?"

"This." He bent low and, from between the diapers, picked out a sheet of paper.

"What is it?" Maribel said.

Dean unfolded and read. As he did, his face seemed to change colors. He went from golden boy to gray boy.

He lowered the note, then handed it to Maribel. "It's not signed."

Maribel set the baby in the basket, then read:

Her name is Brianna, and she's a really good baby. Sometimes she even sleeps through the night. The past three months have been hard, but I want to keep my baby. I just need a couple of weeks to figure some things out. Please take care of her until I come back. Tell her mommy will miss her, but I promise I'm coming back. I left some formula and diapers, and I promise to pay you back for any more you have to buy. She likes it when I sing to her.

"Figure a few things out" could mean anything from drug addiction to a runaway teen.

And this troubled girl had left the baby…with Maribel.

"I swear, I… I don't know who would have done this. I don't even live in Charming. I'm here on vacation."

"She must know you somehow. More importantly, she trusts you with her baby."

"She's trusted the wrong person if she thinks I'm going to allow this to happen."

He narrowed his eyes. "What does that mean?"

"We have to call the police."

"No. We *don't*."

"Just one week ago, I was an employed social worker with the state of California. I know about these things."

"Sounds like you're no longer employed, and we're in the state of Texas, last I checked."

"That doesn't change facts. This is child abandonment, pure and simple."

"Except it's *not*." He snapped the letter out of Maribel's hands and tapped on the writing. "It's clearly written here that she'll be back. She's asked you to babysit. That's *all*."

"Are you kidding me? She left the baby on my *doorstep*. Babysitting usually involves *asking* someone first. An exchange of information. Anything could have happened to her baby. You were upset when I left a bag of *groceries* on the doorstep."

"Is it possible she rang the doorbell, and you didn't hear? You took your sweet time coming to the door for me, and I was about to knock it down."

"It's…possible." She shook her head. "I don't know. We should call the cops. At the very least, get her checked out at the hospital and make sure she's okay."

"No. If we take her to a hospital, too many questions will be asked."

"Those questions *need* to be asked! We don't know what we're dealing with here."

"We know *exactly* what we're dealing with here, thanks to the note. A probably young and overwhelmed single mom is asking you to babysit. You're the one person who could stand between her ability to ever see her baby again."

You're the one person who could stand between her ability to ever see her baby again.

His words hit her with sharp slings and a force he might have not intended. They felt personal, slamming into her, slicing her in two.

"Nice try. But I refuse to be guilt-tripped into abandoning my principles."

He snorted. "Principles. That's funny."

"What's funny about principles? Don't you have them?"

"Principles won't work if there's no real intent behind them. Or is family reunification a myth?"

She crossed her arms. Interesting. Her analytical brain took this tip and filed it away for future use. The man seemed to know a few things about the system.

"Of course it's not a myth. It's the goal, but too many times, the parents are unable to meet their part of the deal. The children come first. Always."

"And the children want to be with their parents. It's the number one truth universally acknowledged. If you call law enforcement, that's going to complicate everything."

"That will simply start the clock ticking, and she'll have forty-eight hours to return."

"I can't let you do that. This mother clearly wants her baby back."

Everything inside Maribel tensed when this total stranger told her what she could and couldn't do. He didn't know how many times she'd had faith in a parent, worked for their reunification, only to be burned time and again. The last time had nearly ruined her. She was done rescuing people.

"I can't… I can't take her."

"You're choosing not to. Do me a favor? Stay out of this. I'll take the baby."

"*You* will. You?"

For reasons she didn't quite understand, the surfing cowboy had strong feelings about this. And she got it. A baby in need brought out universal emotions. She wanted to help, but the right thing to do was to call the authorities. Eventually, if the mother *proved* herself to be worthy, she'd get her baby back through the proper channels. Parents should prove they were capable of caring for their children. That way, all could be reassured this wasn't simply a temporary lapse in the girl's judgment. Everyone could be certain the baby was returned to a safe environment.

Dean took the baby from Maribel, then bent to pick up the baby's basket. He moved toward the front door. "Don't let us bother you."

"Wait a second here. What do *you* know about babies? Have you ever had children?"

"No, but I know enough. The rest I'll learn online."

"Online? So, you're going to *google* it?"

"Listen, there are YouTube videos on everything. I guarantee you I can figure this out. You don't need a PhD to change a diaper."

Her neck jerked back. It was unnerving the way he seemed to read her, to know her, before she'd told him a thing. No, you didn't need a *PhD* to change a diaper, but to understand why people reacted in the ways they did. To meet them in their dysfunction and try to help. The problem was all bets were off when addiction was part of the picture. Then parents didn't behave logically. They made decisions not even in their *own* best interest, let alone a child's. And Maribel didn't know whether this mother was an addict who could no longer care for her child. She didn't know anything at all about this mother, and the thought filled her with anxiety.

She cocked her head and went for logic. "This is going to interfere with your precious surfing time, you know."

She'd noticed him on the beach with his board every day, like it was his religion.

"Not a problem." He turned to her as though giving her one more chance to reconsider. "But if that's an offer to babysit a time or two, I'd take you up on it."

"Babysit? For all practical purposes, that's *my baby* you're holding. She left her for me to take care of."

"And you've said you can't violate your principles, so…"

"I also don't know whether I can trust you to watch YouTube videos and figure out how to take care of a baby."

"Well, damn. Looks like your principles are in conflict with one another."

Really? Tell me about it!

Not long ago, this had been her life. A desire to help but forced to follow rules set in place with the best of intentions. Foster care was never the horrible place pop culture and the news media led people to believe. It was only meant to be a temporary and safe home. Too many negative stories made the press, and did not acknowledge those angelic foster parents who cared for children with what amounted to a pittance of a salary.

"While you cuddle up with your principles tonight, I'll be next door with Brianna." Then he left with the baby.

"Number one!" she shouted behind him, but either he hadn't heard or decided not to acknowledge it.

She wasn't cuddling up to her principles, she was *living* with them. Doing the right thing. And yet…procedure would involve alerting the police. The problem was she seemed to be in a gray area, but ethics were always important, regardless of whether legalities were involved.

You're here to unplug. Mindfulness is the key. You're going to teach yourself to cook. Read feel-good fiction. Stay off your cell, all social media and recharge. You have a major decision to make.

Last month, an old headhunter friend had approached and offered Maribel a position with a six-figure salary. She'd be taking over the caseload of a therapist who had counseled the children of the Silicon Valley elite. Anxiety, depression and ADHD were core issues. Maribel had a knee-jerk reaction to the proposition: no. But maybe she could do some good there. It would be something so different from what she'd been doing for years. A chance to use her education and experience in a different way.

She only had a few more weeks to decide before they looked for someone else.

Maribel went back to her dinner of arroz con pollo, so rudely interrupted by both her neighbor and a baby. As she opened cans of tomato sauce and stirred them into the rice, she relaxed and unwound. Her breathing returned to normal, and her shoulders unkinked. Routines were good to employ in the aftermath of shock. They soothed. They reminded a person life would go on.

On the day Maribel discovered the toddler she'd helped reunite with his mother had been rushed to the hospital with dehydration, she'd brushed her teeth in the middle of the day. Later, she would come to doubt every decision she'd ever made, including the one to become a social worker.

Despite the fact Dean had let Maribel off the hook,

she couldn't ignore the mother's request. The baby was her responsibility, and she never shirked her duties. Not from the time she was working with her parents in the strawberry fields of Watsonville to the moment of her PhD dissertation. She, Maribel Del Toro, was no quitter.

She didn't want a surfing cowboy dude who had to google *diapering* to take care of the baby. And even if Maribel had a good sense of people, she didn't know this man. She'd let him take a baby next door, where he might hopelessly bungle it all. In all good conscience, she couldn't just stand by.

Ten minutes later, she turned off the stove and banged on the door to *his* cottage.

He opened the door, almost as if he'd expected her. But then he walked toward the connected bedroom with barely a glance, simply leaving it for her to choose to walk inside or not.

"I can't walk away from her. It's my responsibility," she said.

Since he didn't say a word, she closed the front door and followed him past the sitting room area, the kitchenette and into the bedroom. He'd emptied a dresser drawer and placed Brianna in it, surrounded by her blankets.

"This is a temporary bed for her." He ran a hand through his hair, looking more than a little out of sorts. "Maybe I should buy a crib."

He'd removed the hat, and she wasn't surprised to find golden locks of hair had been under it, curling at his neck and almost long enough to be put in a short ponytail.

Hands in the pockets of his jeans, he lowered his head to study the baby as if mulling over a complicated algebra word problem.

Brianna cooed and gave him a drooly smile. Aw, she was such a cute baby. Beautiful dark eyes and curls of black hair. Her beautiful skin was a light brown. She could be African American, Latina or multiracial.

"As you said, babysitting her is temporary. You don't need to invest in a crib. Maybe this, um, drawer will do for now."

"You *approve*?"

The corner of his lip curled up in a half smile, and something went tight in Maribel's belly. The cowboy's eyes were an interesting shade some would call hazel, others might simply call amber. But they were no longer hot with anger.

She tilted her chin and met his eyes. "Let's just say I'm in new territory here, but so far, so good."

"You're going to help me?"

"It would be irresponsible of me to let you do this on your own."

He shook his head. "Those principles in conflict again. Pesky little things."

"Don't make fun of me. This is serious."

"Yeah, it is. A baby needs you. I know what I'm going to do. What about you?"

She still didn't know, but maybe she didn't *have* to make an immediate decision. It was entirely possible the mother would be back by tomorrow at the latest, regretting what she'd done and missing her baby. Unfortunately, Maribel was too jaded to believe this a real possibility.

But she wanted to.

"We don't even know if she'll be gone the full two weeks. She could come back sooner."

"Exactly." Dean picked up a diaper. "The way I look

at this, Brianna is going to need more diapers. I already went through two of them."

"*Two?* You've been in here for fifteen minutes."

He scowled and scratched his chin. "She wet while I was changing her. Is that…normal?"

Oh boy. This guy really didn't know a thing. Then again, how often did men babysit siblings, nieces or nephews even if they had them? Not often, at least not in her family.

Dean had already explained he had no children of his own. *That he knew of.*

"It's normal. You're lucky Brianna isn't a boy. Sometimes the stream goes long and wide."

"Okay." Dean crossed his arms and gazed at her from under hooded lids. "Thanks for the four-one-one."

"Um, you're welcome." Self-consciously, Maribel pulled on the sleeve of her sundress and chewed on her lower lip.

She didn't usually wear dresses, and that might be the reason she was so ill at ease here with him. Usually she wore pantsuits, her hair up in a bun. Men were still occasionally strange creatures to her, who had ideas she didn't quite grasp.

Watching this particular man from a safe distance had been comfortable. Easy. She could ogle him all she wanted from the privacy of her own cottage and realize nothing would come of it. Now, standing next to him, there was a charge between them. He'd really *noticed* her. She suddenly felt a little…naked. And a lot… awkward.

"You mind watching her while I go buy some diapers and formula?" he said.

"Go ahead."

A perfect opportunity. While here alone, Maribel

planned on surreptitiously checking out Dean's unit. It wasn't that she had trust issues, no sir, but if he was going to watch the baby *she'd* been entrusted with, she should make sure he could be relied on with any child. She wouldn't call it snooping, exactly. More like a light criminal background check.

"Be right back." He grabbed his keys.

"And don't forget baby wipes."

"Okay. Wipes."

She pointed. "*Baby* wipes. Don't get the Lysol ones."

"Speaking of mansplaining." He quirked a brow and gave her the side-eye before he walked out the door.

Snooping commenced immediately. First, she checked on Brianna, who, with a clean diaper, had gone back to snoozing. Admittedly the drawer was an ingenious and scrappy idea from a man who'd probably had to figure things out in the wilderness when all he had for supper was a stick and a rabbit.

Okay, Maribel, he's a cowboy, not Paul Bunyon.

She knew little of life on the range, where she assumed he lived. Checking through his luggage, she found plenty of shirts and jeans. Interesting. He wore dark boxer briefs. Not even white socks but dark ones. Wasn't that against cowboy regulations?

Put the underwear down and back away, Maribel.

His underwear and clothes told her nothing about the man. Importantly, she hadn't found a gun or a buck knife. She rifled through drawers in each room, finding real estate flyers and Ava's "Welcome to Charming" Chamber of Commerce handout. But nothing embarrassing, dangerous or disgusting. She checked the medicine cabinet and under the mattress for those pesky recreational drugs. On her principles, she'd whisk this baby away in a New York minute even if she found the (ahem) legal stuff. Nothing. So far, he checked out.

Then she found a pack of condoms in his nightstand drawer, and it snapped her back to reality.

What am I doing?

She sat on the bed and stared at the wall, covering her face. If only her colleagues could see her now. They'd no longer have any doubts that she'd done the right thing by resigning from the California Department of Social Services.

They'd no longer have any doubt that she'd lost all faith in humanity. She no longer believed in people. She no longer believed in second chances.

This poor man was trying to do a good thing here, and she'd found his condoms, violating his privacy in every way. None of her business. Hey, at least he was prepared. She could find nothing wrong with the man who'd offered to care for the baby, so she didn't have an excuse to call the authorities. He was right to hope. Maybe. There was a memory nagging at the edge of Maribel's mind, but she couldn't pin it down. Last week, when she'd been to the Once Upon a Book store with Stacy Cruz, Maribel might have mentioned her former career in social services. There had been a teenage girl there looking through the mystery section.

She could give this mother at least twenty-four hours.

One day to regret her decision and come running back for her baby.

The mother would be back, and if she didn't return, *then* Maribel would call the police.

Chapter Three

Dean stood in the middle of aisle fourteen, feeling like a giant idiot. He'd asked for wipes and the clerk sent him straight here, but this wasn't right. These were the Lysol cleaning wipes Maribel had warned him about, as if he didn't know any better. The clerk had simply assumed *he* didn't have a baby, but obviously must have a bathroom or a kitchen to clean. And he hadn't been specific enough. *Baby* wipes.

Maybe babysitting Brianna wasn't such a great idea. If only his pretty neighbor would have agreed to watch the baby and let him off the hook. What was wrong with her, anyway? He expected most women would want to babysit a cute baby, but then again, he'd wager she wasn't most women. It turned out she was a social worker with an inherent bias to mothers who made mistakes.

People like Maribel had changed the trajectory of Dean's life.

He wandered down the aisles and finally found the

baby stuff. There were packages of diapers in all manner of sizes. Newborn, the smallest, and then differing numbered sizes by weight. He had no idea how much the baby weighed. In two seconds, he was overwhelmed. He didn't even know how old this baby was and hadn't thought to get Maribel's cell number so he could text her from the store. What *size*? He wanted to get eight to fourteen pounds because that made sense, but maybe over fourteen pounds would be best. Better to have a bigger size than too small, right? He knew that much, anyway.

The formula deal was a lot easier to figure out, so he picked up a case. The baby wipes, once he found them, also easy. Did not require a size, only choosing between scented, unscented, with added aloe vera and hypoallergenic. He chose the ones for sensitive skin, just in case.

As Dean was holding the newborn size diapers in one hand and the next larger size in the other, a man came rushing into the aisle and began snatching pacifiers off the rack like there might soon be a shortage of them. Pacifiers! Dean should have thought of that. Before the dude grabbed them all, Dean reached for one.

"Those are the best. Orthodontists recommend them," the man said, noticing Dean.

"Is there a sale going on?"

"Is there? Hope so. We're trying to wean her from these, but it's not working. And no matter what we do, we can never have enough of these on hand. We've lost so many of them under furniture, beds, cars, anywhere. I figure when we move, we're going to find a treasure trove of old and hairy pacifiers. They didn't just *disappear*. Must be hiding somewhere. It's like losing a sock in the dryer. No one has figured out where the other one goes. It's a mystery. Well, pacifiers are like clean socks."

"Uh-huh." Dean cleared his throat and examined the packaging. "How many should I get for my baby?"

"How old is she?"

"Um, she's really...*young*."

The man quirked a brow, thankfully accepting Dean's ignorance as to the age of his pretend child.

"You look familiar. You're that beginning surfer who hangs out at the Salty Dog, aren't you? Cole told me about you."

Dean's hackles went up at being referred to as "beginning" anything, but it was an unfortunately fair assessment.

"I'm Dean Hunter. And you are...?"

He offered his hand in a firm grip. "Adam Cruz. Nice to meet you. I'm one of the Salty Dog owners."

"Pleasure." Dean tipped his hat and reframed his story. "I'm, uh, babysitting? My niece. For my sister, she...she forgot to..."

Tell me how old her baby is?

Adam eyed the diapers Dean held. "Leave enough diapers? They go through those fast. My wife and I have a daughter, too. That's nice of you to babysit. I take people up on that every chance I get. I love my daughter, but holy cow, I need more time with my wife. Ya know?"

"Um, yeah. That's actually why I'm doing this. My sister needed some time with the wife." Dean winced, realizing he'd outed his nonexistent, invisible sister.

"And you're probably wondering what you got yourself into now."

Dean chuckled and rubbed his chin. "Ha, yeah. You could say that."

"Don't worry. I was terrified the first time I held my baby, afraid I'd break her."

"Yeah, that's how I feel."

Since the moment he'd called Maribel's bluff and hauled the baby with him next door, he had no idea what he was doing and if he'd somehow do more harm than good. Add to that the anxiety of wondering if the mother would come back as promised or if his next-door neighbor would get to be right. She would then turn him into the authorities right along with the baby.

He took the baby, she'd point and say. *And then proceeded to watch YouTube videos on how to take care of her. It was a recipe for disaster from the get-go. I tried to stop him!*

He could almost see *Rodeo Today*'s front-page headline:

Four-Time World Champ Quits Rodeo Circuit to Steal Someone's Baby

Dean held up the two different sizes of diapers. "Which one?"

"Easy. Unless your baby was delivered just today or premature, the newborn size is going to be too small. I made the same rookie mistake. She didn't fit into newborn by the time she was three days old. I'd get the next one up, twelve to eighteen pounds."

"Hey, thanks, buddy. I appreciate it."

Adam waved and rushed away, taking ten pacifiers with him.

When Dean arrived back to the cottage a few minutes later, the noises from inside sounded like *ten* angry babies in there, not *one*. Panic roiled inside of him, but he had nowhere to run. He was going to have to go inside and deal with this mess.

Maribel paced the floor with the screaming child. "Oh my God, you're back! Help!"

Her face flushed and pink, her eyes were nearly popping out of their sockets.

"What did you *do*? What's wrong with the baby?"

"You assume I did something to cause this? How about if you don't accuse me, and I won't accuse you?"

Somehow, he expected her to be better at this, though it might be unfair of him to assume so because she had a uterus. In his case, he would have done better at delivering this child than he probably would taking care of it. It couldn't be much different than assisting in the birth of a calf. And as a bonus, baby cows didn't cry.

"Make a bottle! Quick! She could be hungry. I've already changed her. You did buy more bottles, didn't you?"

Bottles. He forgot the bottles. Stupid Adam leading him to the pacifiers like they were made of gold when Dean should have focused on more bottles instead.

"She left one in the basket. Get it! Now!"

"Stop ordering me around."

He grabbed the bottle and a can of formula, grumbling the entire time.

What had she been doing when he'd been sweating in the store aisle over diapers? All she'd had to do was watch the baby. How hard could that be? She was a sweet little angel the whole fifteen minutes she'd been in his dresser drawer. Following the directions, he mixed the powder with water and poured it into the bottle, shook it then carried it over to Maribel.

"Did you warm it?"

"I was supposed to warm it? Here, give it back. I'll use the microwave."

"Not the microwave!" She hissed. "Good lord, you don't know *anything*. Here, you take her. I'll warm the bottle."

Dean took the baby, who didn't look anything like

the angelic little bundle from earlier. Now she was a wriggling mess with a wail that would kill most grown men. Her little hands were curled into fists like she was mad as hell. He swore he could see her tonsils.

"Hey, hey. Listen, I'm trying to help you. Look, I know you're mad your mama left, but that's not my fault. She'll be back. I hope."

She better come back. He was willing to give the mother the benefit of the doubt, but someone who would abandon her baby and never return was lower than dirt. He hoped she had a damn good excuse.

Dean did his best to pace, shuffle-walk and swing, imitating Maribel. Brianna stopped crying for one second when she opened her eyes, as if shocked someone else was holding her. Still clearly not the person she wanted. Her silence was a momentary lapse, as if taking a breath and gaining strength. She went right back to crying with rejuvenated energy.

"Okay." Maribel appeared with the bottle and pointed to his couch. "Already tested for temperature. Just sit down with her."

He'd never been this awkward and bumbling in his life, but did as Maribel ordered, resenting every second of her authority. Balancing Brianna in the crook of his elbow, he eased the rubber tip of the bottle into her open mouth. She sucked away at the bottle with fervor.

Maribel collapsed on the couch next to Dean. "Guess she was just hungry."

"Why didn't you feed her while I was gone?" The mother had left one can of formula and a bottle after all.

"Are you *kidding* me? You don't know how hard this is! I couldn't hold her and make the formula. I only have two hands, and she cried louder every time I put her down."

More and more, Dean worried he couldn't do this on his own. And she obviously couldn't, either.

"Are all babies this *loud*?"

"She has a good set of lungs on her. I thought she'd never stop." She leaned back. "Oh, would you listen to that?"

"What?"

"Silence. I never knew how much I loved it until it was gone."

He eyed Maribel with suspicion. "How long has she been crying? She was fine before I left."

"She just took one look at me and started wailing. It's hard not to take it personally." Maribel leaned forward, watching the baby take the bottle.

This put Maribel at his elbow, dark hair so close to him he could smell the coconut sweet flowery scent. Cute Stuck-up Girl smelled incredible. His irritation with her ebbed.

"Aw, she's so cute. Check out her perfect skin." She caressed the baby's cheek with the back of her hand.

If it could be said they were staring at the baby, which they probably were, she stared right back. Her dark eyes were wide as she took them both in. This was one smart baby, alert and aware *something* had changed.

"Thanks for helping me," Dean finally said. "I'm sorry if I sound grumpy. Obviously, I couldn't have done this without you."

"I saw how strongly you felt about this."

"I'd say we both have equally strong feelings."

She sighed and offered Brianna her finger, and the little hand fisted around it. "It's just… I've seen this kind of thing before too many times, and it doesn't end well."

"Never?"

Dean didn't want to hear this. He wanted to believe

the mother would return. Sometimes all a mother needed was for someone to have a little faith in her.

Sometimes that's all anyone needed.

"Not with abandoned babies. There's generally abuse in the home, a teenager trying to hide the unwanted pregnancy." She shook her head. "You don't want to hear the rest."

Dean swallowed hard. "But did anyone ever leave a note saying they'd be back for her baby?"

To Dean, the note the mother had left was filled with hope. He remembered too well the taste of hope. No one should be denied a second chance.

"Not to my knowledge."

"Then it's possible. You just haven't heard of any instances. Granted, I agree this is unusual."

"I want to believe she'll come back, but there have been too many disappointments along the line for me. Addiction is powerful. It overcomes love."

That was one belief Dean would never accept. Not in his lifetime.

"Sorry, no. Nothing can overcome love."

Maribel turned her gaze from the baby to him, forcing him to realize how close she was. She had a full mouth and deep brown eyes that shimmered with the hint of a smile. Damn, she was…breathtaking. Much better-looking close up. He'd noticed her, of course, on the beach wearing a skimpy red bikini, displaying long legs and a heart-shaped behind. They often passed each other: her sitting under the umbrella reading, him coming back from his surfing day. After their disastrous first meeting, she'd been easier to dismiss from a safe distance with a curt nod. Far easier than to remind himself he didn't need or want any complications like the type a beautiful woman would bring into his life.

Get your act together before you even think to ask some-one to tag along.

Her lips quirked in the start of a smile. "That's…certainly not what I expected you to say."

"Why? You think cowboys don't believe in love?"

"Honestly, you'll have to forgive me because I'm not sure most *men* believe in love. Or at least, I'm not meeting them."

"Not sure who you've been dating, but that's a pretty sad statement."

"It is, isn't it?" Maribel leaned back, putting some distance between them, as if only now aware of how close she'd been. "I'm sorry to make such a blanket statement. You're right, there are some men who believe in love."

"But these are not the men you're dating. Why not?"

"Well, it's not like they wear a sign."

He snorted. "They don't wear a sign, but there are *signs*."

She simply stared at him for a moment as if she was still trying to decide whether or not he could be trusted.

"What are we going to do tonight?" She nudged her chin to Brianna. "About her?"

"We? I'll let her sleep in the drawer, or maybe I'll just lay her on the bed next to me."

She narrowed her eyes like she thought maybe this was a bad idea. "Are you a light or heavy sleeper?"

"Light." And lately, he hadn't been sleeping at all. But that was a story for another day. "It's a big bed. I won't roll over on her."

Maribel stood. "Okay. You take the first night, and tomorrow I'll take the second."

"You trust me? What if I'm some weirdo?"

"Some weirdo who wants to take care of a baby so her mother won't lose custody? I guess you're my kind of weirdo."

That wasn't enough for him. He pulled out his wallet and opened it to his driver's license, pointing to the photo. "This is me. Take a photo if you'd like."

She glanced at the ID. "That's you. But I…left my phone next door. I'm actually unplugging this vacation."

Unplugging. What a concept.

"I need your cell number anyway. What if I need you in the middle of the night because I'm in over my head here?"

"Just walk over and knock on my door. But…loudly. *I'm* a heavy sleeper."

"Lucky you." He walked her to the door. "Can we agree not to tell anyone else about the baby?"

"I think that's best. I'll check on you two in the morning."

But between old memories, a helpless baby and a beautiful woman next door, Dean would be lucky to get a wink tonight.

Nothing can overcome love.

He certainly wasn't like the men Maribel met on dating apps.

Maribel mulled those words over as she brushed her teeth and got ready for bed, changing into her 49ers long T-shirt. If she hadn't known any better, she'd have thought those words had come out of her own mother's mouth. Her mother often made such sweeping and general statements, seemingly drawing the world into patches of black and white. No gray.

But Maribel certainly did not expect this Greek Adonis–type man with the chiseled jawline and broad shoulders to utter such words. Or to behave with such tenderness and concern toward a baby. Her heart had squeezed tight watching this big man holding a tiny in-

fant close against his chest, as if he'd single-handedly
protect her from the world. He might think he could,
but Maribel had news for him. It wasn't going to be
easy and almost inevitably result in a pain not easily
overcome.

He'd been surly with her since the moment they met,
his physical countenance often matching his sharp and
pointy words. Narrowed eyes, tight jaw. Rigid shoulders. Until that one sentence, laid out for her like a truth
bomb. When he'd said the words, his eyes were soft and
warm, his voice rich and smooth as mocha.

Is family reunification a myth?

With those words, he'd poured a metaphorical bucket
of ice water over her.

Because she used to believe in families. She once
believed parents could be reunited with their children
simply because of the deep bonds of unconditional love.
Parents were hardwired by biology to love their babies
and protect them. She'd believed with all her heart before she came front and center with the gray area: addiction. Mental Illness. Poverty. Now, she still lived in
those murky shadows. She wished she could see things
differently and, as she had in the beginning, with a hope
and belief that she could change the world. She now realized she could not.

And if the mother hadn't returned by tomorrow
night, Maribel would call the police. Dean wouldn't
take it well, and there was no point in preemptively
starting an argument by revealing her plan. For now,
she'd agreed to do this his way. It certainly didn't mean
he would *always* get his way. By tomorrow night, maybe
this wouldn't be an issue. The mother would be back,
or the baby would be on her way to a competent foster

home with a loving couple prepared to keep and nurture a baby.

She settled on her bed, pulling out her book to read before she went to sleep. Recently, on the advice of a friend who wrote a book and ran a website on avoiding burnout and rediscovering your purpose, Maribel had returned to print. Normally she read everything from her phone app, but according to her friend, she'd inadvertently zapped herself out of the joy of reading. Her goal here was to slow down, take her time, touch the paper pages and flip through them. Reading was an experience for more than one sense. It could be both tactile and visual. She'd somehow lost the joy of taking her time with something she loved.

Last week she'd visited Once Upon a Book with Stacy and loaded up on novels with happy endings. If it had a dog on the cover and a couple lovingly smiling, it got purchased. Some of her friends loved the raunchy and realistic stuff about the agonizing pain of breakups. If a book made them ugly cry, it became a forever favorite. Not Maribel. She'd had enough of real life. When she'd wanted to cry, when she wanted a knot in her stomach that wouldn't go away, all she'd had to do was read her case files.

In the first few days of reading print books again, she became aware of two things: her focus was lacking, and she almost didn't have the patience to slow down enough to *read*. So she continued to work at it one page at a time. This week on the beach under an umbrella. In fact, she'd had a quiet week until the baby showed up.

Outside, the sounds of soothing waves rolled in and out, and Maribel focused on turning the pages of her book. In no time at all, she was in the mountains of Humboldt County, where a handsome farmer had taken in a divorced mother of two looking for a new start. Sleep came easily, enveloping her in warmth.

The next morning, Maribel blinked, stretched and listened through the thin wall connecting both cottages. No baby crying. Hardly any noise at all outside. Only a sense of disturbing awareness pulsing and buzzing through her body that she couldn't ignore. Maribel could almost hear her sister Jordan's voice in her head.

Time to admit a few things.

Okay, yes, I'm attracted to the grumpy man. So what? Who wouldn't be?

He exuded alpha male confidence, and it had always been her lot in life to fall for the difficult men. For the ones with permanent scowls and surly attitudes. She couldn't seem to fall in love with someone sweet and kind like Clark, her nicest ex-boyfriend, who'd told her in no uncertain terms, "I'm sorry, Maribel, but you are sucking the life right out of me."

Ouch.

Maribel wasn't great at dating, having spent most of her childhood studying. It wasn't that she was trying to prove something, but early on, Maribel realized her strengths were in textbooks. Whether it was science, math or history, she slayed it. Testing wasn't an issue for her. Blessed with a nearly photographic memory, academia wasn't difficult. Boyfriends, at the time, were. This meant that essentially, she was a little socially hindered when it came to romantic relationships.

She'd tried online dating, setting up her profile on Tinder and the others. One of the men had turned out to be married, making her paranoid enough to check for wedding ring tan lines from that point on. One man had arrived at their coffee date looking perfectly presentable. Slacks, dark button-down, loafers. A face with good character, if not particularly handsome. No tan line. After ordering, he called himself a naughty boy, said he had to be punished from time to time and wanted a dominant woman.

She left without finishing her coffee, went home and removed her profile from that particular dating app.

Now, she went to the kitchen to make coffee, the quiet of the morning reverberating all around her. Dressing quickly, she walked next door to check on the baby. Dean had left the door unlocked, so she let herself inside. Tiptoeing through the connected rooms to the bedroom, she found the baby sound asleep in the drawer wrapped in blankets, her little fisted hands bracing her face, her sweet mouth softly suckling in her sleep.

Dean lay on his back on top of the blankets, wearing board shorts and—*oh my*—no shirt. He'd thrown one arm over his face like he wanted to block everything out. Suddenly, he sprang up on his elbows, eyes squinting into the brightness.

"What? *What?*"

Maribel startled and took two steps back. She hadn't said a word and, in fact, was barely breathing. He wasn't kidding about being a light sleeper.

"It's just…me," Maribel squeaked and held up both palms, surrender style. "Sorry. I woke up early and wanted to check on you two. Go back to sleep."

He ignored her and instead walked around the bed to check on the baby.

"She's doing fine," Maribel whispered. "You can relax."

"Now she's sleeping better than I did." He ran a hand down his face. It was only then she realized he'd gathered his hair into a short ponytail.

He had a good face, chiseled jaw and irresistible stubble.

Down, girl.

"Rough night?" She swallowed.

"She was up at two in the morning wanting…something. Gave her a bottle, but she just wanted to be… I don't know…held?" He scratched his chin, and the stubble made a low sound.

"So, you didn't get much sleep?"

"No big deal. Haven't slept well in a while. You?"

"Like a baby. A very nice rest, thanks."

It wasn't entirely true. She'd lain awake for an hour thinking about the baby. About Dean. The mother and whether or not she would return. Whether or not Maribel was doing the right thing giving her a chance to return before involving the authorities.

"Got news for you. Apparently, babies don't sleep. Kind of like me. If you slept well, you did *not* sleep like a baby."

"That could be why you're grumpy all the time." She cleared her throat when he gave her the side-eye. "What do you do about it?"

"I don't take medication if that's what you're asking."

"No, there's melatonin, which is natural. Personally, I recommend reading before bedtime. Something light and happy."

He turned to study her then, his amber eyes appearing darker near the irises. Well, if he was going to stare, she would stare right back. She wasn't intimidated by good-looking dudes with hot bodies. If someone looked away first, it wouldn't be *her.*

Let that be him. She met his eyes. With a baby between them and the fact it was morning, she couldn't escape the unnatural intimacy of the moment. She was in his bedroom just as he'd rolled out of bed. He stood at her elbow, arms crossed, so close her bare elbow brushed against his naked and warm skin.

And it seemed that a live wire lay sparking between them.

One half of his mouth tipped up in a smile. "How did I do? Did I pass the health inspection?"

Still meeting his gaze, she cleared her throat. "You did fine, obviously."

The gaze he slid her made bells and whistles go off in her head. Her body buzzed, and her legs tightened in response to the hint of a smile on his lips. Smiling, she'd decided, was overrated. Better than a smile was the start of one. The way it began in the eyes, moving slowly. Like a teaser of "coming attractions."

Damn it!

She looked away first, too unnerved by the blatant invitation in his eyes.

"Okay! I see everything is good in here. I'll make her a bottle for when she wakes up, and I can take her next door."

She thought she heard him mutter, "Chicken," as she quietly walked away.

Don't miss
A Charming Doorstep Baby
by Heatherly Bell,
available September 2023 wherever
Harlequin Special Edition books and
ebooks are sold.

www.Harlequin.com

COMING NEXT MONTH FROM

HARLEQUIN

SPECIAL EDITION

#3007 FALLING FOR DR. MAVERICK
Montana Mavericks: Lassoing Love • by Kathy Douglass
Mike Burris and Corinne Hawkins's rodeo romance hit the skids when Mike pursued his PhD. But when the sexy doctor-in-training gets word of Corrine's plan to move on without him, he'll pull out all the stops to kick-start their flatlined romance.

#3008 THE RANCHER'S CHRISTMAS REUNION
Match Made in Haven • by Brenda Harlen
Celebrity Hope Bradford broke Michael Gilmore's heart years ago when she left to pursue her Hollywood dreams. The stubborn rancher won't forgive and forget. But when Hope is forced to move in with him on his ranch—and proximity gives in to lingering attraction—her kisses thaw even the grinchiest heart!

#3009 SNOWBOUND WITH A BABY
Dawson Family Ranch • by Melissa Senate
When a newborn baby is left on Detective Reed Dawson's desk with a mysterious note, he takes in the infant. But social worker Aimee Gallagher has her own plans for the baby...until a snowbound weekend at Reed's ranch challenges all of Aimee's preconceived notions about family and love.

#3010 LOVE AT FIRST BARK
Crimson, Colorado • by Michelle Major
Cassie Raebourn never forgot Alden Riley—or the way his loss inspired her to become a veterinarian. Now the shy boy is a handsome, smoldering cowboy, complete with bitterness and bluster. It's Cassie's turn to inspire Aiden...with adorable K-9 help!

#3011 A HIDEAWAY WHARF HOLIDAY
Love at Hideaway Wharf • by Laurel Greer
Archer Frost was supposed to help decorate a nursery—not deliver Franci Walker's baby! She's smitten with the retired coast guard diver, despite his gruff exterior. He's her baby's hero...and hers. Will Franci's determined, sunny demeanor be enough for Archer to realize *he's* their Christmas miracle?

#3012 THEIR CHRISTMAS RESOLUTION
Sisters of Christmas Bay • by Kaylie Newell
Stella Clarke will stop at nothing to protect her aging foster mother. But when sexy real estate developer Ian Steele comes to town with his sights set on her Victorian house, Stella will have to keep mistletoe and romance from softening her hardened holiday reserve!

YOU CAN FIND MORE INFORMATION ON UPCOMING HARLEQUIN TITLES, FREE EXCERPTS AND MORE AT HARLEQUIN.COM.

HSECNM0823

Get 3 FREE REWARDS!

We'll send you 2 FREE Books plus a FREE Mystery Gift.

FREE Value Over $20

Both the **Harlequin® Special Edition** and **Harlequin® Heartwarming™** series feature compelling novels filled with stories of love and strength where the bonds of friendship, family and community unite.

HARLEQUIN
PLUS

Try the best multimedia subscription service for romance readers like you!

Read, Watch and Play.

Experience the easiest way to get the romance content you crave.

Start your **FREE TRIAL** at
www.harlequinplus.com/freetrial.